PRAISE FOR TESS WINNETT THRILLERS

"Fast-paced! Riveting! Emotional! Suspenseful! Compelling! Complex! This book brings it ALL!"

"It is not the novel to start reading in the evening or the reader will find themselves losing sleep in your desire to learn what happens next."

"*The Girl They Took* by Leslie Wolfe is so good I can't find the words to describe how good it is. Definitely it is the best Tess Winnett book yet and maybe the best book Leslie Wolfe has written."

"The ending is so astonishing I truly believe no one can predict it."

"Plenty of twists and turns lead the reader to a satisfying conclusion."

"I've read most of this author's books and enjoyed each one, but this one ranks right up at the top, it's just that good."

PRAISE FOR LESLIE WOLFE

"The queen of suspense is back with another gripping installment in the Tess Winnett series."

"Leslie Wolfe has written another great mystery. Thank you for a great plot and outstanding characters."

Powerful! "Leslie Wolfe weaves a compelling story of an FBI agent who looks beyond the rule book in her quest to recover a kidnapped child."

THE
GIRL
HUNTER

BOOKS BY LESLIE WOLFE

TESS WINNETT SERIES

Dawn Girl
The Watson Girl
Glimpse of Death
Taker of Lives
Not Really Dead
Girl With A Rose
Mile High Death
The Girl They Took
The Girl Hunter

STANDALONE TITLES

The Surgeon
The Girl You Killed
Stories Untold
Love, Lies and Murder

DETECTIVE KAY SHARP SERIES

The Girl From Silent Lake
Beneath Blackwater River
The Angel Creek Girls
The Girl on Wildfire Ridge
Missing Girl at Frozen Falls

BAXTER & HOLT SERIES

Las Vegas Girl
Casino Girl
Las Vegas Crime

ALEX HOFFMANN SERIES

Executive
Devil's Move
The Backup Asset
The Ghost Pattern
Operation Sunset

For the complete list of books in all available formats, visit:

Amazon.com/LeslieWolfe

THE
GIRL
HUNTER

LESLIE WOLFE

ITALICS PUBLISHING

$\varprod$ **ITALICS**

Italics Publishing Inc.
ISBN: 978-1-945302-75-6
Edited by Joni Wilson.
Cover and interior design by Sam Roman.

ACKNOWLEDGMENT

A special thank you to Mark Freyberg, my New York City authority for all matters legal. Mark's command of the law and passion for deciphering its intricacies translates into zero unanswered questions for this author. He's a true legal oracle and a wonderful friend.

1

RUN!

The swamp falls quiet when I scream.

My clipped cry, quickly smothered as my shaking hand rushes to cover my gaping mouth, leaves the stage open for the concert of crickets, frogs, and countless other critters that call the Florida Everglades their home. Within half a heartbeat, the cacophony of sounds is back in full force as if I wasn't even there.

Gasping for air, I lean against the thick trunk of a bald cypress covered in Spanish moss and listen intently. Not too far behind, I pick up the sound of a twig cracking. My hand touches my chest in an instinctive attempt to soothe the panic of my thumping heart when I sense his approach, drawing closer with every step.

"Where are you, sweet little Daisy?" His voice, coarse and lewd and repulsive, seems tinged with laughter, but I know better. It's the anticipation of the hunt, the excitement that rushes through his veins at the thought of seeing me bleed, writhing in pain at his feet, begging for his mercy.

And he's drawing closer with every step, crunching rotting leaves and palm fronds under his boots, seeding unspeakable fear in my blood. It takes every ounce of willpower I have to not dash away from there screaming and running as fast as I can. I stand still, holding my breath, knowing that when I set foot out in the open, and he sees me, he'll strike me down mercilessly.

He never misses.

I have the scars to prove it.

My knees are shaking, and my breath, shallow and raspy and shattered, will soon let him know where I'm hiding. I have to move before he gets too close to me. Barely controlling the suffocating sense of dread that rises from my chest, I look for the next tree wide enough to provide some cover.

The closest one is at the edge of some stagnant water, and a gator might be lying in wait near its roots. There's another one, some fifty feet away, rooted entirely on dry land. But fifty feet seems like an unbelievable challenge when he's out there, just a few yards away, hunting for me.

Careful not to be seen, I pick up a fistful of dirt from the ground, then weigh it in my hand, waiting still for him to draw closer. I can hear the limp in his step, in the way he grunts when he puts weight on his right foot, muttering swear words at every step. Still, he's coming.

I catch a glimpse of him as he approaches. I see him only for a split second through the curtain of trees and waterfalling moss. His face is etched in stone, the anticipation of the hunt written in every feature and every line. The half-smile, half-grimace stretching his mouth is an omen of the fate he has in store for me. But my eyes are drawn to the crossbow he carries with ease in his right hand, a small, compact weapon that can send death my way without making the tiniest sound. Only slightly larger than a full-sized handgun, the thing from hell can fire multiple arrows without reloading.

I've seen the damage it can do.

I've felt its arrows ripping through my flesh.

Fear choking me, I shift in place without realizing it, crunching dry leaves under my feet. The noise, barely noticeable under the cover of myriad critters bustling in the falling night, catches his attention from yards away. He freezes in place, searching for me, turning only his head and, with it, the sights of that wretched crossbow.

I hold my breath.

And wait.

Seconds go by, seeming like hours. Insects claim their blood meal from my skin, but I barely notice them. My eyes stay riveted on the silhouette I can barely distinguish beyond layered curtains of moss. The wind picks up just a smidge and shifts the moss chains near me gently, quietly. One tendril touches my face, and I nearly flinch, but I remain still, watching him, waiting for the right time to bolt.

An owl's hoot nearby makes him turn his head in my direction, but he doesn't see me. He looks right past me, licking his lips and grinning.

"Come on, dear girl, show yourself." His voice is almost convincing. "Can't let the night crawlers hunt you." A throaty chuckle. "You're mine."

He takes a few steps farther down the path and stops again, his head slightly tilted, probably listening intently. I look at the dirt in my hand, planning my throw. Hopefully, the noise it will make when it hits the palmettos across the path will get his attention for long enough to allow me to run.

Seeing the black dirt on my skin chokes me. The smells of damp earth, of bog and mist and saltwater and death, snatch my weary mind and fill it with memories too painful to endure.

David.

My husband, the love of my life, is gone.

Images flash before my eyes. His pale skin covered in the dirt that I threw over his still-warm body. His hands, marked by a struggle that ended in blood, rest over his chest. His once vibrant, loving eyes now forever closed.

I am the one who consigned him to the damp earth of the Glades. With my own hands. And I should've been there, buried by his side. Not here, fighting to survive, clinging to a life that makes no sense without him.

A sob climbs forcefully from my chest, demanding to be heard among other creatures' agonizing calls. I manage to stifle it, covering my mouth with the back of my hand and blinking away tears.

For a brief moment, I consider coming out in the open and waving my arms around until an arrow or two extinguishes the pain in my chest. But I know what would happen if I did. I wouldn't find the craved relief of death, only the renewed purgatory of being that brute's prisoner.

I fill my lungs with humid, sticky air and find the courage to throw the fistful of dirt across the path, aiming at a cluster of thriving palmettos where I could've easily hidden.

The hunter freezes in place the moment he hears the sound. Slowly and quietly, he turns in place and takes two steps toward the palmetto bush, studying it intently.

That's when I bolt.

I try to move as silently as I can, but he still hears me. By the time he's ready to fire his arrow, I reach the cover of the big cypress, fighting to slow my breathing just a little.

"Sneaky, my little Daisy girl," he says. Some of the earlier excitement in his voice is now replaced with budding anger. "Enough games for tonight. It's getting late, and I have plans for you." His lustful, bloodcurdling cackles silence the frogs for a moment. "Boy, do I have plans for you? You'll love every minute of it."

His words fill my heart with terror. Whatever he promises, he delivers tenfold. I've learned that the hard way. His words are paralyzing me like the stare of a deadly snake right before the lethal bite.

He starts coming toward me with a decisive, heavy-footed step, favoring his right leg. My heart thumps against my chest as I realize I can't stay put for much longer, and I'm not ready to bolt again. The last remnants of daylight are disintegrating quickly like gossamer blown in the wind, and I can barely see a few feet ahead of me. Moss tendrils wave gently in the calm breeze like ghosts haunting the forest from hell.

My knees suddenly weak, I hold on to the tree trunk and steady myself. "Snap out of it already," I tell myself, an angry whisper between clenched teeth.

I'll make it. I know I will.

I have to.

He's almost close enough to grab my arm when I run as fast as I can, zigzagging between trees, holding my breath and willing myself to not look back.

"Ah, there you are," he says, sending shivers down my spine.

He follows, closing in despite his limp. I don't look back; I just hear his breath and heavy footfalls as I dash desperately left and right, knowing it's my only chance to escape his arrows.

The sound of a cord snapping taut rips through the air like a whip.

I shriek and fall to the ground, breathless.

2

FISHING TRIP

Tide Life was approaching the dock a little too fast.

A light green, thirty-foot center console fishing boat with two powerful engines, she was the pride and joy of her new owner, a long-haul trucker by the name of Tim Haskett. Every buck he'd made for the past three years he'd sunk into that boat and all the after-market gear he'd outfitted it with. Then came the fishing gear, and a man could spend thousands, then lamely rationalize the investment by saying it saved money on food, putting fish on the dinner table every now and then.

Tim and his fishing buddy, Freddie Caufield, had taken *Tide Life* out only a few times before. Whenever they caught a day off from work with decent weather, they met at the ramp before sunrise, where Tim towed the boat with his RAM dually truck, and Freddie hauled the beer in his old Toyota. Freddie didn't have money for boats and trucks and fancy saltwater reels. He had a six-month-old baby girl, a toddler just starting to walk on the old, squeaky floorboards of his ranch, and a third baby on the way. No money left for fun.

A few hours of fishing and drinking under the crisp Florida sun got both men sunburned and more than a little buzzed. It was easy to lose count of the beer cans emptied and crushed before being thrown back into the open cooler, with all the excitement and the wind in their faces, pushing the two Yamaha engines to the max on the gleaming waters of the Gulf.

"Whoa, there," Freddie said, tempering his friend's enthusiasm. "You're gonna hit hard." He frowned at the approaching dock, holding on to the tower and ready to jump on the dock to tie the lines.

"It'll slide right in," Tim said. The doubtful tone of his voice didn't match the reassurance in his words. He held the wheel knob with one hand, while the other clutched the throttle white-knuckled, ready to give it gas. The boat glided on the smooth water in neutral, going fast, carried sideways by strong currents.

"It'll hit!" Freddie shouted, grabbing hold of the tower bar with both hands and bracing for impact.

"Damn it to bloody hell!" Tim cursed, pushing the throttle to full reverse. The engines screamed and started pulling the boat away from the dock at the very last moment. The hull scraped against the dock with a noise that got Tim's teeth grinding. "Son of a bitch."

The boat continued in reverse until it reached a safe distance from the dock, then Tim put the throttle back in neutral. He bent over the port gunwale to look at the damage and promptly released a slew of profanities. "That's thousands of dollars' worth of damage. Bloody hell."

Freddie popped open a can of beer and handed it over to his friend as if it were the supreme panacea. He took it and gulped half of it thirstily.

"It's easier to back into a loading dock with an eighteen-wheeler, at night and in the rain, huh?" Freddie asked, popping another brew for himself.

"Damn right. I can do that in my sleep. But this thing just goes wherever the hell it wants."

"We'll get the hang of it." Freddie raised his sweaty beer can in a silent toast to his buddy. "Whenever you're ready, mate. I'm kinda hungry," he added gently after a while. Unlike his friend, he had a family lunch to show up for, or he'd probably spend the week in the doghouse. Tim had noticed Freddie's wife had started to lose her sense of humor after their second child.

Tim downed the rest of his Heineken and sent the crushed can flying into the cooler, then gave the dock a scrutinizing glare as if it were some enemy ready to meet him with blazing guns.

This time he approached at crawling speed, and shifted into neutral when he was still a few yards away from the dock. The momentum and currents took over and delivered the boat smoothly at the dock, perfectly aligned and without another scratch.

Holding the lines, Freddie jumped on the dock, and quickly wrapped them around the cleats, then hopped back on the boat and started unloading their gear.

A park ranger chose that particular moment to drive through the boat ramp parking lot in his marked cruiser. He slowed down as he drove by the dock, giving them a good sizing up.

"Shit, man," Tim whispered, trying his best to not stare at the ranger. "He better not come here and ask us about our catch."

Freddie shot the approaching ranger a quick look, then closed the lid on the cooler and put it on the dock. "Nah. He'll be on his way soon."

"Told you, we should've dropped it back into the sea," Tim grumbled. "Why risk it? It's bad luck, I'm telling you."

Freddie didn't reply. He just coiled the anchor rope calmly, keeping his eyes on the passing ranger. The ball cap visor and a pair of mirrored Ray-Bans shielded his stare from the ranger's view.

"What do we do now?" Tim asked, shooting sideways glances to one of the boat's storage compartments, where an illegal hammerhead shark was stashed.

"We could leave it there, on the boat," Freddie replied. "We put the blacktips in your truck like that's all we got, get the boat out of the water, and drive off."

Tim seemed to weigh the decision for a while, then nodded. "You driving with me today?"

"Uh-huh," Freddie replied, grinning. It was a long weekend, and they had planned to go out on the water again the following day. No need to drive his car back and forth, when Tim could chauffeur his ass. But Tim loved his company and didn't mind it one bit.

The ranger drove off after nodding in their direction, and both of them breathed with ease.

"All right, let's do this," he said, then hopped on the dock with the keys to his truck jingling in his hand.

A few minutes later, they were driving off toward the city. They had a good hour drive ahead of them on the interstate. That was the fastest route, but Tim was still a little anxious about the illegal hammerhead stowed away on their boat. People went to jail over stupid shit like that. They'd had quite a few beers since sunrise, and it wasn't even noon yet. Choosing the least traveled road, he turned onto the side road crossing through the Everglades instead of taking the route to the interstate.

The road, weaving through thick woods and swamps, was deserted, which suited Tim just fine. The occasional gator stuck its nose out on the asphalt, but quickly withdrew when the RAM approached.

After a couple of miles, Tim relaxed a little more, although he still wished he'd dropped that hammerhead back into the Gulf, instead of giving in to Freddie's request. It wasn't like they weren't going to catch anymore tomorrow or the following week. Freddie and his family couldn't eat as much shark as they took out of the ocean if they tried. Probably Freddie was selling the blacktip for some extra cash and keeping the hammerhead for his family. Tim shook his head slightly, reflecting on his choice to not have a family just yet. He was turning thirty next fall. Why rush? Life was good the way it was, except for that nasty scratch on the port side of his hull.

"Hey, what the hell is that?" Freddie asked, pointing at something on the side of the road. "Slow down, will ya?"

He didn't see it at first, but hit the brakes, nevertheless. Then he advanced slowly until he could see what Freddie was talking about.

A young woman, dressed in bloodied, torn clothes and wearing a pair of oversized rubber work boots, was picking berries from a shrub on the side of the road. Tim hit the brakes again and stopped the truck in place. The woman didn't seem to be aware of their presence, although she was only ten or twelve yards away. She rummaged through low palmetto leaves, picked berries, and threw them in her mouth hungrily, crouched casually in the ditch, seemingly ignorant of the threat of alligators and snakes. She was incredibly thin, probably emaciated by hunger. Her hair, clumped and dirty, ran in long strands around her face, but Tim could still see her face was bruised and grimy.

"What the hell is she eating?" Freddie asked, staring at the girl with his mouth ajar. "There's nothing there, no raspberries, nothing but swamp crap."

"Maybe sea grapes?" Tim said, unable to take his eyes off the girl. "Or saw palmetto berries. Not much else edible here."

"Ugh, they're both terrible," Freddie was quick to reply. "What do we do? There are crocs out there. They'll snatch her."

As if she'd heard him, the girl turned her head and looked straight at them for a moment, but then continued to pick berries and eat them, slowly making her way along the road.

"We should go talk to her, offer some help. Maybe give her a ride?" Freddie said.

Frustrated, Tim turned on the four-way flashers. "No way I'm approaching *that*," Tim snapped. "Don't you see she's been beaten up to hell and who knows what else? Do you think I wanna go to the big house over some piece of swamp trash?"

"Then we got to call the cops, man. We can't just drive off and leave her there." Freddie frowned and took out his phone. "That shirt of hers is barely clinging on to her. And those pants sure ain't hers."

"So you've never seen homeless people before?"

"Not in the Glades, all right? They don't come here, or the crocs get them before anyone gets to see them. But she ain't homeless."

"How the hell would you know that? You're making shit up again."

He let out a quick groan. "Whatever, but I'm calling them, all right?"

"What if they pin this on us? Then what? You got a wife and kids. Wanna go to jail for her? You know cops will be happy to collar the first two losers they find."

Freddie pressed nine-one-one but didn't connect the call. "I still have a conscience, dude. I can't just leave her there for the damn crocs to snack on. Call me an idiot and that's that." He tapped on the screen to connect and the emergency operator picked up immediately.

"What about the shark?" Tim asked immediately after Freddie ended the call. "We should dump it before they get here."

"You'll think they'll search the boat?" Freddie asked incredulously. "Really? Why would they?"

"Listen, this girl ain't okay in the head. No one in their right mind would be doing what she's doing. Who knows what she'll tell them? Let's get rid of the bloody shark already. Feed it to the gators on the other side of the road."

They were just about to hop out of the truck when flashing red and blue lights appeared in the rearview mirror. Tim pulled the truck door shut with a frustrated sigh.

"Told you that shark was bad luck."

3

TRUTH

"Manolo Pruneda Rafael." Tess enunciated the name without looking up from the case file, although she could quote from memory every single detail of the suspect's history. Pretending she struggled with saying his name, she accentuated certain syllables to resemble everyday English words like man and prune, guaranteed to aggravate the suspect a little bit more.

The suspect remained silent, although the effort made him clench his fists. His cuffs were chained to the table, mere inches away from the folder she held open casually on the page with the suspect's photo and extensive criminal record.

Then she looked straight at him. "I'm FBI Special Agent Tess Winnett."

His nose crinkled in disgust. "So what? Want a medal for that or something? You think you're the first fed pig I ever sat across from? Chained like an animal just for the color of my skin?"

"Ah," Tess replied quietly, looking full of mock interest at his record. "That's the play you're betting on, huh?"

"Damn right, *puta*, that's exactly it. Make a note of that in your papers there." He stabbed the table surface with a dirty index finger.

"You were arrested with a kidnapped seven-year-old boy in your car. The little boy everyone's been looking for since you snatched him from his parents' home in Delray two nights ago. You might've seen it on TV."

He flashed a grin enough to show tobacco-stained teeth, crooked and lacking basic hygiene. "I don't know who put him in my car. I told the cops that, but they wouldn't believe me. 'Cause my skin ain't the same color as yours, *tarada*." He sucked his teeth then spat on the floor, but Tess didn't flinch. The stained concrete had seen much worse.

She leaned back into her chair and pulled the case file closer to the edge of the table. "You started young. A couple of gang-related charges, some possession, a gun charge, then you grew up to be a man with particular inclinations." She smiled, a hint of a smile while she locked her eyes onto his. "You were tried as an adult for that gun charge, and that meant no more juvie hall for you." She frowned and whistled softly. "You were barely fourteen. That's terrible." Then she closed the file and looked at him again. "But I think something happened to you at South Bay state prison." His pupils flared, loaded with anger. "Something that made you discover who you really are."

"Shut the hell up!" He slammed his handcuffed fists against the table. Springing from his chair in a fit of unfiltered rage, he tugged against the chain forcefully, but couldn't get much closer to her.

Holding his rabid glare calmly, she whispered, "Sit down." She didn't expect him to obey, but he did, a bit slack-jawed but still angry. "You went from exposing yourself to kids all the way to snatching one. One that we know of. But I believe this isn't the first time you took a kid." He swallowed with difficulty, as if his mouth had gone dry.

So, there had been more.

"Lawyer," he said in a high-pitched tone, defiant and daring. "I know my rights."

"All right," she replied, taking her phone out from her pocket and texting Donovan her coffee order. It was his turn to do a Starbucks run. "There, I called one for you." She waited for a moment, but he only sat there, grinning smugly at her as if he'd won some battle.

A quiet chime alerted her she had a new message. It was just a thumbs up emoji from the analyst. "They're sending for a lawyer right now." She stood and walked slowly, getting his hopes up for a moment that she'd leave him alone, then retaking her seat to his visible dismay. "But I'm supposed to be in here for at least an hour, you know, or my boss will say I don't do my job. I can't ask you any more questions, and please, remember: you have the right to remain silent. Use it." Rafael's grin widened then turned into a smug smirk as he looked around the room as if he had an audience in awe of his brilliance.

She dropped the phone in her jacket pocket and looked at the camera hanging from the ceiling at the far corner of the room. A red dot showed it was working, recording the suspect's interrogation.

Good.

She leaned against the chair's uncomfortable back rest and stretched her legs. "So, you like snatching kids." It was a statement, not a question. His pupils dilated just a tiny bit in response. "Does your mother know what you do for fun?" A beat. "Oh, shoot. I'm not supposed to ask any questions. So sorry." Smiling awkwardly, she added, "It's in my nature, asking questions. But, please, don't answer anything until your lawyer gets here."

His upper lip curled with contempt. He leaned forward as much as he could reach and grinned at her, then mouthed the word lawyer.

"Yeah, yeah, he's coming. Or maybe it's a she, I don't know." No reaction. "For your sake, I hope it's someone good. Otherwise, you'll land up in jail with men who really hate child molesters." She mock-cringed, letting her face express a fear she wasn't feeling. Whatever Manolo Pruneda Rafael had coming was of his own doing and nothing short of what he deserved. "But hey, these lawyers are good. Half our cases get thrown out of court over technicalities."

His shoulders slouched a little, a telling sign he was starting to feel more relaxed, more in control. Less vigilant.

She examined her fingernails for a while. "I'm so sorry to tell you this, but the boy we're looking for, we know where he's at." She tilted her head and winked. He swallowed hard and licked his lips nervously, then clenched his jaws. Muscles danced under his skin in tense knots. His eyes shot a piercing glare. "It doesn't look good." She leaned farther back, her eyes riveted on the suspect's pupils. "You see, feds are thorough. They search everywhere. Your house," she started enumerating slowly, casually, but saw no reaction. "Your mother's place, your car, your workshop—"

There. A flicker of fear dilating the pupils for a millisecond.

"Even your church," she continued, not letting on she got what she needed. "Putting that boy on the stand will do wonders." Another flicker of fear. "Then there's DNA, and no one can lawyer their way out of a charge when there's DNA."

This time, he lowered his eyes and withdrew. The expression of smugness was long gone. Seemingly defeated and scared, he looked as if he was about to start begging for a deal.

No deal for you, Mr. Rafael, Tess thought, leaving the room without another word.

She bounced down the hallway toward her office, mobile phone in hand, rushing to make the call to her colleague at CARD, the Child Abduction Rapid Deployment unit. From the opposite direction, Donovan approached cheerfully with two venti cups in hand.

"Winnett!" Pearson called from across the bullpen. "In here, now."

Hearing his voice, Donovan pulled a quick one-eighty and made for his desk. Tess let out a long, loaded breath of air and changed direction too, heading for her boss's office.

4

THE ROOKIE

Special Agent in Charge Alan Pearson waited for Tess in the doorway, hands propped firmly on his hips. He'd rolled up his shirtsleeves and abandoned his suit jacket on the back of his leather chair, and that rarely happened. SAC Pearson was nothing if not procedural, following the book to the letter, even if he'd written parts of it, and business formal attire was in that book. His shiny scalp, wrinkled by ripples stemming from his deep frown, was covered in tiny beads of sweat.

He wasn't alone in his office. One of the assistant district attorneys for Miami-Dade County sat comfortably on one of the visitor chairs, her slender legs crossed, her three-inch heeled, black pump punctuating the air with the beat of her impatience. Porscha Litchford was her name, and her reputation preceded her in an intense, almost intimidating way. Whispers around the federal building occasionally picked at her name with comments such as, "Our ADA is what happens when your parents really want a sports car but have a baby instead." Tess found that people poked fun at people's physical traits or things they didn't control about themselves, such as their name, when they had little else to pick on. The thirty-four-year-old ADA was feared on the stand as she was behind the scenes, in law enforcement offices throughout the county.

Pearson gestured toward the empty chair, but Tess remained standing, while her boss walked around the desk and sat. "Winnett," he said, "where are we with—"

"I'd like to know why you continued interrogating the suspect after he asked for a lawyer," the ADA cut him off in a cold, unforgiving tone. "When they're going to let him walk because his Miranda rights have been violated—"

"They're not going to let him walk," Tess interrupted. "It's on video. I didn't ask any more questions after he asked for a lawyer."

"But you continued to extract information from him, in your own *unusual* way." She punctuated the word with a flutter of her hand near her temple as if saying Tess's methods were insane. "*After* he'd asked for legal representation."

Tess looked at her unfazed. "There's a child missing, Ms. Litchford," she said coolly. "Maybe that doesn't matter much to you—"

"What matters to me is the law!" She stood abruptly as if the comfortable leather chair had somehow ejected her.

"—And the letter of the law was followed to a T, Ms. Litchford," Tess continued unfazed. "I did my job. Now it's your turn to do yours. Put that sick son of a bitch in a deep, dark hole and throw away the key."

Gasping with indignation, the ADA turned to Pearson.

"Winnett, take it down a notch," he said. "Let's keep it professional. We're on the same team."

Tess nodded once, hiding the fire in her eyes behind lowered eyelids. "Now if you'll allow me to focus on a missing child's safety, I have a call I need to make."

Pearson stood, his face lit up. "He has the little boy?"

"Yeah. In his workshop. And there's DNA evidence on him." She stepped outside and made the call to her contact at the CARD team. When she was done, she almost bumped into ADA Litchford, leaving Pearson's office red-faced and somewhat breathless.

Tess had that effect on people. That didn't change, no matter how hard she tried.

Pearson beckoned her in. "What did they say?"

"They're on their way there. We'll know in about ten minutes."

Pearson stared at her for a long moment, his face carved in stone but his eyes speaking volumes. "Remind me again why you're not joining the Behavioral Analysis Unit at Quantico," he said eventually, running his hand over his forehead as if trying to wipe off the wrinkles carved in it. "They're holding a spot open for you, aren't they?"

She shrugged. "I don't believe they still are. It would be a bad leadership decision to keep the team understaffed in the hope that one day some particular person might join. No single agent is worth that."

He shook his head and smiled to himself but didn't argue.

"Are you trying to get rid of me?" she probed, keeping her face serious. Pearson was not exactly famous for his sense of humor.

"Some days I am," he replied calmly. "Like today, for example. You set more fires than I can put out, Winnett."

She looked at the carpet for a moment, feeling the need to justify her actions and hating herself for being defensive. "CARD asked me to sit with this suspect for a reason. He took another child while he was out on bail, awaiting trial for kidnapping. Everyone knew he was going to lawyer up the first chance he got. I just had to try to find that missing boy, sir."

Pearson raised his hand in the air. "I understand your motives, and why CARD chose you specifically for this interview. But telling ADA Litchford what her job is? Really?" He groaned and sat heavily, looking tired all of a sudden, the corners of his mouth lowered, his eyes weary. Reaching out for a bottle of water, he unscrewed the cap and offered it to Tess.

She shook her head. "Thank you, I'm good."

He drank about half of it thirstily, then screwed the cap back on. "So, why aren't you working in Quantico for Bill

McKenzie, in a role where you can do more of what you did today, and less people interaction and politics? Maybe you'd be happier there."

She gave the idea some thought as if it were the first time she heard it, although it wasn't. McKenzie, her behavioral sciences mentor, had offered the position to her on several occasions. And every time, her answer has been the same.

"This is my home," she eventually said. "Whatever family I have left, it's here."

"Family?" Pearson asked, leaning forward, visibly interested. "I never heard you mentioning family until now. I— I thought you had no one left," he added, seeming a little uncomfortable.

"It's just Cat," she replied almost apologetically. "Not a blood relative, but to me, he's closer than family."

"How old is he, these days? That man never seems to age. He has this Sam Elliott vibe going about him," Pearson added. "As if time has stopped for him. With that hippie hair and that tiger tattoo on his chest," he chuckled. "I never met anyone like him."

A wave of sadness clouded her vision for a moment. "He's seventy-seven."

"Oh." A beat of silence. "How is he doing?"

"Age never forgives anyone. He needs me, even if he doesn't say it, and I'm there for him."

"How about your parents? Are they still alive?"

She nodded, wondering what was going on, why so many personal questions. It wasn't like Pearson to pry. "Just my father, but we're estranged."

"That means you're staying?" Pearson asked, the change in tone of voice so sudden it gave Tess a sense of whiplash. She nodded and smiled hesitantly.

"Good," he continued, sounding almost enthusiastic now, causing Tess to raise an eyebrow. "Because you have a trainee to mentor. A new field agent, fresh out of Quantico."

"What? Hell, no," she blurted before she could control herself. "Please, sir, don't make me train some rookie."

She paced in place restlessly, feeling the urge to storm out of Pearson's office and never look back.

"Winnett, let me—"

"Sir, you don't want me training anyone. I have some shortcomings you don't need the new person to pick up from me, and, please…" She ran out of breath and realized she'd been making pleading gestures, waving her arms around like a lunatic. Discouraged, she let them fall alongside her body and studied Pearson's disapproving face in discouraged silence.

"Winnett," he said, and her name on his lips cracked in the air like a whip. "As long as I'm the SAC here, I make these calls. Got it? Nothing I tell you is open for negotiation."

She lowered her loaded gaze. "Yes, sir, copy that."

"Then, I have to tell you I agree with you," he added, and she looked straight at him, surprised. His eyes were just a bit softer than before and colored with a hint of amusement. "Of course, I'd never place a rookie in training with you. But this young man has requested you specifically by name."

Her jaw dropped just a little while her brow furrowed. "Who is he?"

Pearson gestured toward the door. A young man walked in, dressed neatly in a charcoal suit and white shirt.

"Hello, Tess."

5

ON SCENE

The Miami-Dade police cruiser stopped right behind the boat trailer. Tim waited for a moment, then hopped out of his truck with Freddie doing the same on the passenger side.

"I made the call," Freddie announced, stepping over the boat trailer neck to reach the officer. "Hi." He raised his hand as a greeting but seemed anxious and uncomfortable.

A gold nametag affixed above the cop's left shirt pocket read Patchett. He seemed old, about sixty or maybe even older than that. He wore a poorly trimmed moustache, salt and pepper, with uneven strands curved toward his mouth. He looked butch and jaded at the same time, his face bearing the weathered signs of a difficult life. A bit overweight, Officer Patchett had jowls that bounced when he walked, much like a bulldog's. In fact, if Tim had to give the guy a nickname, that would've been it. Bulldog.

A second cop approached quickly. Dressed in a gray suit and blue shirt, he flashed a badge bearing the insignia of Broward County Sheriff's Office, not Miami-Dade police, although the two men had shared the ride over. That was strange. He introduced himself as Detective Michowsky, and he was no spring chicken either. The suit walked with a slightly crooked gait and his left hand rested on his hip, probably where pain kept him from walking straight.

"Where is she?" Patchett asked. "The girl you called about."

"Over there," Tim replied, pointing at the ditch where the girl kept on foraging, completely oblivious to their presence. Freddie's finger pointed as well, a bit shaky for some reason.

The bulldog pressed a button and spoke into his radio, "Possible 10-41 here, send a bus, stat." Some garbled static came in response. "Stay here," he instructed Tim and Freddie.

Then both cops approached the girl, while the two truckers watched, inching closer out of sheer curiosity.

"Hello, ma'am, I'm Officer Patchett," the bulldog said. "I'm here to assist you. Let's get you out of that ditch."

The girl shook her head vigorously, then turned her back to the cops. Crouched down, she continued looking for berries to eat.

"Ma'am, we need you to come over here," the bulldog insisted. This time, his voice was low, commanding, stern. "Don't make me come in there to get you."

"Just go away," the girl said, gesturing with her hands as if she was swatting flies. "Leave me alone."

"Are you hurt?" the other cop asked. "You're bleeding."

The girl looked at him with a slight tilt of her head, then popped a palmetto berry into her mouth. "Not anymore." From what Tim could tell from about ten yards away, her stare was absent, as if not really seeing the people in front of her.

Detective Michowsky seemed to think the same thing, because he waved his hand in front of the girl's face as if to test if she could see. She instantly pulled away.

"Go away already," she said. "I can see just fine. You busybodies don't have any business here."

Officer Patchett gave the ditch a disgusted look and groaned. "Ma'am, it's not safe to be where you are. As long as you're endangering yourself, we have a duty to intervene."

He reached for her arm and grabbed her, balancing his weight carefully on the side of the ditch. The moment he touched her, she shrieked and pulled away vigorously. Patchett, thrown off-balance, slipped and landed face-down in the ditch. Michowsky rushed to help him, but Patchett stood on his own, brushing off the dirt from his soaked uniform with a deep scowl on his face.

The girl watched them warily from a few steps away but didn't run. The two cops whispered something between themselves, too far from Tim to catch. But he was staring at the girl, whose frayed, torn shirt had come apart even more during the fracas with the officer. Her right arm, now completely exposed, showed scars of cuts and bruises, some recent, barely starting to heal. One wound had been sewn clumsily with what seemed like thick, black thread. Bruises extended on her chest and abdomen, and one of the cuts, caked in dried blood, was fresh enough to start bleeding again from her encounter with the officer. Whatever that girl had been through, it must've been hell.

An ambulance pulled up at the scene, approaching fast with the red flashers on. Patchett beckoned it closer to where the girl was. She stared at them with eyes widened in fear, seemingly paralyzed. The first EMT jumped out of the van and talked briefly with the two cops, then he and the other EMT took out the stretcher.

Without much hesitation, one EMT unfolded a blanket and the other, a young woman with fire-red hair tied in a ponytail, loaded a syringe with expert motions. After a quick look at each other, they jumped into the ditch and approached the girl.

The first EMT wrapped her in the blanket and fought to hold her still, while she clawed and kicked and screamed, letting out guttural gibberish that made no sense. The tone of her raspy voice was heartbreaking, a desperate plea Tim could easily understand even if there were no comprehensible words.

The red-haired EMT found her shoulder and jabbed it quickly. Within seconds, the screams subsided, and coherent words started coming out of her mouth in a weakened but just as desperately pleading voice.

"No, no, I have to go back," she whispered, then she fell listless into the EMT's arms. They loaded her onto the stretcher and strapped her in, every move precise, calculated, efficient. The only thing that seemed out of place was the detective's reaction. Once the girl was on the stretcher, he drew close and studied her intently, gently pulling rebel strands of hair away from her face. Then he said something that sounded like, "I'll be damned," and took a couple of pictures of her with his phone.

As they loaded the girl into the ambulance, Tim turned to leave. "We're done here," he said, eager to put some healthy miles between the two cops and the hammerhead stashed on the boat.

He was about to climb into the truck when he felt a hand on his shoulder, heavy, uncompromising.

"Where do you think you're going?" Officer Patchett said. "We're not through with you two." Then he extended his hand. "Keys."

Tim dropped the keys to the truck in his hand, feeling blood draining from his face. "We need to go," he said weakly. "My friend's family is waiting—"

"They'll be there when we're done," Patchett said. "You, come on over here," he called Freddie. The young man, visibly scared, approached in a hesitant gait. "Now you two get to tell me how you found this girl and what you did to her."

"We didn't do—" Tim started to say, but Freddie cut him off in a high-pitched voice.

"Nothing! We didn't even touch her!"

"Interesting you'd mention touching," the bulldog grinned. "What, you found some poor woman on the side of the road, and figured she couldn't tell us who raped her if she tried?"

"Jeez... no!" Freddie exclaimed, slapping his forehead with his hand. "Tim said we shouldn't stop, because you guys are crazy. And I didn't listen. Can't believe you're trying to pin this shit on us."

"Now, aren't you happy you didn't touch that girl, man?" Tim said, looking straight at Freddie with a disappointed frown on his face. He felt almost parental about his friend. Although Freddie was a year older and an experienced long-haul driver, he lacked street smarts when it came to people. What he lacked though, he made up for with a heart of gold and the naiveté of an innocent child.

"Sure am," Freddie replied, as the cop watched their interaction with the same scowl on his face. "We didn't even get out of the damn truck!" he added, furiously glaring at Patchett. "We didn't help that poor girl because we're so damn afraid of cops like you."

"That doesn't mean you two didn't add to her misery," Patchett replied, sounding just as convinced as before, when he'd accused them of assault without the tiniest bit of evidence.

Tim drew a lungful of air to steady himself. "There's no shred of evidence, not a single trace of DNA belonging to us anywhere near that girl. We didn't get out of the truck. We saw her, we stopped, we called nine-one-one. End of story." He stopped speaking and looked calmly at the cop.

"Let them go," the cop wearing the suit said, and the instant relief felt by Tim resembled a wave at high tide, leaving him spent, shaky. "These two schmucks had nothing to do with it, unless they've been camping here since last fall. Do you know who the girl is?" Michowsky asked. The bulldog's frown deepened. "Kiana Mallery." Patchett didn't show any sign of recognition when he heard the name. "She used to host that popular outdoors TV show, something with swamp in the name, I forgot what it was. But it's her for sure, and she's been missing since September."

6

New Case

Tess's heart swelled when she recognized the voice.

Memories rushed to her mind, dizzying her a little more than she cared to admit. Their bodies, lying side by side on a colorful towel in Miami Beach last fall, relishing the hot sun, eating grapes, chatting after closing a complicated case. She remembered dozing off, feeling safe, yet slowly falling for the Broward County detective who had dreams of becoming an FBI agent.

Then, in her typical manner, she killed the idea of the two of them together, refusing to take his calls or reply more than a couple of cold, professional lines to his emails from Quantico.

And now, she barely recognized him, neatly dressed, clean-shaven, his hair trimmed to match FBI regulations. But the fire in his eyes was still there, untamed, and had the same effect on her.

"Todd Fradella," she exclaimed, her surprised voice a pitch higher than she would've preferred. The concern over Pearson watching faded quickly and she landed in his open arms for a quick hug. "You're back! When did you—"

"Last week," he replied as she pulled away, shooting Pearson an apologetic look. Her boss watched their interaction with undisguised curiosity and a hint of a frown.

A smile lingered on her lips as she studied Todd from head to toe. "You look good. How did you enjoy Quantico?"

He lowered his eyes for a moment, then looked at her intently. Somehow, the world narrowed to just their bubble, and everything else stopped having any meaning. She'd thought all that was in the past, but the feeling was still there, just as strong and overwhelming as it had been on that beach. "Quantico was great, but my home is here." A glint of heat in his eyes as he spoke made her turn away to hide the burning in her cheeks.

"So, I am to assume you're okay training *this* rookie, Winnett?" SAC Pearson asked, his voice tinged with a touch of sarcasm.

She nodded. "Yeah, sure. We go way back—"

"I figured," Pearson replied. "I've seen his name on a number of case reports from last year."

"Yes, sir, that's correct," she added, shifting her weight from one foot to the other, eager to leave her boss's office and catch up with Fradella.

"He finished third in his class," Pearson added. "We're lucky to have him."

"Thank you, sir," Fradella replied.

"Well, then, I have a case for you," he said, opening a blue folder and steepling his hands above it. "Out of Collier County."

"How come we're picking up a Collier case? It's typically Agent Patto who covers that area, isn't it?"

Pearson turned to Fradella. "There are some things I'd appreciate you didn't learn from your new mentor, SA Fradella. Don't even try to ask why Winnett gets away with it, because she doesn't." He shot Tess a warning glance. "Not anymore."

"Understood, sir," he replied calmly.

"Glad to hear someone does," Pearson replied. "And since I have to justify every decision I make, Winnett, then here you go. Again, you've been requested by name."

Pressing her lips in an apologetic line, she waited silently for Pearson to continue. Her career wouldn't be damaged much if she learned not to antagonize her boss every chance she got.

"A Detective Michowsky asked for your assistance with this case."

Fradella struggled to hide a grin that seemed to confuse Pearson. Tess's left eyebrow shot right up. Michowsky worked out of Broward County and was Fradella's old partner. What the hell was he doing in Collier?

As if reading her mind, Pearson added, "Michowsky is on loan there, for a reason I can't recall, but you can investigate that too if you so desire." Tess bit her lip and didn't say a word. Every bit of sarcasm in Pearson's voice she had earned, and the best she could do was not make it worse.

"Detective Michowsky found—"

Porscha Litchford stormed through the door, looking even angrier than before. She didn't step all the way inside. She just pushed the door open forcefully and held on to the handle while glaring at Pearson, then at Tess.

"I checked with my boss, the district attorney for the state of Florida, and he agrees. This case could be thrown out of court easily. All Rafael has to do is tell his lawyer that you continued to question him after he asked for a lawyer. That's all it takes," she added coldly. "And you put a pedophile back on the street."

Tess struggled to stay quiet for a long moment, thinking Pearson might be better suited to handle the irate ADA, but she couldn't bear being accused of doing something she had not done. "I *did not* ask Rafael any other questions after he lawyered up. I specifically told him he didn't have to reply to anything anymore. For the last time, it's on tape. *Watch* the tape. You might find that helpful," she added, regretting the snide remark the moment the words left her lips and made Pearson groan with frustration.

"See what I have to deal with?" the ADA asked Pearson as if Tess wasn't in the room.

"Excuse me," Donovan's voice came from the hallway, from behind Litchford. Scoffing with exaggerated annoyance, she stepped back, allowing the young analyst to come in.

Donovan was beaming and didn't stop his energetic bounce until he reached Pearson's desk. "They found him! The little boy, he was right where Winnett said, in Rafael's workshop, chained to the wall. Forensics confirmed there's plenty of evidence to put Rafael away for life." He held his hand up high, and Winnett met it in the air with a loud clap. Pearson stood and grinned widely, a rare sight.

"So, there, Ms. Litchford, that's why—" Tess said, turning to face the ADA, but she was already gone. Good for her... let her take that piece of news to her boss.

"Is he okay?" Pearson asked.

"He will be," Donovan replied after a moment's hesitation. "It's hard to ever be okay after something like this." He frowned and stared at his shoes, while silence engulfed the room. "But we found him alive, in one piece, so there's hope."

The exhilaration waned within moments after Donovan returned to his desk, leaving Tess and Fradella on one side of Pearson's desk, and the SAC on the other, flipping through the pages of the new case file.

"They found Kiana Mallery Bayliss, the TV host. She's been gone seven months."

"Do they have an estimated time of death?" Winnett asked.

"She's alive, Winnett."

"Oh. I assumed—"

"Yeah, I know what you assumed," Pearson replied coldly. "But this Detective Michowsky seems to believe this case might be right up your alley."

7

THE FEDS

They had airlifted Kiana from the site where she was found, after the EMTs found arrythmia, most likely due to severe dehydration. Her struggle with the EMTs had probably made it worse, taking the last shred of strength out of her thin, emaciated body. They had already loaded her on the stretcher and into the bus, and they were about to drive off, when the technician taking her vitals shouted, "Hold it." A few minutes later, the Mercy Hospital helicopter landed on the highway and took her away.

Michowsky and his temporary partner, Officer Patchett, waited until everyone left before climbing into the Collier County cruiser and headed east, toward Miami. Patchett was unusually silent and grim, a deep frown etched on his brow, his lips pressed together tightly under his unevenly trimmed moustache.

But Michowsky had an idea how to unlock the mysteries behind the officer's crabby mood. He took a slight detour on a small one-way street in Little Havana and pulled into the parking lot on the side of a popular burger joint.

"Come on," he said, cutting the engine. "I'm buying."

Patchett hesitated for a moment, then got out of the cruiser with a groan. He was a bit heavy and struggled climbing out of the cruiser even if he held on to the doorframe for support. A pair of vintage cops, that's what they were, the two of them seemingly way past their expiration date. They'd better not have a perp to chase on foot anytime soon. Michowsky's back had been killing him lately, not letting him sleep well, not even allowing him to walk straight and fake the youthfulness he'd stopped feeling a while ago. He wasn't defying age any better than Patchett.

The place had small tables on a patio behind the main building, and Michowsky chose a remote one with a gesture of his hand. They sat on small, metallic chairs, and set the orders they'd picked up from the bar counter on the sticky table surface. Michowsky allowed himself a moment of pure enjoyment, inhaling the smell of crispy bacon smothered in molten cheddar, a guaranteed artery popper. But life's short. Might as well enjoy it while he could.

The burger was as good as it smelled, or maybe even better. Cheese-loaded herb fries were crispy on the outside and just the perfect soft on the inside, not gooey but puffy and light. A bottle of sweaty Coke chased what had to be a two-thousand calorie meal with some sugary caffeine he needed with every fiber in his body. One quick look at his partner and Michowsky noticed he was coming around some.

"Good stuff, huh?" he asked.

"I can't believe I never ate here before," Patchett replied, talking with his mouth full. His moustache moved angrily when he chewed, fluttering above his mouth like a trapped moth. "It's not my beat, but I come here all the time. My wife's cousin lives just two blocks over."

"Well, now you know," he replied, leaning back on his chair and patting his lean abdomen with a satisfied sigh. Another couple of meals like that and he'd grow a potbelly too.

The earlier scowl returned to Patchett's face the moment the last fry found its way from the greasy plate to his mouth. He didn't say a word though, no matter how much chitchat Michowsky offered as enticement. Not giving up still, the detective led the way to the cruiser and invited Patchett to drive them to the hospital where they'd taken Kiana.

They found her still being seen by doctors, but she had been taken upstairs to one of the rooms. That was a good sign; her condition must've been upgraded to stable. Otherwise, the girl would've been treated in the ER or ICU.

The room was at the far end of a nearly empty corridor. Per Michowsky's instructions, a uniformed officer stood guard in front of the room and nodded when he approached flashing his badge. He seemed to know Patchett personally, because the two shook hands and exchanged quick greetings.

Michowsky stopped in front of the glass sliding door and peeked through the slightly open vertical blinds. The light was dim inside the room, the window blinds completely shut, and only a small ceiling fixture was turned on. Kiana lay on the bed in a light blue gown, seemingly sedated yet restless. Her head turned left and right on the pillow, rhythmically, as if she was trying to break free from a nightmare.

Standing at the foot of the bed, a young, slim doctor dressed in scrubs was giving a nurse some instructions. The nurse, in her fifties, with gray hair tied in a low bun and thick-rimmed glasses, reminded the detective of his high school math teacher, the bane of his teenage existence. Michowsky couldn't catch what the doctor was saying, but the nurse standing right next to her kept nodding and jotting notes on a chart. Then the doctor turned on her heels and slid the door open.

"Doctor, if you don't mind," Michowsky intercepted her, "how's she doing? When can we talk to her?"

Dr. DiDomenico, per her name tag, frowned a little at Michowsky's badge. "She came in with severe dehydration and malnutrition. She has countless bruises, lacerations, puncture wounds, ligature marks, even snakebites. But she's stable now."

"Recent?" the detective asked, although, as little as he'd been able to see at the side of her stretcher, he already knew the answer.

"Some are fairly recent, yes," the doctor replied, giving her wristwatch an impatient look. She was a slender brunette with long, sleek hair tied in a ponytail. She couldn't've been more than thirty years old.

"Any signs of sexual assault?"

"She wouldn't let us examine her. We respect patients' decisions when it comes to their bodies." Michowsky frowned with an unspoken question in his mind. "But I'm willing to bet my career that she's been repeatedly assaulted. If you see the state she's in, it's a no-brainer."

He envied the young doctor's clinical detachment. Sometimes, these cases were too much for him, even if he'd seen a lot in his twenty-five years as a detective. When he thought of his daughters, growing up to be beautiful, attractive young women, luring creeps just by walking down the street, it got to him, twisting his gut. The fear he felt for them, for all women like Kiana felt visceral at times, hard to bear. Without realizing, he clenched his fists until his knuckles cracked and turned white.

The doctor's gaze dropped to the cop's fists. "Yeah, I feel that way too," she said, turning to leave.

"When can we talk to her?" Michowsky asked, under Patchett's inquisitive stare. "We have questions."

"Give her at least another hour," Dr. DiDomenico said with a tinge of sadness in her voice. "And don't expect much. The kind of trauma she's experienced comes with a toll. Dissociation, amnesia, confusion, irritability, bouts of rage. Then we should expect the onset of PTS. It happens more often than not."

Before he could thank her, the doctor walked away briskly, heading for the bank of elevators at the end of the corridor.

"You don't think we can talk to her now?" Patchett asked. "She must remember something."

Michowsky stifled a frustrated sigh. "You were there. You saw how out of it she was. I'd be happy if we can get anything usable out of her, but I'm not counting on it." He sat on one of the chairs lining the opposite wall. Patchett remained standing, his hands shoved deeply inside his pockets.

"We don't have time, and you know it. The perp's in the wind by now."

"We wait," Michowsky stated firmly. That poor girl deserved an hour of undisturbed rest. And the perp's reckoning would come soon enough. He only hoped he'd catch a minute alone with that sicko in some remote corner of the Glades and deliver it to him with his bare hands.

He stood and looked at Kiana through the blinds. She was sedated, barely able to move, but still fighting off the nurse, tugging at her IV, and trying to rip the gown off her body. Not getting any sleep. Drawing closer to the glass, he heard her whimper and moan in a low, guttural voice.

The nurse eventually walked away from her bed and sat on a small lab stool in the corner. Within seconds, the girl fell asleep, an agitated slumber filled with nightmares if Michowsky were to venture a guess based on what he could see. After a few more minutes, the nurse approached the bed quietly and managed to cover Kiana's body with a blanket without waking her up. After adjusting her IV, she went back to her stool with a book in her hand.

"That's why you called the feds?" Patchett asked in a low voice reeking of disappointment. "Because you didn't want to chase this son of a bitch yourself?"

Finally, Michowsky's temporary partner was sharing what had been eating at him. "This perp is not what you think, Patchett. Trust me."

"So, you're saying, Collier County's detectives aren't good enough to work this case?"

"It's not about being good enough," he replied, frowning at the glass door to Kiana's room. "It's about having the right tools to catch someone who does stuff like that."

Patchett scoffed with indignation and walked away a few steps, then leaned against the wall and checked his phone. Two nurses turned the corner and walked past quickly, shooting side glances at the uniformed officer guarding Kiana's room.

"Do you know who's in there?" one of them asked in a low voice, pointing a finger with short, purple-coated fingernails at the glass, but not slowing down. "It's that TV star who went missing last year."

"Really?" The other one replied with barely contained excitement, ogling the room in passing before heading into another room farther down the hall.

Michowsky felt the urge to rush into Kiana's room and close her blinds completely. Soon someone would talk, and the place would start crawling with newspeople and just plain gawkers and trolls, losers who look to spice up their boring lives with sprinkles of someone else's misery.

Patchett returned and stopped in front of Michowsky with his hands propped firmly on his hips. "I don't think the sheriff will be too thrilled to have the feds all over our shit. You should've asked him first. It's his damn county, you know." Michowsky looked at Patchett but decided to let his comments slide. "I think our people are more than capable of working this case by themselves," Patchett added.

"I'm sure they are," he eventually replied, seeing that Patchett wasn't relenting. "This fed is different," he added. "Not like anyone you've ever worked with."

"Different? How so?"

"Her specialty is catching scum like our perp."

"What? Kidnappers and rapists?" Patchett's voice was derisive, almost arrogant.

A beat of tension, while the PA system called a code blue in a room nearby.

"No," he eventually replied. "Serial killers."

Patchett's mouth gaped open. For a long moment, he seemed unable to think of something to say, so he eventually walked away, slowly pacing the mosaic floor, staring at Michowsky occasionally but keeping his distance.

"There you are," the detective heard a familiar voice approaching.

"Hey, Winnett," he said, shaking her hand. Then he turned to the man standing next to her and grinned. "I'll be damned! It's Fradella. I didn't recognize you, kid. All spruced up and with that haircut." He quickly caught the younger man in a bear hug. The two patted each other's backs a couple of times then pulled away. "The FBI looks good on you, partner. Is it better pay?"

"A little bit better, yeah," Fradella replied.

"Then you're buying," Michowsky replied under Patchett's disapproving glare. "For a whole month," he added and winked.

Tess approached Kiana's room and peeked inside, just as Michowsky had done earlier. The earlier smile had waned off her lips, making room for a frown of deep concern. Michowsky approached.

"He had her all this time?" she asked, keeping her voice low.

"That's what I think."

She bit her lip and didn't say anything for a while. She just seemed unusually pale under the indirect sunlight filling the corridor, consumed by something Michowsky didn't understand, something that made her chest rise and fall quickly with shallow, rushed breaths.

He was about to ask, when Kiana sat abruptly on the bed and let out a bloodcurdling shriek, tugging at the collar of her gown. The nurse rushed to her bedside and tried to keep her flailing arms still. Destabilized, the IV stand fell to the floor rattling.

Tess slid open the door and stepped inside.

"Let me try."

8

KIANA

Tess closed the door behind her gently, careful not to startle the girl. She was sitting on the bed, her left wrist held tightly in place by the nurse. Kiana was fighting her off as if in a dream, with flailing, weak movements and guttural, throaty whimpers that sounded more animal than human.

Taking in all the details, Tess shuddered. That could've been her, sitting on that bed and trying to make sense of the surrounding world, all those years ago after the brutal assault that left her within an inch of her life. She hadn't thought of that agonizing night in a while. She'd willed herself to be done with it, to never let it change her destiny. The passing of time, the healing she'd slowly found amid friends and colleagues who knew nothing of her past, and Cat, who knew everything and would've died before saying a word, had somehow made her whole again. But tiny cracks appeared along the scar lines of her mind, when seeing Kiana's bruised body, the despondent look in her eyes, the flicker of madness that too much suffering can kindle in anyone.

That could've been her.

The thought chilled her blood as memories came rushing in. The blows that had made her see stars before her world turned dark. The weight of that man crushing her body. The look in his bloodthirsty, lecherous eyes, the stench of his breath burning her face. Then later, when he left her for dead, her agonizing crawl on deserted streets until she somehow landed on Cat's doorstep. That was fate dealing her a helping hand after the unspeakable ordeal in some weird, nonsensical twist, as if fate was still undecided about her.

A perfect stranger, a sixty-something-year-old Vietnam vet who could barely make ends meet keeping his bar afloat, took her in. He turned off the *OPEN* sign that hung right underneath the neon *MEDIA LUNA* written in bluish cursive by the white crescent moon and kept it off for a week. He risked his life, his entire existence by taking care of her the way she wanted. No doctors and hospitals. No police. So that her assault would never be known and define her entire life. So that she could go on and fulfill her dream of becoming an FBI agent without an unerasable blemish casting a heavy shadow over everything that she could become. She could've died that night in Cat's tiny bedroom, and yet he didn't break his promise to her and selflessly tended to her wounds the best he knew how.

She'd been lucky to find him in her path. A gentle, caring man with a heart of gold, instead of hospitals, cops, media, and a lifelong label she refused to accept at any cost.

Kiana's fate had been entirely different. Seven months she'd been gone. Tess looked into her haunted eyes and saw a flicker of what she'd been through. The unimaginable horror of it.

"You can't be here," the nurse said, seeming torn between the urge to escort Tess out herself, and the need to continue holding Kiana's arm in place so she wouldn't tear off the IV needle from her vein.

Tess raised her hand for a brief second, then approached the bed and said quietly, "He's gone now. It's just us." She touched Kiana's hand tentatively, but the girl didn't pull away. Tess gave the bruised hand a gentle squeeze and continued holding it, watching the girl's shoulders relax a little.

Her vacant stare landed on Tess's face after a moment. "Are you the new girl?" she asked, looking left and right as if checking to see if danger lurked in the corners of the hospital room. "When did he take you?"

"No," Tess whispered, still holding her hand. Kiana's questions sent icicles through her blood. Were there others out there? "This is a hospital and you're safe. He's gone." She sat on the side of the bed and shot the nurse a quick, commanding look. The nurse let go of Kiana's wrist. The girl leaned back against the pillows and closed her eyes.

Tess watched her breathe for a moment, glad she was finally resting. She was ghastly thin, her bones poking through her skin. Her hair was an uncertain shade of brown, still clumped with dirt and dried blood. Frowning, she shot the nurse with an inquisitive glance.

"We're giving her a sponge bath," she whispered apologetically. "She just got here."

A sponge bath wasn't going to cut it; not even close. But Tess was grateful they hadn't given Kiana a bath yet. Moving slowly, she let go of the girl's hand and fished out a small evidence pouch from her pocket. Without a word, the nurse offered her a pair of gloves. She slipped one on and gently picked a few fragments of dirt and leaves from Kiana's hair. Maybe that piece of evidence could help them isolate the location where she'd been held.

Kiana's eyes opened wide, and she sat abruptly. The IV stand rattled a little, the tubing stretched to the max. Tess peeled off the glove and took her hand quickly. "You're safe," she said. "He's gone. You're in a hospital now."

The terror in her eyes waned and her eyelids grew heavy. She still sat, but struggled to do so, wobbling, seeming dizzy and visibly weak. "I have to go back," she said in a pleading whisper. "Please, let me go back."

That request gave Tess pause. Why would she possibly want that? Was she protecting someone? "Would you like to sleep some more? I'll keep watch," she offered. "I promise, I won't leave your side."

"No!" Panicked, Kiana jumped off the bed, landing barefoot on the cold floor. The IV stand toppled over the bed despite the nurse's attempt to catch it in time. "Don't drug me!" she shouted, looking around desperately like a trapped animal searching for a way out.

"You're okay," Tess said calmly, taking her hand. "We won't drug you." Kiana looked at her with pleading eyes. "I swear, no drugs," Tess added. "Here, let's take a seat on this bed, shall we?" She cringed, hearing herself speak to her as if she were a child. That's not how Cat had spoken to her twelve years ago. That's not how he'd gained her trust.

But Kiana followed Tess and sat on the edge of the bed obediently. "I have to go back," she said wearily, her eyes half-closed already. She allowed the nurse to ease her back on the pillow without putting up much of a fight. But that docility ended the moment the nurse tried to cover her with the blanket. "No," she said, pushing the blanket away and tugging at her gown.

"All right, no, it is," Tess said, giving the nurse a quick look. The woman stepped back, looking at her in disbelief. She seemed ready to call someone to have Tess thrown out of the room and her patient sedated into oblivion. "But promise me, if you're cold, you'll tell me, okay?"

"No blanket," she whispered. "You don't understand. I have to go back. Let me go."

"Yes," Tess replied gently, and the nurse's eyebrows went promptly up. "Of course, we'll let you go. You're free. This is a hospital. You leave when you want, or when you feel better. Your choice."

Her words made the girl open her eyes slightly and whisper, "Thank you."

Tess didn't expect to hear that but welcomed it as a sign that she was reaching her. "Why do you want to go back?" she asked. Kiana didn't reply, just stared at her with a haunted look. "What are you afraid of?"

The girl closed her eyes and shook her head slightly, the silent answer to Tess's question. Whatever was haunting her, driving her to return to the hell where she'd escaped from, she wasn't ready to share.

Not giving up, Tess squeezed her hand again and asked, "Do you know who you are?"

Kiana nodded slightly. "I—um, yeah." The whisper was barely audible, weak, hesitant as if she wasn't really sure, but Tess didn't insist. The question she'd asked brought a new wave of sadness on the girl's face.

"How long were you gone? Do you know?"

A tear streaked her cheek and stained the pillow cover. That was her only answer.

Tess waited a moment, but only the low hum of electronics disturbed the silence of the room. "You were gone for seven months. What happened to you all this time?"

9

CELEBRATION

Seven Months Ago

I didn't know people could be so happy.

It was scary. It felt that way, just for a split second.

The thought crossed my mind in a rare moment of lucidity, when I took a short break from what had been months of all-consuming bliss. I still remember that instance, when I was waiting for David to get the valet to bring the car around after our celebratory dinner at *Forte dei Marmi.* We had dined *al fresco,* right by the patio's entrance, and I didn't want the evening to end. I stayed behind, still seated at the table, playing absentmindedly with the seam of the impeccably white linen tablecloth, enjoying the moment. Our dinner had been perfect, the loveliest of celebrations for a major achievement. My TV show, *Swamp Secrets,* was going national. Starting with the next season, it was going to be picked up by a major syndication network. I was, finally, breaking into the major league of documentary television with a hefty serving of reality vibe on the side.

That's what *Swamp Secrets* is, really. Documentary meets reality TV, each episode highlighting a different species from the Everglades and the people who interact with it. Who hunt it to survive or to defend their homes from predators. Who breed it, harvest it, farm it, or, like me, are just passionate about it and want to share their passion with the viewers.

I'd done little else earlier that day other than sign the paperwork the station had piled in front of me, their legal rep smiling unctuously the entire time she shuffled the papers for my quick and effective convenience. Yes, I signed my name on each dotted line. Yes, I agreed to go national. Of course, I did. Yes, I agreed to bring the secrets of the Florida Everglades ecosystem to everyone's living room. Yes, I was so thrilled about it I couldn't stop grinning. When we were finally done signing, I went home and paced the floor in an exhilarated state of agitation until David's key turned the lock.

We've been married for almost three years, after a short and passionate dating period that barely lasted a few months, mainly until we both graduated from college. I took biology, with a major in plant ecology, and he took software engineering, with a major in project management. Worlds apart, but none of that mattered. He's perfect for me, reserved and calmly giving me space to be myself, yet always there, willing to try something new if I wanted. I fell hard and fast and totally, and the day he made me his wife was the happiest I'd ever lived.

Still at the table waiting for the valet, I was reflecting on how different we are, David and me. He's methodical, reserved, rather shy, and painstakingly calm about things, while I, the tomboy who grew up like a swamp wildflower with my adventurer father, am nothing like that. Exuberant and a risk-taker, gutsy and restless, I turned my passionate love for nature and adventure into a career.

By the time I turned twenty-three, I had my own TV show, running on an obscure, local station with very few viewers. It wasn't anything much, but I was thrilled. For about a year or so I had no idea how I'd managed to land that gig, until my producer, Martin Stone, shared that he met me one time when I was fishing by Plantation Island with my dad. I didn't remember it; not at first. He was new to the area back then, a transplant from New York City, and had been on the water all day with nothing to show for it. That's when I happened to pass by in a small boat with my dad. I gave him some pointers and shared my bait. He caught a big redfish within minutes, while we were still chatting. And I caught an agent's call about a year later, and that call changed my life.

And then, four years into the show, came the news of syndication, the heap of signed papers, and the fabulous dinner at *Forte dei Marmi* in Miami Beach, with its mouthwatering branzini and the delicious tiramisu served with a small glass of Armagnac.

Then that bothersome thought, like an alarm signal pulled by fate, a heads-up that happiness is so fragile, so easy to tear apart like a piece of luscious satin, then slip away between my fingers, no matter how desperately I try to grasp at it and hold on for a heartbeat longer.

Yes, people shouldn't be that happy. It's scary, the thought of falling from such heights.

I didn't pay attention back then. I should have, but I just willed the blood-chilling warning away and smiled at my husband who invited me to join him at the curb, where the valet had pulled our Jeep.

I walked over with a spring in my step, despite the high heels and uncomfortably tight skirt. We were dressed for the occasion, but we'd driven over in my vehicle, an all-outfitted Jeep Wrangler with all the bells and whistles that go with what I do for a living. Oversized tires. Light bars. Suspension lifts that made it incredibly hard for me to climb into the passenger seat without ripping the side slit of my skirt all the way up. As it usually happens, my Jeep, painted in camo colors and lit up like a Christmas tree, got a small group of people to gather near the valet desk, chatting, pointing fingers, touching the gritty finish of its push bar.

"Hey," one patron asked, "aren't you the swamp girl?" He was a bulky guy in his fifties, with a red face covered in sweat beads and a stalky blonde hanging on his arm, at least six inches taller than he was.

Boy, was I ever, and then some. National syndication. I grinned and nodded, then waved at him as David pulled away from the curb, heading for the shore.

David squeezed my hand as he drove. "Happy?"

That pang of fear stabbed me again, but I smiled. "With you? Always." Then I rested my head on his shoulder for a moment, while he circled the parking lot at the South Pointe Park, looking for an empty spot.

I left my heels in the Jeep and chose to walk barefoot to the beach. The plan was to stroll down the pier, maybe spend some time sitting on a boulder and watching the moon rise over the waves lapping the shore. David loosened his tie, then, after a moment's hesitation, he pulled it over his head and sent it flying onto the Jeep's back seat, followed immediately by his jacket. Then he took my hand, and we started walking toward the pier, under the thick, touching crowns of a row of live oaks. Patches of silver moonlight lit the asphalt occasionally, lighting our way, a picture-perfect night of whimsical serenity.

We stopped briefly for a passionate kiss. Melting in his arms, I wondered if we shouldn't go home instead and seal the evening making love. David had that power over me, to make me forget everything I wanted to do and just wish to be with him instead.

But he pulled away gently, breathless, still holding my hand, and said, "Shall we?" I smiled, and for some reason, hid my smile from him, the loaded thrill that made my breath shallow and my heartbeats fast. If he could wait a bit longer, so could I, knowing well the wait was going to be well worth it.

"Excuse me," a man's voice interrupted my thoughts. He'd pulled alongside us in a small, beat-up van and had put his head out the driver-side window, smiling apologetically. "Do you know where the boat ramp is? This jalopy doesn't come with GPS." As he spoke, he tapped against the van's door with his open hand. The sound echoed strangely in the dark silence of the deserted parking lot, bringing a chill down my spine.

"No, but we'll figure it out," David replied, pulling out his phone. He was always like that, eager to help, a kind, selfless soul. "Let's see here," he said, flipping through screens until he displayed a map of the area. I put my head close to his, looking at the screen, eager to find where the ramp was, so the stranger could be on his way.

I didn't see the blow coming.

I've been obsessively going over it in my mind, to no end. I don't know when he got out of that piece of crap van or how I could've been so absorbed into looking at the phone to not see the tire iron rising, then hitting David in the back of his head. As if life was playing in slow motion, I remember hearing the sound of metal hitting bone, the heart-stopping crack in his skull, the fine mist of sprayed blood, then the thud of his body falling to the ground. I drew air and opened my mouth to scream, but then my head exploded into a million green stars and the asphalt rushed to meet me.

Almost unconscious, I felt the stranger's hands grabbing me, lifting me, then throwing me inside the van. I landed over David's inert body, the smell of his blood filling my nostrils with a metallic scent and my heart with unspeakable fear. I tried to scream, but only a whimper came out.

Then everything went dark.

10

QUESTIONS

"Why the hell am I hearing about this now?"

Tess pushed aside her laptop with a brusque gesture. The computer slid on the table until it came to a stop, inches away from hitting Fradella's.

They were huddled in one of the small training rooms, on the same floor with Kiana's room. It smelled of stale disinfectant and pine-based cleaning solutions. The weak fluorescent light fixtures above head flickered at times, one lamp yellowish at one end and showing signs of imminent death.

The hospital accommodated their request for a place where they could set up, and that was it. Twenty chairs faced a small table, and a whiteboard was hung on the wall behind it. The windows, as dark as the early morning overcast sky, lit with occasional streaks of red and white whenever an ambulance pulled into the emergency room access downstairs.

They'd been poring over the case details since Kiana finally fell asleep for the night. At first, Tess suspected the nurse had mixed a bit more sedative in her IV, even if the girl had specifically requested no more sedation. But hospitals honored the patients' requests when it came to administering care and medication. So maybe the nurse hadn't sedated her. Perhaps Kiana's exhaustion had eventually burned through the adrenaline, and she'd fallen asleep at last. An agitated, nightmare-ridden slumber, haunted by the horrors of her past, but still healing and much-needed after seven months of hell.

Tess had watched over her just like she'd promised. After a while, seeing she wasn't waking up, she found a senior hospital administrator and secured the small training room for her, Fradella, and Michowsky to start working on Kiana's case. The hospital brought sandwiches and soda, and a Keurig coffeemaker with a few doses of much-needed caffeine.

"What are you talking about?" Michowsky looked at her with a confused gaze under a ruffled brow. He took off the glasses he wore when he worked on his computer and rubbed his eyes thoroughly, probably to scare off the tiredness written all over his face.

"She's married to a David Bayliss, thirty-one," she replied, aware of how frustrated her voice sounded. "I'm saying, we should've probably known she went missing with her husband, but only Kiana was found. Don't you think? And where the hell is this David Bayliss?"

"Let me see," Michowsky approached, looking at the screen. Then he tapped with the tip of his index finger where the officer taking the report had entered his name. "Officer Tate. I know this guy, fresh out of the academy last year, just a kid. He probably didn't know any better. He filed two reports for two different persons instead of one for both." He scoffed and shook his head. "Greenhorn mistake."

"The husband wasn't listed in Kiana's missing person report?" Fradella asked. Out of the three of them, he seemed to fare the best, as if lack of sleep did nothing to the young, energetic rookie. It was his first case as a federal agent. Tess hid her smile when she recalled her first days as an FBI special agent; she was so excited to be finally working her own case, she could've gone without sleep for a week.

Tess pulled the laptop closer and looked at the screen, scrolling through the pages of Kiana's missing person report. The husband's name was there, buried in some description of where she was last seen. The officer who took the report was probably a fan of Kiana's, focusing entirely on her disappearance and not her husband's. But Tess had missed it also, and for that, there was no excuse.

"Damn it," she muttered, reading the notes on the missing person case again. "This changes things. We have to look at this differently." She ran her hand through her hair, pulling the scrunchie that held it tied neatly in a bun and rubbing her scalp until she felt the tiredness lift off her brain like fog under the early morning sun. "You take the case notes," she told Fradella, "and I'll go through witness statements."

"How?" Fradella asked.

"Huh?"

"Why does it change things?"

"It's obvious," she said, a little impatient and somewhat uncomfortable with her role as a mentor. But Fradella waited patiently, and she steadied herself. She had learned these things too, and back when she started, Bill McKenzie had been graceful about it, supportive, a true mentor. "It's one thing to kidnap a woman, even if she's an outdoor adventurer and fit. Still, she could've been easily overpowered. It's an entirely different ballgame to snatch a man in good physical shape, six-two, buck-eighty-five. Grabbing both without anyone seeing or hearing anything, from a busy Miami street? Damn near impossible." She pressed her lips together, wishing there was still some coffee left in her cup. "This isn't the unsub's first rodeo." She sat with a groan and started reviewing the case file again, careful with every tiny detail.

"And that's exactly why I called for you," Michowsky grinned. "Where do you want me? How can I help?"

"Can you please find out when is Kiana's doctor due back? I want to speak with her first thing."

Michowsky left the room with a crooked gait he was trying his best to hide. Silence took over the dreary room, while Tess read through the witness statements affixed to the case.

Kiana had last been seen having dinner at the *Forte dei Marmi*, an upscale place in Miami Beach. Her husband's credit card was swiped there at 9:42 P.M. Witnesses recalled the couple's fancy Jeep and had more to say about the vehicle's accessories than the state of mind of its driver and passenger. One witness recalled how Kiana was dressed, in a long, shimmering, blue-satin dress tight on her hips and a high slit on her thigh. Of course, he remembered that. The higher the slit, the more accurate the witness's account of the victim's attire, and that was the rule for most witnesses and most victims. Such a detail made people pay attention, letting their gaze linger for a bit instead of just mindlessly wandering away.

Tess flipped through several pages and found the linked report for Kiana's husband, David Bayliss, from South Miami. He was a handsome man in the photo attached to the case file, with blue eyes and light brown hair combed back sideways over a tall forehead. Tax records showed him employed as a software engineer for a downtown bank. The reports had been filed by David's parents and Kiana's father.

Tess scrolled back to the beginning of the record, where a photo of Kiana filled the screen. She remembered her vaguely from television, although Tess wasn't the least bit interested in the type of show she was hosting. Outdoors life in the Glades was the stuff of nightmares for Tess; she couldn't bring herself to understand why people would choose to live there, surrounded by myriad critters who could kill a human being in under a minute. But Kiana smiled widely in the picture attached to her file, a photo her family must've brought with them. It was taken on the set of her show, while she was talking with a bulky man covered in tattoos, a snake hunter by the looks of it. He held a large boa by the neck with a strong, steeled grip, and the snake's body hung listless, coiled at his feet. Kiana had a spark in her eyes, seeming her entire body relished being there, doing her job. She wasn't just hosting a TV show about the Florida Everglades and being reasonably good at it. She was thriving.

"Interesting," Tess muttered. "Maybe that's why she survived."

Fradella looked up from the screen of his computer. "What do you mean?"

Tess hesitated for a moment. "Kiana knows the Glades inside and out. Unlike most women, she's not afraid of the habitat. She loves it, understands it. Knows how to survive in it."

"You're saying otherwise she would've been dead?"

"I don't know what I'm saying," Tess smiled awkwardly. "It's just my gut." He kept looking at her, visibly interested. "On one hand, the unsub was skilled and bold enough to snatch two people without leaving a trace of evidence or a witness. On the other hand, you have Kiana, who resurfaced after seven months, alive but severely malnourished. What if there were others? And where the hell is her husband?"

A quick rap against the door disrupted Tess's thoughts. The door opened and a tall brunette walked in. She carried a manila folder under her left arm. "I'm Dr. DiDomenico, Kiana's attending." She held her hand out, and Tess gave it a quick squeeze. "You have questions?"

Michowsky entered the room and closed the door, then leaned against the wall. He seemed a little out of breath. Tiny beads of sweat covered his forehead. He'd probably struggled a little to keep up with the slender physician.

"Thanks for stopping by," Tess said, inviting her to sit with a hand gesture. The woman remained standing. "I need to understand what this girl went through. What kind of injuries, how severe, how old, and if there's anything unusual about her wounds, something we could use to narrow down our search."

"She's still not talking, is she?" the doctor asked. Tess shook her head. "I'm not surprised. I don't anticipate she'll talk anytime soon." Dr. DiDomenico set the folder on the table and opened it. "We were able to take some photos of her wounds, before she became more grounded in reality and refused to let us examine her anymore." She flipped through a few pages of handwritten notes, then pointed at some photos, detailed, close-up images of Kiana's wounds. "This is a puncture wound of unknown origin," she pointed with a perfectly manicured fingertip at a photo showing a round scar. "On her left thigh. Seems to be at least three or four months old. It was made by a sharp, penetrating object with ragged edges. There was a corresponding exit wound on the other side of her leg."

"A through-and-through bullet?" Fradella asked.

The doctor shook her head. "I don't think so. You see these jagged edges here? That's not what a bullet hole looks like."

"Then what was it?" Tess asked.

"I'm not sure. I haven't seen anything like it in all my years of practice in an emergency room."

Tess gave the doctor a scrutinizing look. She didn't seem old enough to cite all her years of practice; she was probably still working through her residency rotations. It was time to call Dr. Rizza.

"This is a snakebite," she pointed at another image. "Three of them, actually. Clustered together."

"Multiple snakes?" Michowsky asked, raising his eyebrows.

"One snake, multiple bites," she replied confidently. "There's no rule that says a snake cannot bite more than once. That's a common misconception. Most snakes bite as many times as they want until they feel safe from the threat." She traced the pattern of healed puncture holes with the tip of her finger. "See here? Same bite pattern, same jaw width. Same snake."

"Venomous?" Tess asked, repressing a shudder.

"It's been a while, but the tissue doesn't show signs of past necrosis, so I'd venture an educated guess and say, most likely no. Three envenomation bites by a common venomous Glades snake like the water moccasin or the diamondback rattler could've killed her in the absence of proper emergency care and antivenom administration."

"Anything more recent?" Tess asked, looking at the images the doctor fanned out on the table. They told a harrowing tale.

"In a minute," she replied, stopping on a close-up of Kiana's feet. "You should see this first. There are some rat bites on her feet and a recent black widow bite, still darkening her skin. And the soles of her feet are a mess of splinters, burrs, and cuts, as if she spent months walking barefoot through the Glades. How long was she missing?"

"Seven months," Michowsky replied. "But she was wearing boots when we found her."

The doctor bit her lip and didn't say anything. Instead, she flipped through her folder and extracted two more photos. One showed Kiana's wrists, covered in rope burns and scars. The other one, her ankles, bearing similar ligature marks. "She was repeatedly bound, tightly, her blood flow restricted. I can tell you she fought against these restraints until she split her skin open. You see this pattern here, under her thumbs? It's very likely her hands were bound like this," she demonstrated bringing her wrists together as if she wore handcuffs, "then she was hung from the rope, her own weight causing these rope burns here and here," she punctuated with her finger.

Tess looked at the photos, visualizing Kiana's ordeal with every single image. "And this?" She pointed at a close-up of Kiana's arm.

"This is fairly recent," Dr. DiDomenico replied. "Another through-and-through puncture wound with ragged edges. But here, we see clearly there's a triangular pattern to the edges of the wound."

"An arrow," Tess whispered. "A broadhead, large game arrow." She clenched her teeth until her jaws hurt. "The son of a bitch is a hunter."

Silence took over the room for a moment, while Dr. DiDomenico stared at Tess with her mouth slightly gaping. Then she collected her photos and closed the folder. "I don't envy you," she said quietly, "and the job you do. The things you see."

"When do you think she'll want to talk to us about what happened?" Tess asked half-heartedly. She already knew the answer; if Kiana was anything like her, that would be never. She would never willingly talk about what happened.

"Scans didn't find any brain trauma. Physiologically, she's fine, and she should remember. I believe I mentioned this before to your colleague," she gestured toward Michowsky, who nodded. "Psychologically, that's a different story. She might not be able to remember what happened until she's strong enough to handle the trauma."

"When can she be discharged?"

"She's not in any immediate danger. Hydration remains a priority, and her electrolytes are still out of balance. But I'd like to keep her under observation for at least another forty-eight hours, make sure she gets plenty of fluids." She looked intently at the closed folder in her hand as if something were written on its cover. "Is she able to care for herself? Feed herself?" Tess didn't reply, just lowered her eyes. "I'd rather she stays with us a while longer."

They shook hands again, and Dr. DiDomenico left. The door whooshed to a close in her wake, bringing a whirlwind of questions to Tess's mind. One question rose above all others with the power of an unfinished thought, of a moment's sudden panic.

"Is her husband still alive?"

11

ASSUMPTIONS

The sun pierced the stuffy air in the room, peeking over the horizon and through the double-paned window. Tess squinted and rubbed her eyes, then resumed reading the missing person case notes.

Fradella stood and turned off the ceiling lights. The low hum disappeared, leaving the room perfectly silent. Distant, muted PA announcements were starting to gnaw at that silence more and more frequently.

"They did a good job working this case," Tess said, a hint of disappointment in her voice. She'd hoped she could find something they missed, something she could use.

"Who? The Miami-Dade detectives?" Fradella asked.

"Yeah."

Michowsky stood and stretched, propping his hands on his hips and leaning back. His spine cracked loudly, earning him a raised eyebrow from Tess.

He shook his head. "Old age," he quipped, feigning amusement badly. Tess could see the tension in his mouth, the poorly masked grimace of pain still lingering on his face after he'd got up from his chair. "But don't let me hear you repeat that to anyone."

"Your secret's safe with me," Tess replied. "But since we're in a hospital, you might want to make some friends in the orthopedics department."

He waved her off with a hand gesture. "Some other time."

"Okay," she conceded, knowing Michowsky too well to assume his stubbornness might've somehow disappeared since the last time they'd locked horns. Maybe it was an issue with men of a certain age. They just got stuck, in their beliefs, in the way they did things and looked at life and handled everyday challenges, not realizing the damage they did to themselves and others. But Tess wasn't Michowsky's therapist; his back pain wasn't the reason she'd been up all night, staring at computer screens. "Let's revisit what we know about Kiana and her husband."

"I looked into David's background," Michowsky offered, visibly relieved Tess had moved on from the subject of his arthritis. "He's a software engineer, and married Kiana almost four years ago, three at the time of their disappearance. He was born and raised in Dade County and met Kiana in college. They both went to South Florida."

"Crime scene?" Tess asked. "What do we know?"

Fradella pulled his laptop closer and leaned forward. "David's parents filed the missing person report the following evening, when the couple failed to show up for a family dinner. Kiana's father was there too. When they couldn't reach either of them, they made a few calls and learned neither Kiana nor David had shown up for work that morning." He flipped through some screens. "Dade County cops found their Jeep in the South Pointe Park parking lot."

"Evidence?"

"Nothing. David's jacket and tie were found on the Jeep's back seat, soaked." He checked his notes quickly. "A pair of high-heel shoes were also found in the car. But that's where the trail ends. It rained heavily that night, erasing everything, even their footsteps after leaving the Jeep."

"How do we read this?" Tess asked.

Michowsky frowned a little, seemingly confused for a bit. "They weren't pulled out of the car by force, that's for sure," the detective replied. "The guy takes off his jacket and tie, and the wife her shoes, that's a no-brainer. They went for a walk on the beach."

"Sometime between 9:42 P.M., when they paid for their dinner with credit, and 1:07 A.M., when weather services said the rain started," Fradella said. "They left their Jeep topless," he added quickly. "It's in the notes; it was a fast-moving storm."

"And that's where the trail ends," Tess said with a long sigh. She stood and started pacing the room. "Dade police tried everything. They had a K9 unit deployed, but after the heavy rain, the dog couldn't pick up any scent. They tried to locate their phones, and both were offline. So was Kiana's watch and fitness tracker. Those phones were never turned on since."

She stopped and looked out the window, not seeing the warm colors of morning reflected in the distant ocean waters. Something was nagging her, an annoying little thought bouncing around in her mind like a mosquito buzzing when trying to get some shuteye.

"Family dinner in the middle of the week?" she asked. "*Forte Dei Marmi* dinner the night before? Do we know what was going on? Was that their habitual lifestyle?"

"No," Fradella replied. "David's mother, Linda Bayliss, said in her statement they were celebrating. Kiana's TV show was going national. It's kind of a big deal."

Tess held her hands in the air. "Stop for a second." She walked around the table until she reached the whiteboard on the wall, then picked up a marker. "Let's start jotting down what we know." As she scribbled, the marker made squeaking noises on the whiteboard and filled her nostrils with the pungent smell of its ink. "He disposed of two expensive phones, latest models, and a six-hundred-dollar watch."

"What if he changed SIM cards?" Michowsky asked.

Tess refrained from smiling. The Broward County detective hadn't kept up with the latest in device monitoring.

"They could still track the devices, the moment they get powered on. New technology," she added. "I believe we can assume the unsub is smart and forensically astute. He might also be financially comfortable."

"You mean, rich?" Fradella asked.

"I mean, all we know is he didn't feel compelled to risk getting caught by selling the hot devices on the black market to make next month's rent. Destitute unsubs have a certain pattern of behavior we're not seeing here."

"Got it," he replied.

"Miami-Dade detectives encountered a whale of a problem, and we are nowhere near solving it. Where did the unsub cross paths with the victim?" She turned her laptop around so that the two men could see the screen. It was playing an episode of *Swamp Secrets.* "Anybody could've seen this. Anyone out there. There's no tracking down the victim's last few days to try to figure out where the unsub saw her and decided she was the one worth taking. There's no real way to profile the unsub geographically, because we simply don't know if he didn't choose her by watching her show."

"But you're assuming the unsub targeted Kiana, not David?" Fradella asked.

"I'm one hundred percent positive about that," she replied calmly. "All evidence in support of my assessment is written in scars on Kiana's body. We're dealing with a sexual predator, a hunter, and a torturer. He's bold enough to grab his targeted victim, even if he didn't catch her alone, and skilled enough to do it in the middle of Miami Beach and not leave a trace of evidence or a single witness."

"And David Bayliss?" Michowsky asked. "What do you think happened to him?"

A chime coming from her phone interrupted her before she could answer. It was her seven o'clock alarm. "I want to be there when she wakes up," Tess said, rushing out the door.

12

HANDS

When Tess reached Kiana's room, Dr. DiDomenico was already inside, talking with her. From a distance, the girl seemed stronger than the day before, more determined, more lucid.

Fradella and Michowsky caught up with her, but something on their faces told her they had bad news. "What happened?"

Fradella showed her his phone. The screen displayed a newscast airing on a local TV station. He turned the volume up as Tess watched in disbelief.

"Formerly missing TV host Kiana Mallery Bayliss was not available for comment. Sources close to her stated she's being treated for injuries and dehydration at Mercy Hospital. The same sources stated that the FBI has now taken over the investigation that had led to zero viable suspects in the past seven months since Kiana, twenty-seven, and her husband David Bayliss, thirty-one, were taken from a Miami Beach parking lot. Stay tuned for the latest in this developing story."

"Damn it to bloody hell," Tess snapped. "How the hell did this happen? I wish I could get my hands on that source." She forced a deep breath into her lungs, then released it slowly. "Let's get Miami-Dade Police to double her detail. As of right now, the unsub knows where she is. My guess is he'll do anything in his power to keep her from talking."

A couple in their sixties approached from the elevators, holding hands tightly as if to encourage each other to take a few more steps. Tess watched them curiously, a little wary of their presence, as if no one else had any business being on that hallway. The two walked right past Tess and the two men, not paying any attention to them.

The woman had been crying. Tears still stained her cheeks, overflowing from her red and swollen eyes. The man, tall and seeming vaguely familiar, kept his lips pressed tightly together and supported the woman's arm under the elbow, his fingers intertwined with hers in a white-knuckled grip.

They stopped in front of Kiana's room and approached the uniformed cop guarding her door with hesitant steps. The cop firmed his stance and reached for his sidearm as if to check it was still there.

"Do you know if they found our son?" the man asked. His voice was breaking despite his straight back and determined facial expression.

The cop shook his head. "No, I'm sorry. Not that I know." Then he shot Tess a quick glance.

She approached, flashing her badge. "Special Agent Winnett, FBI." The two turned to face her with the light of hope in their eyes. From up-close, she recognized David's features in the white-haired man standing in front of her. "Are you David's parents?"

The woman nodded. "Yes. Have you found him?"

"We're still investigating," Tess replied, hating herself for giving such a heartless, cliché answer. Truth was always better. "So far, we didn't—" She stopped talking when she noticed movement inside Kiana's room and turned to watch.

Transfixed, the girl stared at her in-laws for a breathless moment, then slid off the bed and started walking toward the door. The IV tugged at her arm, but she removed the needle without hesitation and slid the door open before her attending could stop her.

Mrs. Bayliss started sobbing and opened her arms to welcome Kiana. "Oh, sweetie… what happened to you?"

Kiana dropped to her knees and raised her arms in an imploring gesture. "Please, please, forgive me," she cried. "It was my fault. Mine… and now, I can't do anything—" she gasped, looking at her hands with an expression of disgust on her face. "Please," she whimpered, curling up on the floor at their feet.

David's mother stared at her with her hand over her gaping mouth. Tears flowed on her face silently. Mr. Bayliss crouched down and reached for Kiana's hand. The moment he touched her, she flinched.

"No! Don't touch me," she said, pulling away and staring at the back of her hand. "You don't know what I've done," she sobbed, still curled up on the floor. "You don't know. Don't… don't touch me."

Tess glanced at Dr. DiDomenico quickly, expecting her to intervene. She was watching the scene carefully and held her hand up in a calming gesture when she caught Tess's eye, urging her to let the scene play out.

"Tell us what happened to David," Mr. Bayliss asked gently, his gaze on her loaded with infinite sadness and pity. "We need to know, hon. Just… tell us."

Kiana looked at them briefly then lowered her head and winced as if the demons she was battling had landed a deathly blow. "I can't tell you. How can I tell you? No… no… please, don't make me."

Mrs. Bayliss let out a heart-wrenching wail. Her husband wrapped his arms around her. "He's gone," she sobbed, her face buried in his shoulder. "My son is gone."

Kiana didn't show any sign she'd heard her. She stared at the back of her hands as if they weren't hers, studying them, then wiped them against her gown as if they were dirty.

Tess looked at Dr. DiDomenico, who nodded slightly, then approached Kiana and put a firm, reassuring hand on her shoulder. "Let's go," she said, and Kiana looked up at her with fierce, cold determination.

"I have to go back," she said calmly.

Mr. Bayliss crouched down again and took Kiana's hand. This time she didn't pull away. He stared at the scars marking her wrist, then asked, "Tell me, is my son still alive?"

"I'm so sorry," she said, looking at him for a moment while her eyes pooled with tears. "Please, forgive me. I—I had to—" Choked, she gasped for air, bitter sobs strangling her, making her fight for each breath.

David's parents looked at each other for a moment.

"We'll take you home with us," Mrs. Bayliss said, wiping her tears with the back of her hand. "We'll take care of you. And it will be all right, you'll see."

"Where's my daddy?" she asked, her voice tiny, hesitant. "Can he come?"

"Oh, baby," Mrs. Bayliss said, crouching to be on the same level with Kiana and touching her hair with a tentative caress. "Why don't you come home with us? It's your home too."

"I can't," she said, struggling to stand. Her bare feet slipped on the shiny tiles. Her father-in-law helped her up, but she still avoided making eye contact with him, keeping her head hung low. As soon as she was stable on her feet, she let go of Mr. Bayliss's arm and hid her hands behind her back as if to make sure he wasn't going to touch her again. She took a couple of steps back until she bumped into the wall.

Then she looked at Tess with an intensity in her eyes that didn't use to be there before. "You don't understand. You have to take me back where you found me. Now."

13

DAVID

When I came to, the first thing I noticed was David, calling my name in a low whisper. Relief brought tears to my eyes and swelled my chest. He was still alive.

Then the bleak reality kicked in.

I was tied to a chair with plastic zip ties so tightly bound they were cutting into my flesh, each wrist secured to a thick wooden armrest. My ankles were bound to the chair legs, so rigidly I couldn't move an inch. David sat a few feet away from me, bound in a similar fashion. Terror rose in my chest and came off my lips in a breathless whimper, the intensity of it written in my eyes and reflected back in David's panicked gaze.

Then I looked around.

It was morning. While I was out of it, the sun had come up, sending its low rays through a small window stained with years of collected dust and grime. It lit a dreary room with wooden floors that had never been swiped clean, at least not in recent years. The rotted floorboards were covered in layers of stains and grime, and the occasional insect wandered aimlessly by.

Behind David's chair, an old worktable on uneven, jaggedly sawed two-by-fours was free of any objects and far less dusty than the rest of the things in the room, as if it had been used recently. A reddish-brown stain covered its edge, the shape of it seeming to point to a liquid that once had dripped from that edge onto one of the worktable legs.

It looked like dried blood.

The thought made me shudder. I remember how I noticed that worktable that day, not knowing then its purpose. It just stood out, a clear surface among heaps of rusted tools and discarded items.

The one thing that stood out the most about that table was a flower, so out of place in that bleak room. It was a freshly picked daisy, still crisp and white with a bright yellow center, stemless, set flat on the table near the center. Somehow, the sight of it brought a shiver down my spine.

"What do we do?" I whispered, looking at David.

He looked at the crooked door for a moment. It was still shut. The place was eerily silent. Only the distant sounds of the Glades came through the grimy window in a muted concert of croaks and chirps.

Without a word, David started throwing his weight to the side, trying to get his chair to tilt. It didn't budge that easily; it was massive and probably too heavy, but it started tipping to the side more and more with each of his awkward strains. With an uncanny sense of balance and rhythm, he leaned to one side and then the other, his body swaying in sync with the chair. A visible grimace distorted his features as he drove the chair toward the tipping point. With a final, gut-wrenching lurch, he sent the chair pitching dangerously to the side, every muscle in his body tensed in anticipation of the impending crash.

He landed hard on his side and pulled against his ties, hoping the chair had broken under his weight. But it was intact, just as solid as it was before.

Then the door opened, and the man I still remembered loading us into his beat-up van entered, stomping heavily in mud-stained boots.

"Nice try," the man said, stopping inches away from David's face. "You ain't going nowhere," he announced matter-of-factly with a chuckle that gargled in the back of his throat like a growl.

He was in his mid-thirties and exuded an air of sheer power and intensity that was terrifying. I didn't remember noticing that when he'd stopped to ask for directions, but in the light of our current situation I was paying attention closely. His muscular body bore the unmistakable marks of an active, intensely physical lifestyle, his arms strong enough to crush me with one blow. His rugged features were weathered, and his skin touched by the elements, tanned and lined by sun and wind. His hair was short but unkempt, and his beard was trim but appeared clumpy. I'd seen his type before, in the prize-seeking snake hunters of the Florida Glades, often guests on my show. But had I seen *him* before?

I couldn't tell.

He wore cargo pants in a camouflage pattern and a faded gray T-shirt, the typical attire of swamp dwellers, even when they were featured on my show. He didn't have any ink on his arms or neck, as much as I could see. I wasn't entirely sure, but almost all the snake hunters I'd met before had lots of tats. This man didn't. So maybe I hadn't seen him before.

Dark, merciless eyes sized me up, then turned to David with a glint of hatred. Effortlessly, he righted David's chair with him still bound to it. "Don't try this again."

I couldn't see David's face. The man stood between us with his back at me, towering over David in a menacing way.

Then the man turned toward me with a crooked, loaded grin. "Now, what have we here?" He walked around me while I held my breath, trembling under his lusting scrutiny. Then he stopped at my side and touched my face with calloused fingers smelling of stale tobacco.

I flinched, recoiling from his touch with a whimper and turning my head away from him. "No."

The word I uttered in despair made him laugh heartily. He toyed with a strand of my hair, tracing the length of it from roots to ends, twirling it around his fingers, all this time looking at me with an intense gaze I couldn't escape. It reminded me of a snake, the petrifying stare a cottonmouth gives its prey before it lunges and delivers the fatal venom. I couldn't look away, couldn't breathe, couldn't move.

"Take your hands off my wife, you son of a bitch," David snapped, pulling against his restraints.

The man turned at him. "Or what, huh?" A lopsided grin stretched his mouth. "You gonna cuss me to death?"

"You're a damn coward, that's what you are," David said. "Let me out of this chair and fight me like a real man."

I could see the man's jaws clenching. I wished David could shut up and not rile him up anymore. It only made things worse. David was just as desperate as I was, probably even worse, his powerlessness drowning his reason.

But the man didn't punch David. He just focused all his attention on me. For an endless moment, he arranged my hair, studying me as if he was trying to achieve a certain look. Then his fingers started moving lower, brushing against the silky fabric of my blue evening gown.

"No, please," I whimpered again and pulled away as much as I could.

My efforts made him grin with excitement. "You and I will have a good time, I promise."

I desperately shook my head, without thinking. Panic had taken over every fiber of my being. "No, no, please," I implored. "We have money. We can pay our own ransom. Only don't hurt us."

Another throaty cackle. "You think this is about money? That's a new one." He pulled a knife out of the holster at his belt and twisted it slowly in the air. The serrated blade glinted in the filtered sunlight, turning my blood into ice. "Stop trying to negotiate. You have no power."

Lightning fast, the blade sliced into the fabric of my bodice. I screamed and sobbed loudly, barely aware David was shouting endless threats that meant nothing for our captor.

"Oh," he eventually said, crouching by my side and tracing the hem of my skirt's side split with his fingers. His touch made my bare skin crawl. "You're a shy one, aren't you? You don't want hubby to see what we're doing here?" He grabbed my chin with his fingers and lifted it, forcing me to look at him. "That's why you say no?"

I remember whimpering senseless words, begging him to stop, to let us go. He listened for a while with apparent interest, the glimmer of lust in his eyes still sparking, fueled by my vulnerability. Then he eventually stood and walked over to David, still holding the knife in his hand.

With a lightning-fast move, he stabbed David in the stomach and pulled away, blood dripping from the blade of his knife.

David gasped, his mouth agape, his eyes rounded in unspeakable fear looking at me. I screamed, my shriek turning into a bitter wail.

"No, David, no, please." I sobbed so hard I couldn't breathe, pulling against the restraints senselessly until my wrists bled.

David's eyes, rounded in shock, were fixated on me. Blood gushed from his wound, dripping on the soiled floor.

The man wiped the blade on his pants and put the knife in its holster. Then he looked at me with an indifference in his cold eyes. "Make no mistake. This is all your fault. You didn't want to please me with him present, and I understood. That was your choice, not mine." He looked briefly at David and smirked. "Give or take a few more minutes, and your problem is solved."

"Please," I sobbed, "I'll do anything. We can still save him, please. If you call an ambulance, they could still—" I choked and coughed and struggled to breathe under the pressure of the pain rising from my chest, suffocating and searing. "Please, let him live. I'll do anything, I swear."

"Baby, no," David whispered.

Without another word, the man left and slammed the door behind him.

"No, David, no," I cried. "This can't be happening. You can't leave me. Hang in there." I said all that, but I couldn't think of anything that could happen to save his life. Knowing he was about to die while I watched helplessly was excruciating. I couldn't even touch him, hold him in my arms. I was losing my mind, seeing the pallor starting to discolor his beautiful face, watching the light of his love slowly disappearing from his eyes as life left his body.

I screamed and called for that man to come back, to do something. Then I just sobbed, wails burning my chest from the inside as if my heart was going to break open.

"Listen," David whispered. I held my breath and nodded. "I don't have much time left," he added, bringing a new sob on my lips. "I love you."

"I love you, David," I whispered, barely able to see him through the vale of tears. "I've loved you since the day I met you."

"Be strong," he whispered, as a tear rolled down his face. "I've always loved that about you. Your strength. Your passion for life, for nature, for this godforsaken place." He breathed shallowly and struggled more and more to speak. "You must survive this, you hear me? Kiana, you have it in you to survive, to live. Promise me."

"Uh-huh," I said, unable to articulate words that made sense until I took a deep breath of air. "I promise. I love you, baby, so much." I heaved and struggled to contain my sobs when his breaths started to turn labored, rattling. "I'm right here, David. Right here with you."

Then I started calling his name, over and over.

He never answered me again.

14

No Right

"Where is your husband, Kiana?" Tess asked the moment she closed the hospital room behind them.

Kiana didn't look at her and didn't say a word. She sat on the side of the bed, her hands limp on her lap, her stare vacant. Slowly, she lifted her hands and looked at them, focusing her gaze until her eyes looked alive again, yet shadowed by unspeakable pain. Then she started weeping silently while she stared at her hands as if she were looking for something that wasn't there.

"What happened to David?" Tess asked gently.

Kiana's gaze, more and more focused, turned toward Tess and became steeled. "You had no right. I wasn't breaking the law. I wasn't bothering anyone. Yet cops found it necessary to abduct me, lock me up against my will, and drug me. You're no better than that sick son of a bitch." She hopped off the side of the bed. "Well, this ends now. I'm leaving."

Astounded, Tess considered her options before responding. She couldn't believe the girl didn't want justice for what had been done to her. Yet in some twisted way, it reminded her of herself, all those years ago, when all she cared about was to keep her ordeal a secret. "Please help me catch the man who did this to you," Tess said. "The man who killed your husband." A beat of loaded silence. "You owe David that much."

She lowered her eyes for a moment, then looked back up at Tess. "You don't know what you're talking about. And you don't believe me when I say I must go back." She looked around as if looking for something. "How long have I been here?" A touch of worry streaked her forehead.

"Since yesterday morning," Tess replied. "Do you know how long you have been missing?"

She frowned and looked away, as if ashamed. "You told me that already. Seven months."

Tess nodded. "But do you remember being gone that long?"

She squeezed her eyes shut. A tear escaped from the corner of her eye. She shook her head as if to will it away and wiped it with the back of her hand. "I'm done here. I just need some clothes." She shrugged, her thin shoulders poking through her gown. "Or I'll leave dressed like this. I don't care."

"Let me get you some clothes," Tess offered, touching her arm briefly. She expected her to pull back, but she didn't. She just stood in the middle of the room, seeming lost, confused, as if gathering the strength to go out there and find her way back to the hellhole she'd managed to escape from.

But why? Why would anyone want to go back to the kind of hurt her scarred body proved she'd endured? Was there someone else still captive out there? Was her husband still alive?

And if she wanted to go back so badly, why wasn't she storming out the door already? Why wasn't she making a run for it? Maybe it was the meds, or perhaps the recent months of being trapped without escape had eroded her willpower to almost nothing.

Whatever the case, Tess knew she couldn't let Kiana go. Not before she had some answers, some inkling of a chance to find the unsub. If there were others Kiana wanted to go back for, that brought a dire sense of urgency to finding the unsub and his lair.

"If you promise me you won't leave until I get back, I'll bring you some clothes. Some shoes too." Tess searched her eyes. Her stare was vacant again, but the girl nodded. "You're about a size eight?"

Kiana nodded again. "I promise," she whispered.

"Maybe you can take a shower while I find you some clothes," Tess suggested, looking at her clumped hair and mud-smudged skin on her neck.

"Why?" she asked without looking at Tess.

"Only if you wanted to," Tess said, backtracking. "I won't be long."

Kiana sat on the edge of her bed, staring into thin air. A grimace of agony slowly landed on her face. Dissociated, she'd given into her nightmares, haunting memories of her trauma taking a toll.

Tess slipped out of the room, closing the door silently. "Don't let her leave," she told the officer guarding the door.

Then she took a few steps down the corridor to put some distance between her and Kiana's room and pulled out her phone to call Pearson.

"Sir, we have to bring her in," Tess blurted the moment her boss picked up. "We can't let her go."

SAC Pearson let out a loud breath of air. "And by her, you mean Kiana Mallery Bayliss, your victim?"

"Yes, sorry," Tess rushed to apologize. She hadn't called with an update the night before, like she was supposed to. "Let me give you a status on this case."

"Don't bother," he replied coldly. "Fradella did that part of your job for you."

"I see." A moment of tense silence on the phone, while Tess regrouped. "We need to hold her until we get some answers. She refuses to give any information about the unsub."

"Do you have a profile?"

"Based on what?" she snapped, instantly regretting it. "We don't have nearly enough information for a profile. All we know is he was bold enough to grab both of them without leaving any witnesses. This isn't his first kidnapping. Oh, and he's a hunter. That's all I have."

"What about the husband?"

"That's exactly it, sir. Kiana won't say. That's why I need to bring her in. She wants to go back to where she was found, and I'm willing to take her, but I want to question her first."

"Take her back? Are you out of your mind? Since when is traumatizing and endangering victims our standard operating procedure?"

Tess ran her hand through her hair and started pacing the floor anxiously. "If she won't give us anything about the unsub, taking her back to the Glades is one way we could get to him. I just think I can reach her before we have to do that, if only I had a little more time. I believe we're starting to connect."

The tense silence returned for a moment. "Winnett, this woman isn't a lost puppy you get to take home from the pound. She's a victim, an adult citizen with rights, a free person unless there's a warrant issued for her as a material witness in the disappearance of her husband." He cleared his voice and continued, "I'm going to take a leap of faith here and assume you haven't filed any of that paperwork." A beat. "Have you, Winnett?"

Tess bit her lip before answering, steadying herself. "No, sir, but I'm about to."

"Good, you do that. And when the request lands on my desk, I'll give it proper consideration before approving or denying it." Then he ended the call without another word.

That statement sounded too much like a threat for Tess's liking. Pearson could still refuse to sign it. The case had already caught enough media attention to allow them any mistakes, and perhaps Pearson was right to be wary. Tess could see the headlines in her mind. *Surviving victim, freed after a seven-months ordeal, is held without cause by local law enforcement.*

A career killer. For both of them.

But maybe there was another way.

Her next call was to Donovan.

"Hey, D," she greeted him.

"Winnett," he replied gravely. With her analyst, she never knew what mood she'd find him in. "I heard we're chasing another serial killer."

"Who told you that?" Michowsky had voiced his suspicions about the unsub but not in Donovan's presence. In her gut, she felt it was true. She'd refrained to use the words because they didn't have any murder victims and this didn't meet any of the criteria used to classify an offender as a serial killer, except the sadistic nature of Kiana's wounds. Her mentor, Bill McKenzie, had taught her to look beyond the number of victims and see the pathology in the unsub's actions, motivations, and signature.

"Um, no one, just my gut. Are we?" Donovan asked, lowering his voice as if someone was eavesdropping on his calls. "Looking for a serial?"

"Maybe." She rubbed her forehead for a quick moment, gathering her thoughts. "Let's work this as if we were. I need some data."

"Shoot."

"See if anything fits what this unsub could've done if he's really a serial offender. Other missing girls still missing or found dead after being held for a while. Any survivors who match Kiana's story. Any cases involving torture that match this unsub's signature: broadhead arrows, snakebites, rat bites. Let's start there."

"You got it. How do you know the snakebites and rat bites weren't incurred when she fled?"

"It's a safe assumption, because they're not all recent. Oh, and please find out where Kiana's father is. How come he's not here, demanding to take his kid home?"

"On it," Donovan confirmed, then ended the call.

Her next stop was the nurses' station, where she asked to have Dr. DiDomenico paged. The tall woman appeared after a couple of minutes, walking briskly from the elevator bank.

"What can I do for you, Agent Winnett?"

"You were right, Doctor," Tess said, cutting to the chase. "Kiana needs to remain in the hospital for at least another forty-eight hours."

"And?" the doctor asked impatiently with a quick shrug. "I already signed off on that. I don't see a problem."

"She wants to leave. Now."

Dr. DiDomenico pursed her lips and a look of concern washed over her features. "In that case, we must release her. It's unfortunate, yet we can't hold her against her will." Tess looked at the doctor with an unspoken, pleading question in her eyes, challenging her statement, asking for her help. "Um... Not unless she's a danger to herself or others," the attending replied hesitantly.

"I am concerned she could be a danger to herself or others," Tess said with confidence. "She's still in shock after a terrible ordeal. She insists on going back to the place where it all happened, thus endangering herself. Please, Dr. DiDomenico, is there anything we could do to help her?"

"Sure," the doctor replied, sounding a bit more reassured. "We can hold her under the Baker Act. That will give you forty-eight to seventy-two hours to figure out what happens next. Until then, she will be moved to a mental health—"

"Could we keep her here, though? I believe it's important for her well-being to not know her mental faculties are under scrutiny. It might throw her off her precarious balance and make things worse."

The doctor crossed her arms at her chest. "What you're asking me is highly unusual." She seemed to consider options for a moment, and Tess didn't interrupt. "I guess her case is highly unusual too. Let me see what I can do."

Tess thanked the doctor and walked toward the elevators. On the way, she made another call to Donovan.

"Hey, what would it take for us to search the Glades? Figure out how big of an area we'd have to search, starting from where she was found. Use your famous satellites. There must be something you can find. How many people live in that swamp, anyway?"

15

CHARGE

Back in the training room the hospital had provided them as temporary office, Tess watched one of Kiana's *Swamp Secrets* shows. The room smelled of stale pizza, but she found the smell appetizing. Without taking her eyes off the laptop screen where the show was playing, she reached out for the open pizza box. Fradella pushed it her way and she grabbed a slice. It was good. Or maybe she was hungry. She tried to remember when she'd eaten last, but it wasn't relevant.

On the screen, Kiana interviewed several alligator hunters, then explained for the viewers the differences between alligators and crocodiles, and why one was permitted to be hunted, while the other was a protected species. The show host moved freely and leisurely among bearded, brawny men covered in tattoos and dressed as if they'd been sleeping with the gators. She was stunning with her long, silky brown hair with honey highlights, wearing a tight, white tank top and Daisy Dukes with alligator cowboy boots.

"Beauty and the beasts," Tess whispered, taking another bite of pizza.

"I know, right?" Fradella reacted. "She has her crew with her, but it makes you wonder."

"Yep. We need to run background on all the people who appeared on her show before she was taken." She took another bite, regretting the pizza wasn't still warm. "It could've been someone on her show." She patted her lips with a napkin and drank some water, staring at the rugged faces of the hunters appearing on the show. "Hell, it could be any of them."

"Just because they're hunters?" Fradella asked, tossing the empty pizza box into the trash can by the door. "Or the way they look?"

"Looks don't matter at this point. We don't have a composite for the unsub. But these men aren't just hunters. They're Everglades hunters," she replied. "If anyone knows the area and likes it enough to want to live there, this is their profile."

A quick rap against the door, and Donovan entered, carrying a Target shopping bag and his laptop. "Ooh, I smell pizza." He grinned and looked around searching for the source of the smell with excitement in his eyes. His grin instantly vanished when he spotted the empty box in the trash. "Story of my life," he muttered. "Always a little too late."

Fradella shook his hand. "There's more where that came from," he offered. "I can make a call."

"Later." He dropped the shopping bag on the table next to the one Tess had brought a while back, then fired up his laptop. As he was logging in, he looked at Tess briefly. "Kiana's father had a stroke about a month after she vanished. He's in a nursing home."

"Damn," Tess muttered. That girl needed a break, and she wasn't catching any.

"She has her in-laws," Donovan added, shooting Tess another sideways glance. "Pearson said I should mention this to you. He didn't say why."

Of course, he did, Tess thought, stopping short of rolling her eyes.

"She won't go with them," Fradella said. "She seemed unwilling to be left alone with them. I wonder why."

"Guilt," Tess offered. "Over what happened with their son and she's not willing to talk about."

"So you think David Bayliss is dead?" Donovan asked.

"There's no reason to assume otherwise," Tess replied, but still thinking about it. "There's one tiny shred of a chance he's still alive and he's the reason she wants to go back. Yet nothing in her demeanor and her body language speaks to that. There's no real concern or panic. I don't believe that's the case." She circled the table and stopped behind Donovan, where she could see his screen. "All right, show me what you have."

"I have very little about Kiana that could make a difference," Donovan said. "Before she was taken, she lived a low-risk life, if you don't count the critters of the Glades she seems to really like. A very low profile for a television celebrity." He flipped through some screens. "She graduated cum laude from the University of South Florida with a biology degree, and immediately went to work for Big Cypress Wildlife Management. About a year later, she landed her TV gig." He changed the screen to Kiana's Facebook account. "Older photos show her with her father, fishing, hiking, lots of outdoors stuff."

"How about her mother?" Fradella asked.

"She died when Kiana was eight years old."

"Who were the people in her life?" Tess asked. If she had any chance in reaching Kiana, people she cared about could be the key.

"Her husband, of course, and some of her work friends. Her producer, Martin Stone, shows up in a few photos, some with her father. Stone is about the same age as Kiana's dad. I did some background on him; he's a former New Yorker with zero affinity for the outdoors, yet he somehow ended up producing *Swamp Secrets*. Then Kiana's assistant producer, Belinda Santillo, is showing up in lots of girlie pics."

Tess couldn't help a chuckle. "What the hell are girlie pics, D?"

"This stuff." He tapped on the screen with the tip of his finger, while slowly scrolling over a collection of images showing Kiana and a slender, young brunette in all sorts of situations. Laughing while Kiana was having her makeup done on the set. Holding hands before jumping into the water, somewhere on the beach. Eating ice cream from cones topped heavily with whipped cream, their noses dipped in white foam. Seated outdoors at a Starbucks coffee shop, venti cups in front of them. Driving in Kiana's Jeep with the top down, wind blowing in their hair.

A good life, filled with love and friendship and sunshine.

Maybe not all of it was gone.

"She really liked her Glades show," Donovan added. "She was good at it too."

Tess frowned a little. "Did you speak with someone?"

"No, just read the reviews online, and some of her private messages on her Facebook Messenger. I was hoping the unsub stalked her before striking, but there's no sign of that on any of her accounts."

Tess took out her phone to look at the time and frowned. Her battery was almost completely depleted. She plugged it into the wall and grabbed both shopping bags.

"While I do this, let's look at local missing persons who might match Kiana's physiognomy and the manner she was taken. When Michowsky comes back—"

"Where is he, by the way?" Fradella asked.

"I sent him home," Tess replied. "He could barely stand on his feet."

"And he went willingly?"

"I had to twist his arm to the breaking point, but I need him fresh. Both of you. As soon as Donovan has a list of potential matches, you two are going to put in a lot of leg work."

"Yes, ma'am," Fradella replied. Something in his voice caught her attention. Their eyes locked and she saw a glimmer of what she thought she'd lost when he left for Quantico. Long-distance relationships weren't her specialty. Better said, no relationships were her specialty. But the spark she remembered was still there, charging the air between them. A hint of a smile fluttered on Tess's lips before she looked away, heading out the door.

16

UNBEARABLE

Moments later, Tess entered Kiana's room, finding her sitting on the side of the bed as if she hadn't moved in the hours Tess had been gone. A flicker of recognition lit the girl's eyes when she approached, but quicky went away, leaving her gaze blank, expressionless.

Tess set the bags on her bed and started taking out the items she and Donovan had bought, setting them neatly on the bed. From the gift shop she found in the hospital lobby, she'd picked up a light gray, hooded sweatshirt with a full zipper, a pair of sweatpants to match, a white T-shirt, a pair of white socks rolled up in a ball and sealed in rustling cellophane, and some lingerie. The Target bag revealed a pair of white sneakers she laid neatly next to the clothing.

Kiana touched the sweatshirt with her fingers, gently, as if afraid to, and whispered, "Thank you." She wiped a tear from the corner of her eye with a quick hand gesture, then stood by the bed, looking at the clothing items. "The color is all wrong," she said, touching the white fabric, "but it will do."

Wrong? How could white be the wrong color for a T-shirt? Why did color matter? The unvoiced questions brought a frown on Tess's brow. "Should I get you another one? What color would you like?"

"No need," she replied, picking up the panties and the bra with hesitant, slightly trembling fingers. "It's fine."

"Let me give you some privacy," Tess said. Before she could head out the door, Kiana dropped her gown to the floor without reticence and stood perfectly naked, aloof and composed as if her behavior were entirely normal.

Tess froze in place, taken aback by the girl's demeanor. It was as if she didn't care Tess was there, or maybe she didn't want her to leave. She stood by the door, ready to step outside at the slightest indication that Kiana would rather be alone.

Moving quickly and effectively, Kiana dressed herself without making eye contact with Tess. Her stare had gone back to being vacant, although she did, occasionally, focus on what she was doing, when picking a clothing item from the bed or opening the socks' wrapper. Finally, she sat on the bed and put her shoes on, her fingers nimble and quick with the laces.

"Thank you," she repeated. "Now I can go. I'm ready."

"I'm afraid you can't leave just yet," Tess replied gently. "The doctors need to work on you some more. The hospital will hold you two more days." She regretted her choice of words when she saw Kiana's reaction. Regret with a hint of despair, then anger, building slowly but surely behind her blue irises.

"Then what's all this?" she snapped, pointing at her sweatshirt. "Why bother?"

Tess took a couple of steps toward her, but the girl stepped back holding her hand up. She stopped, weighing her options for a moment. "Even if you have to be here for several more days, there's no reason why you couldn't be dressed like a—"

"A normal person? That's what you were going to say?"

"No. I was going to say outpatient." Tess smiled encouragingly. "I'll be here with you, all the way. I promise you."

"The hell you will. I don't care what the hospital has to say. Have you ever heard of getting released AMA? That means against medical advice, and it's perfectly legal." Kiana closed half of the distance between them and faced Tess with her hand propped firmly on her hips. "Thanks for all this," she gestured at her clothes. "If you give me your contact information, I'll send you a check. But I'm leaving now, and you can't stop me."

She tried to move past Tess, but she grabbed the girl's arm, noticing how thin it was under her grip. Kiana whimpered and looked at Tess with fear.

"Yes, I can stop you and I will," Tess replied, speaking as gently as she could, and letting go of her arm. "You're a material witness in the disappearance of your husband. The warrant is on its way."

In a split moment, all the fight vanished from her face. She stood frozen in place, staring at Tess in disbelief. "I'm going to jail?" she whispered, her voice streaked with inflections of panic and despair.

"Or you can stay here instead. This is the best I can arrange for you. You accept treatment and evaluation for two or three more days, and that keeps you out of the FBI interview rooms for a while." She nodded, her head hung low. "And you answer my questions."

Tess looked at Kiana and saw herself twelve years ago, wounded and bleeding and aching with every fiber of her body, in an alternate scenario where she would've been questioned and interviewed to no end by pushy law enforcement, made to share details she never wanted to remember. What she was doing to Kiana was nothing short of heartless, yet the only thing she could do.

Or was it?

For a moment, she was tempted to just tell Kiana she was free to go. Then what would happen? They'd have a next-to-zero chance to catch the unsub, without Kiana's statement, a composite sketch, or any information that could help them narrow down the search. And the unsub could be coming for Kiana, to silence her, to tie up the loose end who got away. She wouldn't be safe out there, by herself.

No, she had no other option but to play hardball with the victim. Sometimes, her job sucked. Other times, it was just plain unbearable.

Tess looked at the girl still standing in front of her, trying to hide how much her heart ached for her. She was slightly trembling as if the temperature in the room had dropped a few degrees. Disheartened, she was staring at the floor, kneading her fingers incessantly.

Tess sat on the edge of the bed and patted the blanket next to her. "Why don't you sit down?"

The girl obeyed without speaking a word or raising her eyes. She folded her hands in her lap and waited.

Before speaking, Tess allowed for a moment of silence to happen. Then, when she asked her first question, she made her voice as gentle as she possibly could.

"Tell me what happened with David."

17

GOODBYE

I must've fainted.

I don't recall when my terrifying reality had turned to oblivious darkness. The sound of a shovel hitting the floor hard with a loud rattle brought me back. The first second of consciousness ripped through my heart and left me gasping for air while a sob suffocated me. I remembered.

David.

He was gone.

His body hung listless, still tied up in the chair, and the man who had taken his life stood silently, watching me trying to get a grip. I was lying on the floor at David's feet. No longer bound to the chair. The skin on my wrists, split open by plastic restraints as I'd fought to free myself, had stopped bleeding.

"Bury him," the man said. I gaped at him in disbelief. "Right now," he added, kicking me in my side with the tip of his boot. The pain knocked the air out of my lungs. "Move it," he ordered, getting ready to kick me again.

I withdrew, pulling myself away from his boots, and stood up shakily, holding on to the table with one hand. It helped if I didn't look at David's body. I couldn't look, not yet. Part of me still hoped I'd wake up from this nightmare and find peace and comfort in his loving arms.

He kicked the shovel, making it clatter when it hit the chair.

Stifling a sob, I managed to whisper, "Where?"

He pointed at the open door behind him. "You're not too bright, are you? Out there, by the big cypress."

I looked through the open door hesitantly. A dark corridor led to a door, wide open, letting some sunshine in. Beyond that door there was freedom, if I could only get to it. A speck of hope started to build on that distant ray of sunshine, on that open door. But where would he be while I buried David's body?

The thought of dragging him out there, of laying his body in the ground tore my heart open. A crushing wail left my chest, filling the room with the sounds of my despair.

In two large steps, the man drew close and raised his hand. When it came down on me, the blow exploded like wildfire across my face. Heat engulfed my face, burning, throbbing, as I saw stars. I remember tasting my own blood while my ears started ringing with a high-pitched sound. My head reeled from the shock while my balance faltered. I reached and grabbed the edge of the table to steady myself.

"I don't like noise," he said calmly. "Get it done and clean up."

For a brief moment, I thought of attacking him, of scratching his eyes out with my bare hands, or maybe picking up that shovel and aiming at his head. I didn't think I'd defeat him; no, that could never happen. But maybe I'd get him mad enough to kill me where I stood, to end my misery. To bring me peace and the quietude of the land of no suffering.

But David wanted me to live. To be strong, to survive this. He'd be so disappointed in me. Aching with sorrow and despair, I looked at his body. I couldn't leave him there like that. I just couldn't.

Covering my gaping, bleeding mouth to keep the offending sobs quiet, I picked up the shovel. "Show me where," I whispered.

He grinned, satisfied. "Atta girl." Then he walked out of the room, and I followed, dragging the shovel behind me.

The corridor was narrow and devoid of any furniture. A large, stuffed Burmese python hung in all its impressive twelve-foot length on the wall, the snake's head propped out above my head as if it was going to strike. It was an award-winning capture, its midsection thick as my thigh. A gold medal hung from the snake's neck on a dusty yellow ribbon. It must've earned that brute a nice grand prize, I realized, recognizing the medal from a couple of features on my show.

But I didn't recognize *him*, the hunter who had captured us.

He stepped out of the dwelling and into the filtered sunshine, then turned and waited for me impatiently. As I caught up, he pointed at an area a few yards farther to the left. "There." Then he disappeared inside the dwelling, leaving the door open.

I breathed and looked around quickly, trying to identify something that could tell me where I was. The house was small and very old, made of wood, showing signs of rot swell and decay near the base, around the windows and doorsill. Don't imagine a log cabin; no, it was probably some engineered wood paneling finished with wood siding, the way the cheaper seventies houses were built. Windows were small and dirty. There was no garage, but farther in the back, behind the house, I could see the front end of a large, black Chevy truck. To the side, a barn or a storage shed of sorts had been erected closer to the water. It was newer than the house, the walls in better shape, although also made of wood. The roof was corrugated metal.

Between the house and the barn, a small section of a few yards in length by about two in width had been turned into a garden and planted with daisies. There were many, about two feet tall, in all stages of blooming. It was the strangest thing to find in the middle of the Glades; daisies don't natively grow there. They require a more temperate climate and well-drained soil, not marshy. Back then, I didn't pay any attention. My weary, desolate mind couldn't care less about some damn flowers.

I had other priorities.

As far as I could see, there was no one who could help me. No roads, no people, no houses. Nothing but wilderness. Cypress trees and very distant, occasional pines told me I was roughly in the central or northern half of the Everglades expanse; otherwise, I would've seen sawgrass marshes. Closer to the coast, I would've encountered mangroves and tidal pools of water.

I was probably somewhere between I-75 and Highway 41, in a twenty-mile-wide stretch of wilderness. I was surrounded by cypress trees, clumped together on a stretch of dryer land, reminding me of the Skillet Strand North Trail, south of Big Cypress National Preserve, by Highway 41. I could've been somewhere close to that.

Before thinking of running, I had to decide in which direction. Was I north of 41? How far north? In that case, I should head south and hope I run into some traffic on the almost deserted stretch of highway. But if I was south of 41 and I headed south, I'd soon find myself knee-deep in water crawling with venomous snakes and alligators, in the middle of sea marshes that went on for miles and miles. Still, in my gut it felt right to head south.

But not yet.

Before thinking of making a run for it, I had something else I needed to do, even if just the thought of it broke my heart.

The snake hunter had pointed in the direction of a big tree, when showing me where I should bury my husband. With hesitant, barefoot steps on the sandy ground, I drew closer, the blade of the shovel leaving a trail behind me as I dragged it along.

Closer to that tree, I noticed several places where the ground had been disturbed. It wasn't even as soil is expected to be, because it's made of layers of mud, sand, and organic matter that quickly set level after floods or hurricanes. Several elongated mounds span toward the water. For a brief moment, I couldn't think what those were. Then, as I realized, my blood turned to ice.

Graves.

My poor David wasn't going to be the first to be laid to rest in that forsaken place.

The sun had dropped behind the tree line by the time I finished digging. To this day, it was the hardest, most heartbreaking thing I ever had to do. Many times, I stopped, pleading with David in my mind to just let me die, to let me follow him wherever he was going.

When I was done and had climbed out of the hole I'd dug, steeling my will for the next part, I couldn't see straight anymore. I'd wept so long and so hard I could barely stand upright. But I had no doubt what would happen if I sat down or refused to do the task I'd been charged with.

"About bloody time," I heard the man's voice behind me. Startled, I turned to face him just in time to see he was carrying David's body on his shoulder like it was nothing. He threw it in the freshly dug grave and rubbed his hands against his pants. "There. Finish it up."

For a while, I stood and looked at David's face as if stunned. How could I cover him with dirt? How could I leave him there, alone, in the never-ending darkness? Blinded with grief, I let myself slide into the grave and held his hand for a while, not feeling how cold it had become or how slick with blood. After a while, I folded his arms over his chest like I'd seen it done at my mother's funeral. I placed one last kiss on his pale forehead and froze again, unable to leave him there.

I must've spaced out for a while. The hunter grabbed me by the shoulders and lifted me out of the grave, then threw me on the ground like I was nothing. "Finish it already," he spat, then turned away and left. From inside the house, I could hear the sound of the television with a ball game on.

I grabbed the shovel and loaded it with dirt. A sob climbed up in my chest, suffocating me, but I let the soil find its way into the grave. And the next shovel, and the next, not able to look anymore as it started covering David's body. When I finished, I dropped to my knees by the side of the grave and steepled my hands as for prayer. They were stained with his blood and covered in black dirt, contrasting with my pale skin, red and black joined together in eternity. I kept staring at them senselessly, finally understanding the meaning of the phrase, blood on one's hands. Yes, I had David's blood on mine, and nothing would ever wash it clean.

"Dear Lord," I whispered, "if you're really there, please take care of him," I said after a while, when no other words came to my mind. That was the best I could do for prayer to a God who'd allowed that to happen.

Then I stood and searched around until I found two small branches, I then tied them into a cross with the scrunchie in my hair. I placed that improvised cross at the head of the grave, then looked around, listening carefully.

Television sounds came from inside the house, and a loud belch, followed by the sound made by an empty can hitting the floor, and another one popped open. If there was ever a time to run, that was it.

I knew where south was. It was still dusk; for a while, I could still see where I was going, then I could wait it out till dawn. I wasn't dressed for it; I still wore the blue satin evening gown I'd put on for our dinner, eons ago. Now it hung in shreds, stained with blood and tears and mud. And I was barefoot.

But it didn't matter.

I grabbed the shovel and bolted, moving quickly and making a run for the cypress woods I could see in the near distance, with the remnants of the setting sun at my right. The woods would give me some cover, some dry land to spend the night on.

I made it to the cluster of cypress trees and stopped for a moment to catch my breath, careful to not be seen from the house. I chose a path visually, before dashing again farther into the woods.

The moment I stopped again, an arrow sliced through the air and pinned my leg against a tree trunk.

18

CONFESSION

Tess watched Kiana battling her demons silently for a while and didn't press. She deserved a few moments to gather her thoughts. She kept kneading her fingers in her lap, with gestures that reminded Tess of a surgeon scrubbing thoroughly. But her hands were clean, at least on the surface.

The nurses had given her a sponge bath while she was out, but her hair was still grimy and clumped together with what looked like mud or maybe dried blood. The samples she'd taken were in Doc Rizza's hands by now, taken to the morgue by Michowsky on his way home.

She felt tempted to ask Kiana to take a shower, to help her relax a little, but decided against it. She gave her a little more time, watching the unspoken battle that was going on in Kiana's tormented features. Slowly and gently, she reached out and squeezed her hand in a gesture of reassurance.

"What happened to David, Kiana?" A tear sprung from the girl's eye and streaked her cheek. "You're safe here," Tess added. "It's just you and me, and nothing you say will leave this room if you don't want it."

She'd said that countless times during interrogations, mainly because cops are legally allowed to lie to obtain information. Only this time, she meant every word.

"He's gone," Kiana eventually said in a low, tear-filled whisper. "He died the day we were taken." She stared at the back of her hands for a moment. "And it's all my fault."

"I'm sure you don't mean that," Tess said. She recognized the burden of guilt the girl was carrying since she'd watched her interaction with David's parents.

"I—I do," she stammered. "You don't know what I've done. I just couldn't—"

She choked on her own words and stopped talking. Tess allowed her a bit of time to continue, but she didn't.

"Where did that happen, Kiana?" Tess asked. "Where did he die?"

She seemed confused by the question for a moment, then looked at Tess with a clear, assertive glance. "You need to let me go. I have to go back."

"Do you know where?"

She shook her head forcefully, her hair whipping the air around her head. It smelled of grime and mildew. "I'll find my way. You just let me go. Please."

"How did he die?" Tess asked. Kiana just squeezed her eyes shut. "Was he killed by the man who took you?"

She nodded, but at the same time whispered, "It's my fault. I killed him."

She'd said it before, but Tess doubted she meant it literally. That sweet, deeply damaged girl wasn't a killer.

"Where were you all this time?"

Kiana shot her another glance, this time a bit confused, as if she didn't know where she was anymore.

"You were gone for seven months," Tess said gently. "What do you recall of all this time?"

As if ready to make a run for the door, Kiana hopped off the bed and started pacing the room angrily, impatiently. Then she stopped squarely in front of Tess and propped her hands on her thighs. "What do you want from me? He kept me locked up, now you do the same. You're nicer, seem friendlier, and so far, you didn't make me bleed. But you don't let me go either. So, pardon me for not wanting to entertain you with my epic story."

Perfect, Tess thought, barely refraining from smiling. Angry was good. Angry was rooted into reality, and very much alive. She could work with angry.

"Fine, don't tell me your epic story. Just tell me what the man who took you looks like. If you know his name that would be great. Tell me where I can find him, and I'll have his ass thrown in jail before the next serving of green Jell-O lands on your tray table. Can you do that?" Tess looked at Kiana openly, with an encouraging smile.

She didn't react the way Tess had expected. She seemed to battle the decision for a moment, while biting her lip and looking past Tess, out the window at the distant Miami cityscape. Then a glimmer of something fierce shone in her eyes and she replied simply, "No. I have nothing to say to you."

Tess felt her blood starting to boil. "How can you possibly not want your husband's killer punished? The man who held you captive and tortured you for seven months, you want him to go free?" She stood and just stared at Tess quietly, unfazed. "You don't want any justice?"

The glimmer sparked again, but she lowered her eyelids for a moment and erased it. When she looked at Tess again, she was serene, perfectly composed, and seemed a little bit annoyed. She'd gathered strength in the past day she'd been in the hospital, and she was steady on her feet, exuding self-confidence and stamina. Only it lasted for a few minutes at a time, as if the reserves of her fortitude were still depleting faster than she could rebuild them.

"Yes, I do want justice," she eventually said, the breath under those words deflating her as if it were the last bit of energy holding her together. She sat on the edge of the bed, seeming defeated again. "There will be a time for justice."

Tess frowned, studying her in detail. She was nothing like the girl she'd seen in a white tank top and denim shorts, lighthearted like a butterfly among all those rugged men on her show. That girl, the TV show host, was the young and innocent version of Kiana Mallery Bayliss. The woman sitting next to Tess with her bony shoulders poking through her sweatshirt and her now vacant stare, was the mature, wounded warrior, returning to a land she didn't recognize as home anymore. She shared behaviors with POWs, which was no surprise, considering her detention and the scars marring her body.

"When I first met you," Tess said, "you asked if I was the new girl." Kiana flashed her a concerned glance, then immediately looked away, biting her lip. "What was that about?"

She slipped off the edge of the bed, only this time she didn't pace the room like a caged animal. She went slowly to the window and looked outside, with her back turned to Tess.

"People don't know what they're doing by holding me here." She wrung her hands together until Tess heard her joints cracking.

"Well, tell me then! Work with me. Tell me what I need to know, and I swear I'll take you back where you were found. I'll drive you over there myself."

"Now?" Kiana asked, the excitement in her voice a mismatch with the flash of anxiety in her eyes. She became invigorated, crossing over the room in a few decisive steps and stopping in front of Tess. "Okay, just ask me what you need to know, and let's go."

"Why did you ask if I was the new girl?" Tess asked gently. Kiana's excitement vanished, leaving her face pale and burdened. "Whom did you think I was?"

Her hands, slightly shaking, found each other and her fingers intertwined, clasped tightly. Her chin trembled as if she was going to break down in tears."

I killed them," she whispered, wrapping her arms around her thin body as if she was suddenly freezing. "It's all my fault."

19

PREY

Lying down on a dusty floor, I endured through the woman's rash gestures. She patched my wound as best she could, doing better than I could've done. The arrow had pierced my thigh, leaving a bleeding, gaping hole in its wake after the woman removed it with a quick, unforgiving yank.

"You had to run, didn't you?" she muttered, not seeming to expect an answer. She was immersed in her work, cleaning my wound quickly and applying gauze and tape she took from an old, discolored first aid kit. The gauze instantly stained with blood. "I need something to apply pressure with," she said, standing and looking around at the variety of yard tools and old hardware littering the barn.

We were in the barn; that much I knew, because the roof was made of corrugated metal. A dim, yellowish bulb hung from the ceiling, with one of those chain switches dangling from it. A small, barred window overlooked the side of the house, so dirty I struggled to see if it was light outside. I didn't recall how I got there; only the intense pain that burned through my leg when his arrow pinned me against that tree. Then his hand around my neck, choking me, holding me in place while he snapped the arrow in half, leaving the point embedded into the tree trunk. I'd screamed in excruciating pain, silencing the wilderness for a mere second.

"You cost me a perfectly good arrow," he'd said before I passed out.

"Hey," the woman called, yanking me back into reality. "I need to apply pressure, or the bleeding won't stop. Any ideas?"

I looked at my blue silk gown with unspoken bitterness. Had I known what I'd be doing while wearing it, I would've never pulled it off its hanger. I grabbed the skirt at the split and yanked sideways as hard as I could, but the fabric refused to be torn.

The woman handed me one of those tiny scissors that come with first aid kits, and I used it to cut into the fabric. Then I grabbed the two sides and pulled apart forcefully. The silk shrieked in protest, but soon much of the length of my skirt was separated from the gown in a section of rectangular fabric. The woman grabbed that from me and ripped a narrow section of it, then used it to tightly tie my thigh wound. I winced, then whispered, "Thank you."

She didn't reply, just focused on gathering the things she'd used to tend to my wound. The remaining gauze, the tape, the crappy little scissors, she sealed all that into the first aid kit, snapping the plastic lid closed.

Then she rummaged through a crate in the corner of the barn and came back with a dirty white T-shirt and a pair of jeans. They felt musty to the touch and smelled of mildew and wood rot. A termite crawled from one of the pockets and found a quick death under Carolyn's foot. "Here. These might fit."

I took them and slipped them on, sitting crookedly on the floor, afraid to put any weight on my wounded leg. The jeans were a bit large, and the T-shirt was torn in places, but they worked better than the remnants of my evening gown, now discarded in a pile of blue, bloody satin.

I looked at the woman with gratitude, but she didn't seem to notice.

She seemed younger than me or about the same age. Her hair was naturally blonde, not like mine. I used to get expensive hairdos every week, and the TV station was happy to pick up the tab. Recently, I had changed my look, going for something more in line with viewer preferences. My hair, about mid-back length, was now bleached blonde and treated with highlights and lowlights to give it dimension. But that seemed like eons ago, in my previous life, before we were taken.

"What's your name?" I asked, shifting in place and trying to ignore the throbbing pain in my thigh.

"Don't you know there's nowhere to go?" she asked, instead of answering my question, as if no time had passed since she'd started scolding me. She shot me a quick, disapproving glance. Her eyes were dull, as if life had been extinguished out of them some time ago. Feeling a chill down my spine, I wondered how long she'd been there.

"I had to try," I whispered apologetically. "I can't just—"

"It's hell to pay when he drags you back here." She wiped her hands against her shirt. It used to be bright yellow imprinted with tiny flowers, but the color was now faded and stained, the fabric thinned out from wear. Her jeans were ripped above the knee and just as dirty, both items a couple of sizes too large for her. Maybe they weren't even hers. "It's hell for you and for me," she added. "He'll punish us both."

"Tell me about yourself," I asked, pushing the darkness ignited by her words into a remote corner of my mind. "Who were you before this?" I gestured with my hand vaguely, but she knew exactly what I was referring to.

A sad smile tugged at her lips. "I used to hate my job," she said, walking slowly to the window and looking outside. The dim light coming through that window had increased gradually, lit with hues of orange and yellow. It was morning; the sun was rising, lending her pale face a shred of color. "Waiting tables at Luca's Sports Bar downtown, with its hollering drunks and catcalling and ass grabbing. What I wouldn't give to be waiting on those tables right now." She wiped her nose with the back of her hand and sniffled. "It's true what they say. We never know what we have until it's gone."

How infuriatingly true that was. Her words made me think of David. I swallowed a sob and put my hand over my mouth for a moment, silencing my tears. "My name is Kiana," I said. "I'm twenty-seven. I work in television."

She didn't reply for a while, but then looked at me from the window and said, simply, "Carolyn."

"Carolyn," I repeated. I always liked that name, but maybe it wasn't the best time to tell her that. We weren't exactly chatting at some fancy coffee shop. "Thank you for taking care of me."

She turned to face me, looking at me intently. "Don't do it again, all right?"

I didn't say yes; there was no point in lying to her. I knew I was going to try to escape until the last breath left my body.

"How long have you been here?" I asked, fearing her answer.

"Too long," she replied, her voice a little irritated. "Do as he says, and you'll survive," she added grimly. "Maybe." She drew closer to me and leaned over to look at the stain blooming through the fabric of my jeans. Blood must've soaked the gauze and the strip of silk used to tie it tightly in place. "Bleeding should stop soon," she said, sounding unconvinced.

From up close, I could see scars marring Carolyn's skin, cuts on her arms, one near the corner of her eye. Her left brow ridge had been fractured and had healed with an indentation that made her eyebrow seem crooked.

Seeing her scars was like a dark, ominous glimpse into my future. My throat feeling parchment dry, I licked my lips tensely and asked, "Does he... um, will he—" I choked, afraid to even say the word, as if speaking it out loud would somehow make it true.

She shook her head in disbelief. "What do you think we're here for? To do his laundry?" A look of unmistakable pity colored her glance. "My goodness, girl, you're so naïve."

Breath caught in my lungs. A moment of sheer panic flooded my brain, and I struggled to stand, feeling the irresistible urge to run. But Carolyn placed her hand on my shoulder, holding me back.

"Don't be an idiot and try to run away again. They didn't name him The Hunter for no reason." Her lip curled in disgust. "That's what gets him off. Hunting us in those woods."

I breathed again, slowly, willing the panic gone. "Who's they?" I asked, my voice fraught with fear. Every new question I asked cracked open the door to the abyss a tiny bit more, but I couldn't stop. I had to know.

Moving slowly, as if in a slow-motion movie, Carolyn pointed at the window.

I stood with difficulty and walked over there, limping and wincing.

On the windowsill, a fresh daisy was missing a petal. Just like the one in the house, it seemed fresh and was stemless.

But I didn't pay any attention to that.

Underneath the sill, someone had written three words in blood.

I AM PREY.

As I read, my blood turned to ice. Tears sprung from my eyes, stinging, blurring my sight. It wasn't real… it couldn't be. I stared at the traces left by someone's finger, dipped in their own blood to make that statement on the wooden wall, and saw myself there, writing on that wall, wounded and bloodied and captive. Eerily, as if I'd traveled in time, sometime in the future but also coming from the past, not clear if it was a near or distant reality but surely harrowing.

Carolyn approached and looked out the window. "Them," she whispered. "The poor souls buried out there."

I followed her gaze, and, through the soiled window, I could see several of the graves, including David's. Seeing the raw earth I'd heaped over his body, now lit by the early morning light, filled my heart with renewed grief. I started sobbing. Carolyn walked away, while I rested my head against the glass.

It moved.

I opened my eyes and stared at the window, surprised. Tentatively, I pushed against the glass, and the window opened. The bars were affixed to the exterior frame and moved with it. I gave the window a critical look, wondering if I was going to fit through the opening.

Barely.

But I could at least try.

Carolyn grabbed my arm. "No," she whispered. "Please don't. There's no telling what he could do this time."

I looked at the woman's pleading eyes. She was desperate and afraid, holding on to my arm with thin fingers turned white, unwilling to let go.

"Don't think I haven't tried to run," she said. The apprehension in her voice was unmistakable. "Many times." A tear rolled down her face, staining her cheek. "Each time he caught me it got worse. And you're hurt and barefoot. You can't even walk straight."

I freed myself from her grip, gently, and looked her straight in the eye, my hands squeezing her bony shoulders. "Listen, I have to try," I said, and with every word I spoke, panic grew in her tearful eyes. "I know my way around the Glades. I could bring help and end this nightmare. I promise I will come back for you. You just have to let me try."

I still held on to her shoulders, firmly, hoping to instill some of my waning courage into her weary heart. But her eyes broke contact, downcast, and I felt a shiver rattling her body.

"You'll get us both killed." There was resigned acceptance in her voice, not a trace of fight left, of hope nor of fear. "But I guess it's better than this life."

I hugged her tightly, even if she was reluctant, and whispered in her ear, "I promise I'll come back for you."

I still remember how tiny and scared and lost she looked when I left her standing there, in the middle of that barn, shivering in the humid heat of the Everglades morning.

Then, trying to ignore the pain searing through my thigh with every move I made, I managed to slip through the narrow window and disappear into the early morning mist.

20

OTHERS

Tess ignored the vibration in her pocket. She'd turned down the ringer volume of her phone, but messages kept coming in, at least three over the past few minutes. She didn't want the fragile connection between Kiana and her to be torn to shreds over some stupid text message.

She gave the girl some time to collect her thoughts, but she seemed to have slipped into a dissociative state, staring into empty space, slight twitches on her face the only evidence of the horrors she was reliving.

"Who is them?" Tess asked gently.

"Huh?" Kiana asked, looking at Tess briefly with the confused facial expression of someone awakened from deep slumber.

"You just said you killed them, and that it was all your fault." Kiana nodded, then let her head hang low, her face shielded by strands of hair falling around her shoulders. "Do you remember saying that?"

"It's true," she whispered, wiping a tear with the back of her hand.

"Who is it you say you killed?"

A quick rap against the door cut Tess off. She barely refrained from cursing. She looked at the door frowning, with an unspoken question in her eyes.

Fradella slid the door open just a few inches. "Need to talk to you."

"Not now," Tess replied. If there was ever a wrong time to interrupt an interview, that had to be it.

"Yes, now," Fradella insisted.

She looked at him intently for a moment, as if to ascertain how serious was the reason she was called away from Kiana. He didn't budge, just nodded almost imperceptibly.

"I'll be right back," she said to Kiana, but the girl had already slipped away again, staring vacantly at some point on the wall.

She closed the door to Kiana's room, and the uniformed cop retook his position guarding it.

"What's going on?" she asked, following Fradella who walked quickly toward the training room they'd been using as an improvised office. "Victim interviews are a sensitive process. An interruption could cost us hours, even days of progress."

"Don't you think I know that?" he threw over his shoulder, sounding a little insulted. He held open the training room door for her, then said, "Just wait and see what Donovan has to show you."

The room still smelled of stale pizza, probably from the cardboard box in the trash can, but the air conditioning had kicked in and the room was pleasantly chilly. Donovan was seated at the big table, hunched in front of his large laptop screen. When she entered, he turned it her way and pointed at a list of names with the tip of his finger.

"There are others, just like you assumed," he said. "I went back five years only, and looked at still open missing person cases, with disappearances in the same geographical area and a similar MO."

Tess felt a chill down her spine. "How many?" She leaned closer to the screen. The list was long.

"Eleven so far, not including Kiana. Never heard from again. But let me show you this." He changed the view he was displaying on the screen. Instead of names typed in block letters, now Tess could see the photo of each missing person, affixed to their original report.

With rhythmic taps on a key, Donovan ran through all eleven missing women. "See? They're almost identical. Long, blonde hair, blue eyes, twenty-five to thirty years old at the time of disappearance."

"The bastard has a type," Fradella added.

"But Kiana is not a blonde," Tess said.

"Not now," Fradella replied with unmistakable excitement in his voice. "And not last year, when she filmed the shows we watched earlier. But take a look at this."

Donovan changed applications and displayed YouTube, where one of Kiana's *Swamp Secrets* episodes was ready to play. "This aired seven months ago, right before she was taken. This was her last episode." He tapped on the PLAY arrow and Tess watched about a minute of Kiana's performance on the show. She was chatting with some old fishermen by their boats. Her hair was blonde with lighter, almost white highlights, wavy and silky, blowing in the breeze as she moved around from one contestant's boat to the next.

She looked just like the other women. They could've all been sisters.

Slack-jawed for a moment, Tess stopped the playback and looked at Fradella. "What does that tell us?"

"That she somehow escaped a serial killer?" Fradella offered.

He was right, but that wasn't all. "The time frame when the unsub could've seen her has just narrowed dramatically. If he has a type, and we're inclining to assume he does—"

"Inclining? Why aren't we positive about this?" Fradella asked.

"So far, we have nothing tying these eleven missing women to Kiana's unsub, just circumstance. And the bias of our profession. But people disappear in Miami-Dade all the time, all kinds of people, all ages, races, and physiognomies."

"Yeah," Donovan replied, his fingers dancing above the keyboard at an incredible speed. "Last year, 1,257 people went missing from Florida, and 768 of them in Miami-Dade only."

"Okay, I'll give you that," Fradella said, frowning at Donovan's screen. "But it's too much to call it a coincidence."

"And we're not going to," Tess said. "We'll proceed with it as if we were certain, but at the same time, remembering we have made assumptions. Our work is based on assumptions, on leads we follow, on hunches and coincidences we refuse to dismiss. Then we look for evidence to support or eliminate them." She sounded so strange to her own ears when she was explaining herself for Fradella's benefit. She wasn't used to doing that; she'd never done it before, just acted on her instinct and her logic, and at the end, closed the case with a collar or a toe tag for Doc Rizza to catalog in his morgue.

Every. Single. Time.

This unsub would make no exception.

At the same time, she didn't want to come across as condescending. Fradella was an experienced detective, even if a rookie FBI agent.

"But you know all this," she added quickly, just in case. "If the unsub has a type, the next assumption we can make is that he targeted Kiana sometime after she changed her hair color. Let's find out when that happened. But don't forget, he could've seen her on TV, like who knows how many other people have."

"Only one episode was filmed with her new hairstyle," Donovan said. "I already checked." He sounded proud of his work and had every right to be. She couldn't've asked for a better analyst.

"We can get the exact date from her team," Fradella added. "How do we validate these eleven cases in the absence of bodies, killer signature, and evidence? Do you want to narrow down the list somehow? Or just proceed with the eleven?"

"That's where victimology kicks in," she replied with a quick smile. "Okay, this is great work," Tess added. "Let's find out if there are any commonalities among these women. Map the places where they were taken from and let's see how those dots line up. Find out who they were before their abductions, and let's hope we can narrow down the place or circumstance where the unsub set his eyes on them."

"You got it," Donovan replied.

"Any luck with the satellite view of the area where Kiana was found? Are there many possible locations where she could've been kept?" Tess's voice was fraught with impatience. She'd thought by now they'd have the addresses of the few people dwelling in the depths of the Glades, ready to visit with a few questions.

"You're not going to believe this, but there are about thirty thousand people who live in areas remote enough to have pulled this off."

"You have got to be kidding me," Tess muttered. "Who are these people?"

"Some are descendants of the Seminole and Miccosukee Tribes. Others are residents of small cities and towns neighboring the Everglades who I couldn't discard, because of their access to—"

She raised a hand in the air. "Okay, I got it. They're too many to do a door-to-door canvas. How about satellite?"

He shrugged. "Looking for what? For a remote dwelling of sorts? There are quite a few."

She bit her lip for a moment, then reached for a drink of water from a small bottle she emptied with a few thirsty gulps. "Then victimology is all we have for now. And Kiana."

"I have the sketch artist standing by," Fradella offered.

"Let him go home," she replied, throwing the empty water bottle into the can. It bounced off the empty pizza box and settled on the edge of the can. "Kiana's not ready to talk yet. She's holding something back, and I can't break through her walls."

"I would've expected her to be eager to give us the unsub," Fradella said. "I can't think of another case where something like this happened."

I can, Tess almost blurted, but kept her thoughts to herself.

After surviving her assault twelve years ago, she would've rather died than give testimony about the atrocities she'd endured, knowing very well it would've changed her existence forever. Everything about her would've become about that dreadful night that still haunted her nightmares. Cat had held his promise and never whispered a word to anyone. He nursed her back to health without expecting anything in return, without asking a single question. She'd made her choice of silence back then, knowing it meant letting her attacker go free, at least for a while. Her choice had given her a chance at a normal life. Maybe Kiana had made the same choice. Perhaps she could do for Kiana a little of what Cat had done for her.

Or maybe Kiana was protecting someone. One or more of the eleven missing women might still be alive, trapped in the middle of one of the most hostile habitats known to man. That would explain why she was so adamant to go back there.

There was something else about Kiana's behavior that seemed out of place. Most survivors look for family, for loved ones to be close to, eager to let the healing process begin in the safety of their presence and the comfort of their homes. Not Kiana. She'd shown no interest to go home, to be with her loved ones, other than a quick mention of her father she'd never since repeated. Surprisingly, she seemed to avoid them. That behavior was aligned with her noticeably crushing guilt for things she'd done, seen, or survived.

She grabbed the door handle, ready to leave. "Ask Doc Rizza if he could swing by to take a look at Kiana's medical records. There's a lot this girl isn't telling us."

"You got it," Donovan replied, jotting down a quick note. "Anything else?"

"The unsub kept Kiana for seven months. There's no reason to assume he'd keep others less or more. When was the most recent of the eleven women taken?"

Donovan flipped quickly through the many databases he was using. "Oh, crap... only three months ago. Ashely

Nettleton, twenty-six, a hotel receptionist from Hialeah. Before that, Carolyn Ladson, a twenty-five-year-old waitress from Miami, taken four months before Kiana."

"They might still be out there," Fradella said, seeming ready to bolt out the door.

He'd voiced her own thoughts, but not entirely. There was no telling what the unsub had done after Kiana's escape.

Tess squeezed the handle and exited the training room without voicing her concern. Until a body was found, they operated under the assumption that Ashley and Carolyn and everyone else from that list was still alive. As long as there was still the smallest chance, she wasn't going to give up. With these thoughts in mind, she made for Kiana's room with a determined stride.

She found the girl exactly as she'd left her, as if she hadn't moved an inch or done anything else since but stare into thin air.

Tess cringed at the thought of pressuring Kiana to talk, but there was no other option. Not when there could be other girls out there going through the same hell Kiana had survived.

Then she approached her and touched her shoulder to get her attention. The girl flinched and stared at Tess with widened, fearful eyes for a moment, as if she didn't recognize her at first.

When she spoke, Tess's voice was cold, stern, determined.

"I know about the other women. It's time to come clean with me."

21

SOUTH

I used to like this place.

No… I used to *love* it. My father's love for it instilled mine. The time we spent together after my mom died, going out there every weekend and exploring another corner of it marked my life. It turned me into who I am today.

Growing up, I wasn't the kind of girl who played with dolls. I was an unruly tomboy, happy to be gutting fish in the back of Dad's old boat, while he found us another perfect spot, slowly navigating the shallow waters. I can still hear his voice calling, "Knife down!" each time before turning on the engine and setting the boat in motion.

Sometimes we went for largemouth bass or catfish in the sweet water inlets, on an old and rusty flatboat he borrowed from a neighbor in the old days, when he and I barely scraped by on his blue-collar wages. Other times, we went out on saltwater, angling for red fish or spotted seatrout, and sometimes bringing home the occasional snapper.

We fished for food more than for sport. A day out on the water filled the freezer with enough to last us a week or two. Not a single morsel went to waste. Dad's not much of a cook, but he can grill with the best of them.

It wasn't just fishing over the weekends. If we got lucky and took enough fish out of the water to last us the week, Dad used to take us exploring the Glades. This is where I have to mention I call the Glades everything south of I-75, the entire southern tip of the Florida peninsula, except for the Miami-Fort Lauderdale metro area, of course. Pavement doesn't interest me much; never did, never will.

Dad upped the challenges with my age. At twelve, we hiked the Pinelands or the Mahogany Hammock. At fourteen, he took me alligator hunting. Dad had a permit and all, but I let the beast live after having it in my sights for a while. He wasn't upset, although he loved alligator meat chili; he just ruffled my already unruly hair and said, "Only when you're ready, and only if you have to. Today, we don't."

At sixteen, I drove an airboat for the first time, and those things are as tricky to drive as they look exciting in movies. That saltmarsh fishing trip was one of the last I remember taking before college. Soon thereafter I started dating a boy in my school, and I became overly preoccupied with my hands smelling of fish when he kissed my fingers.

The love for the Glades remained strong in my heart, and I took it to the next level with my choice of college program. Then, after meeting David, I happily resumed taking the occasional fishing trip with Dad, not because I didn't love David enough to care if my hands smelled of the day's catch, but because *he* didn't care. He was just as completely engulfed in his passion for technology as I was in mine for everything nature. It's also true around that time I had discovered vinegar and its annihilating effect on fishy smells.

Standing behind a tree trunk and gasping for breath in the slowly rising mist, I realized all those weekends spent in the wilderness would probably save my life. Before daring to head out farther into the cypress woods, I sent a thought of deep gratitude to my dad, wishing more than anything that he were there by my side to hold my hand as I ran for my life.

Now my love for the Glades was tarnished, tainted by the harrowing memories of the past couple of days. I tried not to think of that. Instead, I focused on the distance I was putting between me and the snake hunter's house, on staying alive and getting the hell out of there.

The early morning mist was lifting, and with it, my cover was disappearing. But the sky above was covered in a layer of threatening clouds, thick enough to hide the sun completely. To head south, as I'd decided earlier while I did my best to figure out where I was, I needed to keep the sun at my left until it crossed over my head, then at my right. With the sky covered in gray, and while crossing the moss-covered woods, heading south was becoming a challenge.

At first, I navigated as I'd learned in my hiking days with Dad. Yesterday, when the sun was shining, I was able to figure out where south was. The hunter's house faced south. Limping heavily and gritting my teeth in pain, I headed into the woods in that direction and followed it until I almost couldn't see the house anymore. Then I looked in the opposite direction and chose a certain, distinctive cypress tree as the next milestone, knowing it was south from where I was. Then I'd choose the next and the next after that.

At least that was my plan.

But the soil turned moist under my feet, and that meant water could be near. And water I couldn't cross, not barefoot. If I were wearing full gear and a portable GPS or could at least see the sun, I'd head into the shallow waters of the preserve without a trace of hesitation and feel right at home.

I stopped again, looking at the landscape around me, trying to figure out where to go next. The sky had darkened more, and the distant rumbling of thunder made it clear the sun wouldn't be shining anytime soon.

Then I tried to find my milestone cypress, the tree I had determined as my target destination. And I couldn't. After taking my eyes off it for mere minutes, all the cypress trees looked the same. Panic rose the bile in my throat. I could be going in circles... I could become lost and die out there, possibly a mere mile from breaking free.

Panting heavily, I stopped and leaned against a tree trunk, borrowing from its strength to replenish mine. I slowed my breath, counting the seconds, finding my calm and the survival training notions I'd forgotten for a moment.

I could still make it.

If I couldn't get oriented under the sky cover, I could wait out the storm right there, by that tree, and then find my way the moment I'd start seeing the sun. And maybe I'd make it out of the Glades before nightfall. With so many trees around me, it would be impossible to navigate by the stars.

But I could be miles away from anything. I might not last that long without food or water. My gut turned into a knot while fear ran amok through my mind, weakening it every time I thought I had this handled.

I closed my eyes for a moment and listened to the sounds of the wilderness, eagerly awaiting to hear the warblers chirping, a sign the storm has passed. Instead, I heard a rustling near my feet.

I shuddered and opened my eyes, willing myself deathly still. It could've been a snake or a gator sneaking up on me. I looked around and didn't see anything for a while. Then something moved again, the same rustle getting closer.

A black racer raised its curious head and looked straight at me.

I held my breath and stared back. After an endless moment, it slithered away, disappearing into the landscape.

As soon as the racer vanished, I started looking for ways I could climb up that tree. At least alligators don't climb trees, even if snakes do. And mosquitoes tend to stick closer to the water-pooling grounds they breed from.

After giving the tree next to me a critical and disappointed look, I shifted my attention to the next in a visual search for a trunk with lower branches or knots I could use to climb. Cypress trunks grow smooth and tall, impossible to climb without a strap. Climbing a tree was a great idea… if only it were practical.

I flinched when thunder rolled, much closer and louder than before. Resisting the urge to flee, I stood still, looking at the sky for a trace of sunlight peeking through the clouds, but all I got was raindrops on my face. I held my hands out, collecting a few, then licked them thirstily. Then I tilted my head back and opened my mouth.

A snapped twig ended my brief moment of enjoyment just as the rain started falling heavily, its sound muting out everything else. I listened intently, noticing how much the complex, multifaceted sound of rain resembled that of crackling fire.

Barely discernible under the barrage of falling raindrops, I heard another rustling noise, this time closer. Then another. It wasn't a smooth rustling, like the snake's movement against the leaf-covered ground. It was rhythmic, heavy, and eerily familiar.

Footsteps.

I froze in place, holding my breath, while my heart thumped in my chest like a caged bird. *He found me!*

I could hear him approaching slowly, probably listening between steps just like I'd done earlier, wary of where I was going and where I'd put my bare foot down next. His footfalls sounded heavy, crushing the ground cover forcefully. He must've worn boots.

I looked at myself in the gray, dim light of the storm, noticing how my skin glowed in the bluish, distant glow of lightning. My white T-shirt stood out the worst, drenched as it was, the only speck of white in the entire wilderness expanse.

Breathing shallowly, I listened for his footsteps. He continued to approach, only a few yards away, on the other side of the tree that hid me from his sight. He kept on going, moving past me in the same deliberate, achingly slow pace.

"Hey, little girl," he called in the raspy, lecherous voice I recognized and loathed, "why are you leaving so soon?"

Tears burst from my eyes thinking that he'd caught me. I screwed my eyes shut, expecting the blow to come. But it didn't. Instead, he continued searching for me.

I breathed, my tears washed off by the falling rain, and summoned my courage to run. I just needed him to put a few more yards of distance between us. So I waited.

A critter found its way up my leg, crawling onto my skin, probably seeking shelter from the rain. I clenched my teeth and stood still, resisting the urge to slap it dead through the fabric of my jeans. It was too large to be a chigger or a tick. Must've been a spider, a black widow or maybe a brown recluse if I was really out of luck. It moved quickly, meeting no resistance up the large pant leg. If I could've at least stomped my foot, maybe it would've fallen off. But I couldn't make a move. Not when the hunter was mere feet away.

Yet I couldn't stay there anymore, not with the hunter stalking me, not with the critter crawling up my leg.

Moving incredibly slowly, I unzipped my pants and let them fall to the ground under the weight of their soaked fabric. I stepped out of them, getting ready to run in the opposite direction the hunter went. Rain washed the dried blood on my leg, slightly soothing the throbbing pain, but bringing the renewed promise of infection.

After a few tense moments, his footsteps faded into the distance. The rain was falling hard, providing a cover I hadn't hoped for. I took off, zigzagging between trees I used for cover, not even noticing the pain in my thigh as I desperately wanted to get as far away from him as possible. The memory of his arrow slicing through my flesh terrified and energized me at the same time.

Every step I took I looked over my shoulder, expecting him to appear behind me, ready to strike. I knew better; instead, I should've looked where I stepped.

Something raspy roped around my right ankle and I shrieked as it yanked me high up in the air, dangling head down in the pouring rain.

"Gotcha," the man laughed, a mere three yards away. He'd been trailing me all along, knowing exactly where I was, toying with me. Bitter tears choked me as I cried hopelessly for no one to hear but him.

He took out the serrated knife I'd seen before, and with a quick slice through the rope, I came hurtling down. Hitting the ground hard knocked the air out of my lungs and I gasped, my entire body agonizing in pain. He stood next to me, grinning widely, rain pasting his hair on his face and lending his eyes a maniacal spark.

I started pushing myself away from him, writhing and flailing my arms, desperately seeking something I could grab as he drew near.

Then he raised his hand, and my world turned dark and deathly silent.

22

LIES

"I have nothing to say to you," Kiana said. She looked at Tess with determination in her eyes. The glimpse of fear that had lit her eyes earlier had vanished the moment the girl recognized Tess.

"I promised you I'd take you back if you answer my questions," Tess replied. "Why the change of heart?"

"Because you're lying to me." Her voice was cold, detached, factual. "All you care about is to keep me here. If I thought you'd be capable of speaking the truth, I'd ask you why." She plunged her fists into the sweatshirt's deep pockets. "I'm not going to bother."

The change in Kiana's attitude was too dramatic to be blamed on her emotional frailty. Tess reached out to touch her shoulder, but the girl withdrew.

"What happened?" Tess asked, her hand frozen midair for a moment before finding her jacket pocket.

Kiana shrugged, glancing briefly at her before looking away.

"I can assure you I have no idea what could've upset you this much," Tess insisted, softening her tone a little. "Whatever it is, I'd like to fix it if I can."

Kiana glanced at her again, her eyes telling Tess she didn't believe a word she was saying. "Why would you?" she eventually said. "It's your own doing."

Taken aback, Tess pulled away. "What's my own doing?"

"The idea of holding me here under observation for at least two days."

Tess gritted her teeth, frustrated as hell. How on earth did she find out about that?

As if reading her mind, Kiana added, "A shrink wandered by and informed me of my status. I was deemed a danger to myself and others and placed under mandatory psychiatric hold." She looked at Tess with eyes filled with contempt. "Don't stand there and tell me you didn't know about it."

"I can make it go away," Tess replied. "I can sign you out of here under my responsibility."

"And be your prisoner instead of theirs?" She scoffed bitterly and lay down on her bed, curled on her side, her hands slipped between her knees as if to keep them warm. She closed her eyes as if to push Tess farther away. "How about I wait it out, the two days the shrink mentioned, in complete silence?"

"Kiana, I—"

"Save it," she whispered. "I called a lawyer. A good one. You talk to him."

Tess drew breath sharply. Her entire plan was falling apart. "You didn't need a lawyer. You're not under arrest."

Kiana jumped off the bed with her fists near her chest, as if ready to fight. "Enough with the damn bullshit!" she shouted. The uniformed cop guarding her door turned his head and looked inside, visibly curious. "Either I'm free, and I'm walking out that door right now, or I'm in some form of custody that my lawyer will sort out." She propped her hands on her hips, the fire in her eyes reminding Tess she wasn't just someone she could easily coerce into cooperating. There was an inner steel core to that girl, something that not even the unsub had been able to break in seven months of torture. Tess respected that more than she cared to admit to herself.

"I understand," she replied calmly.

"So, which one is it?" Kiana asked impatiently, taking two steps toward the door. "Can I go?"

Tess sighed. "Technically, yes." She kept her voice level and honest, as if she were speaking with a friend.

Kiana grabbed the door handle and slid it open a few inches but looked at Tess as if awaiting her reaction.

Tess didn't move. "Practically, there are several things to consider." She paused for a beat, and Kiana waited. "One, I could take you back where you were found. On your own, you'd struggle finding the place."

"Less than you'd imagine," she replied coldly. "What else?"

"You stated you killed someone. As a federal agent, I can't let that slide." Panic lit Kiana's eyes for a moment, then disappeared under her lowered eyelids. "Even if I doubt it's true." Her statement made Kiana look straight at her with unshielded surprise in her blue irises. "You're right, I lied to you. I *did* ask for the psychiatric hold. I thought you'd be more comfortable in the hospital, instead of the federal building. I believe we've been through this, haven't we?"

Kiana let go of the door handle after closing it with a muted thump, then slipped her hands into her pockets. She remained standing by the door, still ready to bolt, but something held her back, and Tess needed that something to turn into a renewed bond between them, a connection she could use.

"When you make a statement like that, you can't expect to be released. I'd be willing to do that if you gave me anything I can use to justify letting you walk."

"What do you need?" she asked quietly.

"The truth about what happened to you out there. About the other women."

A shudder shook her thin body. She licked her dry lips and wrapped her arms around herself. "I'll try."

Doc Rizza's face appeared on the other side of the glass door. He looked inside and nodded when he caught Tess's attention.

"Who's that?" Kiana asked.

For a moment, Tess considered lying to her, but then said, "The coroner. He's a good friend of mine. He could help me understand how to best help you."

She shrugged, her arms still wrapped around herself. "Sorry to inform you, I'm not coroner material yet. I'm still alive." The cynicism in her reply shed some light on what gave Kiana her remarkable strength. She was bright and had a sense of humor that helped her navigate the most unexpected situations like no one Tess had met before. "But go on," she said, waving Tess off. "Your friend's waiting."

"How about you?"

Her body wasn't as tense as it had been earlier, the fight-or-flight instinct waning. She wandered aimlessly for a moment, pacing the small room slowly, then sat on the edge of the bed, seemingly resigned.

"I'll be here," she replied. "You made me a good offer. Now I have to hope you weren't lying again."

Tess let that slide. "How about your lawyer?"

Kiana's lips fluttered in a tentative smile. "There's no lawyer, but now I know what I need to do if you screw with me again."

Tess shook her head and chuckled. "You're amazing, I'll give you that." She walked over to the door and opened it. "I won't be long."

23

STOCKHOLM

Just outside of Kiana's room, Tess gave Doc Rizza a hug, then looked at him from head to toe. He looked tan and a little healthier than the last time she'd seen him. For the past few years since he'd lost his wife, she'd known him to spend nights in the morgue, enjoying liquid dinners and passing out on the leather sofa he kept in his lab. Now he looked different. Clean-shaven and with a recent haircut, he smelled of fresh laundry and aftershave, not stale booze. She liked the transformation a lot but decided not to mention anything about it right away.

"Thanks for coming," she said. "I appreciate it."

"Anytime," he replied, following her lead as she walked down the corridor headed for the training room. "It's an interesting case, although it's not my usual kind of patient."

"Did you see her records?"

He nodded. "Uh-huh, yeah. And I spoke with her attending, a Dr. DiDomenico," he said, faltering a little saying her name. "For some reason, I called her Dr. DiDemonico by mistake, and she didn't take it too well." He scratched the short tuft of hair left behind at the top of his head by a receding hairline, seeming a little embarrassed still. "I would've guessed it had happened to her before, but nope. She seemed genuinely surprised. And offended."

"So, what do you think?" she asked, stopping a few feet short of reaching the training room door. "Why isn't Kiana talking to me? Why doesn't she want the unsub caught?"

Doc Rizza sighed. "Slow down a little, will ya?"

She let the air leave her lungs with a bit of frustration. She couldn't slow down. All those missing women didn't have the time.

"If you came at the poor girl this hard, it's no wonder she won't open up to you. This is not a suspect you're grilling to make him 'fess up, Tess. This is someone who's been hurt within an inch of her life, for months on end."

She stared at the floor mosaic, her face burning. Doc Rizza was portraying her like a monster. "I *am* compassionate, and I understand what she's going through more than you think, but—" His eyebrow shot up. She was making excuses for herself. Lame. "Could this be Stockholm syndrome after all?"

"Why after all? She spent enough time with the unsub and was tortured, two things that seem to be the fundamental building blocks of the syndrome, together with captor kindness to minimize the pain and screw with a prisoner's mind. We don't know if that happened, unless she told you?"

Tess shook her head. "But Stockholm is supposed to be fanatically protective of the unsub," she added, thinking fast and knotting her fingers while she spoke. "I would've seen signs of attachment to the captor, and I've sensed nothing of the kind." She bit her lip for a moment. "It really throws me off she doesn't want him caught. But she adamantly wants to go back to where she was found. Do Stockholm victims ever want to return?"

"Sometimes," Doc Rizza replied, placing his hand on her shoulder in a gesture of encouragement. "Mostly because the routine of captivity had become their new normal, and they feel lost without it. For a while at least, until they get help and recover. It's overwhelming, Stockholm. It wreaks emotional havoc, and it comes neatly packaged with guilt, shame, fear, even grief for the captor. Are you seeing that?"

Tess tilted her head slightly, focusing intently on a deep scratch on the door. It helped her think. "I've seen lots of guilt and self-incriminating statements, such as, 'I killed them,' when speaking of her husband and other victims. And I've seen grief I thought was for her husband. You're saying it could be for the loss of her captor?"

"It can happen, yes. In this case, she'd be protective of him, refusing to say anything that could lead to his arrest. Is she?"

"She's not talking to me yet, but there's a fierceness in her determination to return. Her eyes... there's an intensity in them when she talks about it. I wouldn't call what I see attachment, no."

Doc Rizza searched her eyes and looked at her for a moment, as if to see if she was really paying attention to what he was about to say. "Tess, if you suspect this woman has Stockholm syndrome, she needs professional help immediately. Otherwise, there's no telling what she could do."

Tess nodded. "That's what I'm trying to ascertain. I was thinking, maybe you could speak to her? It could also be the onset of PTS. I've seen her space out and relive her nightmares without even realizing. When she wakes up, she's confused at first, reactive, afraid for her life. She thinks she's still out there, captive."

"What medications is she on? Do you know?"

"Nothing, not even hydration. She refused treatment adamantly."

Doc Rizza let out a long breath of air. "All right, I'll speak to her."

He turned to leave, but Tess grabbed his elbow.

"Doc, she knows you're the coroner. And she's okay with it."

Doc Rizza's mouth slacked for a split second. "All right, I got that," he said, heading back toward Kiana's room.

24

COMPETITION

"And… cut!"

The director's voice still resonates in my memory, a faint echo of that sunny day in the Everglades, when we were shooting the Florida Python Challenge episode of *Swamp Secrets*.

The last episode I got to shoot before we were taken. Before David was killed.

I rack my brain searching through glimpses of the snake hunters' faces, faded through time, wondering if my captor was indeed one of them and I can't recall. It's useless. I just can't remember.

For some reason, the sound of the director's voice at the end of the early morning segment is still fresh in my mind as if it happened only yesterday. Those two words set the entire crew in motion and released the hunters from their positions. We'd just wrapped up the greeting segment as we call it, the first few minutes of the show where we introduce the week's theme, the contestants, and I give the viewers a minute-long background on what they're about to watch. The week before, it was baby alligators. No hunting involved, just filming them in their natural habitat. The week before that, we showcased pink American flamingoes.

But it's the snake-hunting competition that gets the most viewers, and I've always been thrilled to shoot episodes that get larger audiences. Not because I'm hungry for fame or anything. It's only because I get to share my love for the Glades with more people. That's what matters to me. Or used to.

It was still early, the sun barely above the horizon, and we were filming on location in the southwestern part of the peninsula, by Hell's Bay Canoe Trail just off State Road 9336, where the Burmese snakes are most common. Just like the rest of the crew, I was covered in insect repellent and didn't mind the buzzing and the occasional swat, but my makeup artist was new to my show and was handling it badly. She was a tall, slender redhead with big eyes that darted fearfully left and right as if tracking the flight of invisible monsters. By the time she finished touching up my mascara and ruffling up my mid-back, blonde hair, she was almost in tears.

Sensing her weakness, a snake hunter walked by her with a dead python around his neck, holding its enormous head in his hand, showing off his catch like you'd expect him to. He wandered a bit too close to her. That did it for my poor makeup artist. She bolted back to the car sobbing, shoving the cameraman forcefully out of her way. The man nearly dropped his portable broadcast camera into the swamp.

"Son of a bitch," he muttered, regaining his balance and looking at the disappearing redhead. "You shouldn't be here, sweetheart," he said, long after she'd run past, for himself really, because she was already out of earshot.

But the seventeen snake-hunting contestants laughed, the roaring cackles startling birds into taking emergency flight from the sea marshes spanning around us for miles.

I walked over to the man wearing his catch on his broad shoulders and stopped squarely in front of him, hands propped firmly on my hips.

"You're an asshole," I informed him calmly, then walked away under the director's puzzled stare. I knew his kind of people, swamp people as some Floridians call them more or less irreverently. They didn't intimidate me one bit. To me, they were like distant family, troublemaking cousins you occasionally invite for the family Fourth of July barbecue while praying they won't embarrass you in front of your neighbors. Some of them I knew from last year's contest, while others were new to me but still felt familiar somehow.

Either way, an asshole is an asshole, and that man needed to know who and what he was. Well, if he'd woken up that morning dreaming of how he'd be featured on my next show, he was out of luck. I never feature people like him. Even if I film them without knowing what they are, when I find out, they're gone. I'd rather voiceover a stretch of B-roll than inflate their chauvinistic ego.

"Can't believe that prick," my assistant producer said. "Too bad we can't kick him out of the contest. That would really hurt," she added with a mischievous grin.

Belinda Santillo, or Bella for short, has been my assistant producer since *Swamp Secrets* was first filmed deep inside the Glades at an isolated chickee by Whitewater Bay. From the day we met in the show's studio, she's been my best friend. We instantly clicked. A fiery brunette with sleek, long hair and a slightly crooked smile that seems to take the entire world on a dare, Bella can make things happen with the speed and efficiency things need to happen in television. She just does, and makes it seem easy; it's her gift.

"Don't worry, Bella, something tells me this loser's just a loser, nothing more."

She eyed the hunter sideways, her nose slightly crinkled. "Did you see the size of that snake? He might actually win."

"It's the number of snakes that gets the big prize, not the size." I looked at the hunter in question. He wore a red, sleeveless shirt that revealed part of a snake tattoo on his neck. Our eyes met and I looked away. There was something sticky about him, repulsive, and it wasn't about his choice of game. I wasn't afraid of snakes, not since my dad taught me how to tell venomous ones from nonvenomous. I had this cautious respect for snakes, for Burmese pythons in particular, since he'd told me that one could kill you instantly as soon as it wraps its body around your rib cage. Your heart can't beat anymore. That's it... that's how stronger prey than humans, faster, more agile animals like deer and alligators, fall victims to the Burmese's deathly grip. In an instant.

But that didn't mean I'd hesitate to shoot one dead. They're an invasive species, threatening the fragile ecosystem of my beloved Everglades. Python-hunting competitions like the one we were covering usually brought big prizes. Ten thousand dollars would go to the winner, seventy-five hundred to the runner-up. And every single dead snake brings its hunter a nice four hundred dollars. The biggest snake caught also brings a special prize, a thousand bucks and a medal.

That's why seventeen of the Glades' most experienced and courageous snake hunters had lined up that morning, standing at the water's edge by their flat-bottomed boats. Some had brought pirogues. A younger man I'd never seen before had arrived in a small airboat, inciting comments from the other hunters. Not because it was faster and would give its owner an unfair advantage. Quite the opposite; most of the hunters believed the noise of the powerful fan used for the airboat's propulsion might scare snakes away. Side glances, giggles, and bets started flying around but that man didn't seem to care.

I'd greeted all of them in the earlier segment. They each got to say their names and a little something about their experience hunting snakes in the Glades. I had to choose three men I would feature prominently in the show. I would actually ride along with one of them, taking only the camera crew with me, and shoot some live action deep into the swamp.

"I'll do your hair," Bella offered. "There's no time to get someone else to cover makeup."

"It's fine the way it is, don't sweat it," I said, looking at the hunters, still trying to decide which one I would team up with. Perhaps the better choice would be the one with the biggest boat, so that the new cameraman, his assistant, and me would fit alongside the hunter and his catch. On the way back, burlap sacks with coiled snakes would take up some of the boat's capacity. "Who do you think?" I asked, knowing Bella understood what I was talking about.

"Him, maybe?" she pointed discreetly at a six-foot-four hunk. The man noticed her looking and grinned widely, making an inviting gesture with his hand. Flustered, Bella looked away. "I don't know, girl. All I know is who *I* want to team up with tonight," she whispered and winked. "If you know what I mean."

"Ooh, Bella, pray tell," I quipped. She was always looking for a date. Beautiful and sassy, she should've been the center of attention but wasn't, as if men found her too intimidating and moved on without even trying to see what she was like.

"Oh, you don't know?" she lowered her voice and leaned over, shooting glances to make sure no one could hear us. "And you call yourself my best friend."

"That I am, but not a mind reader," I replied, instilling humorous, exaggerated wisdom in my voice.

"It's him," she said with a quick gesture toward the man standing a few yards away from us, balancing the camera on his shoulder.

So, my BFF had found herself a new guy. I grinned. "The cameraman? Really? Where are you guys going?"

"Don't look!" she commanded harshly with a whisper. "I don't know where we're going." She flashed a quick lopsided grin my way. "The moment he asks me out, you'll be the first to know." I chuckled. "What do you think? Is he the one?"

"How am I supposed to tell? I don't know the guy," I replied in my defense. "He's on loan with our crew." I resisted the urge to stare over my shoulder and size the guy up.

"You don't need to know him. *I* need to know him. Let me have this one, please. I really need a life. Even if he's the strong, silent type, and... meh. Facial hair is so not my thing." She bit the tip of her finger, shooting side glances to the guy. "Who knows, maybe it tickles. You know, down there," she added in a laughter-strangled whisper.

I laughed. She spoke as if I were the ultimate maneater. "Have at him." I looked over my shoulder briefly. He was tall and broad-shouldered and seemed okay. He was dressed neatly in a long-sleeved white shirt and jeans. The baseball cap he wore had the Gators logo imprinted in red and green. A pair of mirrored Ray-Bans shielded his eyes completely. I couldn't tell if he was on to my bestie's blatant flirting.

He seemed totally absorbed by his camera, tinkering with its settings and focusing on several areas of the landscape while making adjustments, completely oblivious to Bella's interest. "What's his name?"

"Jim," she said in an apologetic tone, shrugging as if embarrassed the man of her dreams didn't have a better name. "Don't be sad. You can have all seventeen of them macho hunters."

"Ugh," I exclaimed, then we both burst into laughter so loudly almost everyone looked in our direction. "No, thank you very much. You can have them too, since I see you're into beards lately."

Bella shot the cameraman a quick look, curling her lip. She wasn't head over heels with that guy; he seemed more like a no-other-option kind of guy to her. "Well, no one's perfect." We laughed again and carried on chatting lightheartedly while the competition organizers affixed numbers on the hunters' chests and backs.

"Who won last year?" I asked Bella. The break was over. We were back to work.

"That guy, number four. John Barstow. I can't believe how bad you are with faces." She pointed him out with a perfectly manicured finger. "Wanna go with him?"

"Nah," I replied. "He had enough face time last year. Let's go with number ten, the guy in blue cargo pants."

"Hank," she said, after checking briefly on a list of names. "All right, I'll get everything set up." She gave the rising sun a critical glance. "Let's get things done before it gets too hot. Who do you want as collaterals?"

That was an inside joke. The full term for it was collateral damage. She meant the other two men I'd feature on the show.

"I wish we had a woman to put in front of the camera," I said, looking at the hunters from a distance with a critical eye. They all looked the same. Bulky, sweaty, bearded, with unkempt hair and worn-out clothing, but apparently strong enough to knot a python with their bare hands. "You know, to offset a bit of this extreme masculinity."

"Not going to happen," Bella replied, looking at her list of names. "Number eight maybe? Shane Delaney?" She looked up from the paperwork, looking toward the water's edge for that contestant. It was the guy in red, the asshole who'd cost me the assistance of my makeup artist. "Hell, no," she said the words before I could. "How about number fourteen instead? He's ex-Army. His name is Tom."

The veteran was really tan and somewhat thinner than the others, but his arms were like knotted steel wire, crossed at his chest, bulging through the taut sleeves of his drab camo T-shirt. From across the parking lot, his eyes drilled into mine, his expression unreadable. I'd probably be safest with him. "Okay. How's six for the second interview?"

"Perfect," Bella replied. "Josh is last year's runner-up." She held her fist up and I bumped it with mine.

We were ready. One more segment to shoot, then the official start of the competition in exactly nineteen minutes.

I approached the edge of the water, where the contestants were loading their boats, securing their gear, getting ready to start the hunt. I spoke briefly with number ten, Hank Blackwell, who was thrilled to hear I would be joining him for the hunt.

Then, as I was walking to speak to one of the collaterals, I heard someone say behind me, "Do we have to grab that ass to make some dough here today?" A couple of men chuckled.

I froze in place then swiftly turned around. Only one of the men stared at me in an insulting kind of way, licking his lips and threading his thumbs through the loops of his jeans as if to draw attention to his crotch. His gaze shifted ever so slightly from lustful to vicious, giving me the chills.

Number six, last year's runner-up.

Before I could say anything, the director approached him and said, "You're off the show."

The man grumbled, then looked at me again with a certain vileness in his eyes I can't forget.

Number two, the guy with the airboat, ended up on my list, and I actually opened my segment with his interview. He was articulate and polite, speaking at lengths about the choice of a boat to cross these marshes while looking for snakes, the type of boots most suited for the lime-bottomed shallow waters, and his overall confidence that he would win.

Number two did great in the interview, and so did the veteran, number fourteen. Yet my mind clung to number six, the look in his eyes, the savagery in them, the lust for blood.

Mine.

But he wasn't the man who took me.

25

SHORT LIST

Each missing girl's address was marked on the map with a colored pin. Another, a darker shade of the same color, showed the place where they went missing or were last seen. Bright red and burgundy were the colors reserved for Kiana's home address and the Miami Beach parking lot where she and her husband had been taken from.

In total, twenty-four digital thumbtacks were scattered all over the South Florida map, resulting in a crowded, hard-to-analyze image displayed on Donovan's laptop screen.

One could hear a pin drop in the stuffy training room while Tess leaned over Donovan's left shoulder, studying the map, looking for patterns. The missing girls came from every area of Central and South Florida, from Tampa to Orlando to Miami. One was from as far as Jacksonville but had just moved into a dorm at USF in Tampa, only three days before she vanished.

"Do you see anything?" Fradella asked.

She took a step back. Sometimes it helped to look at the locations from a distance, rather than at street level. "Maybe," she said, not liking one bit the hesitation in her voice. Everything about the case had been unusual, a break from the norm in more ways than she cared to admit. "D, can you remove home addresses, and leave us with the disappearance sites?"

"You got it," the analyst replied, punctuating his reply with a few quick taps on his keyboard.

Half the colorful thumbtacks vanished from the screen.

"There," she said, pointing at the screen with her index finger. "See this line along the coast? From South Beach, where Kiana was taken, to Wynwood, and all the way to Miami Shores, along the coast."

"Yeah, I see it," Fradella replied.

Six of the pins were clustered together in a tight grouping, while the others were randomly scattered in various points south of St. Petersburg on the west coast and Cape Canaveral on the eastern seaboard.

"Let's focus on these cases," Tess concluded with a quick, light tap of her fingernail against the screen where the colorful dots almost touched one another. "Pull everything you can. Full victimology, history, whereabouts in the twenty-four hours prior to disappearance, the works. If we're lucky, these victims have crossed paths before." She patted Donovan on the shoulder, smiling encouragingly. "You're the best, D."

"Don't I know it," the analyst quipped, already immersed in his work.

"Let's go," she said to Fradella, who followed her through the door with a raised eyebrow.

Walking quickly through the corridor and noticing it was swarming with people rushing in both directions, she led the way to Kiana's room, hoping she'd find Doc Rizza still talking with her.

The coroner stood outside the girl's room, observing her through the glass pane. The vertical blinds were half-open, gently swaying under the jet of conditioned air flowing from the ceiling vents.

Inside the room, almost all light had been filtered out by opaque blinds that managed to keep the sun's rays from barging in. A large flower arrangement complete with *Get Well* balloons and a plush teddy were set by the bedside on a small table. There must've been at least two dozen, long-stemmed red roses in that vase, seemingly floating on a cloud of baby's breath. A large card was set half-open by the vase.

Kiana slept on the bed, struggling through what seemed to be an agitated, restless slumber filled with terrors.

Tess approached Doc Rizza and whispered, "How did it go?"

The coroner shot her a quick glance then looked at Kiana. "Not as well as you'd hoped. She didn't want to speak to me any more than she did with you."

"So, you have nothing I can use?" Her tone escalated a bit, drawing the uniformed cop's attention.

"I may be a coroner, Tess, but I'm still a doctor. One thing I'll never do is torture one patient for the potential good of others. This girl doesn't need an interrogation; she needs medical attention and time to grieve, to heal, to find herself after what she's been through." He bit his lip for a moment, then shot Tess a pleading look. "In peace."

Tess looked at Kiana's frail body writhing in her sleep, her heart secretly breaking for the girl. "She's been gone seven months, Doc. And she escaped. The unsub didn't kill her. Either he hasn't evolved to killing yet, or she ran away before he could end her life. Do you know what that means?"

Doc Rizza listened but remained silent after she asked her question.

"It means one or more missing women could still be alive, Doc. It means we have no time to waste, as much as I'd love to give her the time she so desperately needs."

Doc Rizza looked at Kiana for a brief moment. "She won't talk to me, Tess. There's nothing I can do."

Tess stared at the high ceiling for a brief moment, then looked into the coroner's tired eyes. "At least, could you tell if she's got Stockholm?"

He seemed to hesitate before speaking. "In my line of work, we must leave all assumptions for the investigators. Medical examiners stick to science and forensically proven facts, to numbers, evidence, and data." A moment of silence, while the doctor seemed to make a decision that must've required some thought. "But if I were to place a bet, I'd say she doesn't have Stockholm, no."

"Thanks, Doc," Tess said, squeezing the man's warm hand.

"That doesn't make her okay," he added as she turned to leave. "You know that, right?"

"Yeah, Doc, I know that," she replied, choking as she spoke. It would be years before Kiana would be okay again, if ever. She blinked away a rebel tear that burned her eye with the threat of explanations she didn't want to give. "Are you planning to hang around for a while?"

"Yeah, I'll be here a while longer. Maybe she'll change her mind and talk to me after all." He shrugged as if to justify why he didn't believe a word he was saying. "You?"

Tess checked the display of her phone. It was getting late already. "My gut tells me the people she worked with might be able to shed some light. So far, everything about her disappearance seems to be connected with her show."

"You mean, because it was called *Swamp Secrets* and she was held in the swamp?" He had a puzzled expression on his face.

She groaned, feeling the pinch of self-doubt. "If you put it like that, I got nothing, really. Nothing, except my intuition."

26

STONE

The drive to the studio was short, under ten minutes despite the heavy traffic Tess weaved through expertly, with flashers on. Fradella sat quietly in the passenger seat, looking sternly ahead.

"It's okay to talk, you know," she said, taking the off-ramp with squealing tires.

Fradella looked at her surprised and a little flushed. "I know that." A beat of silence. "I guess I'm learning the same job I used to do can be done in an entirely different way. I'm just—"

"It's not that different. We're still looking for means, motive, and opportunity. The same basic principles of criminal investigation still apply. We use forensics, look at evidence the same way, and conduct witness and suspect interviews just like you used to before Quantico." She smiled as she was pulling into the studio's parking lot. "We just focus a bit more on behaviors and try to understand why unsubs act a certain way and how victims are chosen."

He nodded and smiled awkwardly but avoided looking at her. "I'm still learning."

Tess cut the engine and climbed out of the black Suburban. "Faster than you realize," she said as they entered the lobby. The receptionist looked at Tess's badge for a split second, then rushed on clacking three-inch heels to lead them into the producer's office.

He wasn't alone, but quickly suspended his meeting to greet them.

"Martin Stone," he introduced himself, shaking their hands. "Please, have a seat."

Tess sunk into a cushy leather armchair that smelled faintly of orange oil, unable to resist the urge to admire the setting. The producer's office gleamed with sleek luxury. Polished metal accents sparkled against a backdrop of clear, floor-to-ceiling glass windows, revealing the bustling city outside. A glass-topped desk, strewn with top-of-the-line tech, anchored the room, mirroring the cold precision of a steel shelving unit showcasing an array of awards. Comfort met austerity in the plush, metallic-leather executive chair. It was a space that reflected power and success, blending elegance with the hard-edged hues of entertainment industry mainstays.

Stone was in his fifties, an attractive and charismatic individual who moved with ease in that stunning setting. Dressed in an elegant charcoal suit and a white shirt with a tie in shades of metallic gray, he radiated self-confidence in a nonabrasive way. He was effortlessly pleasant and graceful, yet his eyes shimmered with determination from across the desk.

"Thank you for seeing us, Mr. Stone," Tess said. "As you might have heard, Kiana was found—"

"Yes," he interrupted, his voice riddled with excitement. "We're all thrilled she's back. Tell me, how can I help?"

"What happened to the show after she disappeared?" Tess asked, rather abruptly skipping over the small talk. Her question got a flicker of a raised eyebrow from the producer.

"We were stunned. *Swamp Secrets* was about to go national when she vanished. Not sure you knew this, but Kiana had just signed a syndication deal. And we went from that to a hard stop."

"No one replaced her after she vanished?" Fradella asked.

"No." Stone stood and paced the space between his desk and the vast windows overlooking the city. "You see, Kiana *was* the show. It's not like other shows where you can take any promising young talent and train her for a couple of weeks, then kick off a new season with a new host." A sad smile bloomed on his aristocratic lips. "She had a passion for nature that came across with every word she said on that show. She was killing it. She had a knack for keeping it rolling, even when the wild got... well, wild." His eyes lit with admiration as he spoke. "She wasn't afraid of anything. And talk about being prepared... she had every critter behavior down." The smile widened. "She even taught me how to fish, can you imagine?" He stopped his pacing and stood by the window frame.

Tess looked at him sternly. "She's still alive, you know."

He seemed taken aback by her comment. "Of, course, I knew that."

"And yet you speak of her in past tense."

"Oh," he whispered, smoothing his tie with a quick gesture. "I apologize... I meant the past tense that is the show, *Swamp Secrets*, unless you think she'd be coming back soon?"

A cloud darkened Tess's eyes and, for a moment, she didn't trust herself to speak. How could she come back, after everything she'd been through?

"Tell us about her crew," Fradella asked, after shooting her a quick look. "Were there any issues with anyone?"

He drew closer to the desk and looked at Tess intently, then at Fradella. "You mean to say you still don't know who did this?"

"We're not at liberty to discuss the details of an ongoing investigation." Fradella's tone was uncompromising.

"What did she say?" Stone asked. "She must've said something. I heard on the news that her husband is presumed dead. Is that true?"

"Mr. Stone, I believe it would be best if we asked the questions," Tess said.

The producer sat on his chair, an expression of dismay on his face. "Whatever you say."

"Were there any issues with Kiana's crew?" Fradella asked.

"Not that I know of." He rubbed his forehead with the tip of his fingers. "We kept talking about it here, at the studio, after she disappeared, trying to figure it out ourselves. There was one small incident, one of the snake hunters on her last shots gave her a hard time, but it was nothing."

"Really? What happened?" Tess asked.

"Nothing major, just some rude comment that the director overheard and addressed on the spot. Kiana never complained about it; a cameraman mentioned it a while after she went missing. But if you want to know more about the incident, speak to Bella Santillo, Kiana's former assistant producer. She was there that day. My assistant can take you to her."

"You don't normally go, um, where the show is recorded?" Tess asked, painfully aware she knew very little about how those hours of recorded entertainment came into existence.

"Me?" Stone touched his chest with a perfectly manicured hand. "I never set foot in the Glades."

"Oh? And still, you're the producer of this show," Tess said with a slight frown. "You created it, right?"

"Yes, I did." The smile reappeared. "One of my biggest achievements in television. Won me an entire shelf of awards." He pointed loosely at the gleaming steel shelving on the wall at his left.

"For someone who's never seen the Everglades, why *Swamp Secrets*?" Tess probed, continuing to drill into the one detail that made no sense whatsoever.

"It was all Kiana," he replied warmly. "I've lived my entire life in New York, until I decided to retire to South Florida. I moved down here, bought a house in Key Largo and a fancy boat. Then I met Kiana, one day when I was about to return from a fishing trip completely humiliated. It was out by Plantation Island, so, I guess I have come close to entering the Glades, but didn't, not really." He cleared his voice quietly and took a sip of coffee from a white mug kept on a warmer. "Then this girl shows up in a beat-up, rusty old boat with her dad, gives me some pointers and some bait, and I pull a big one out in minutes. I never forgot how she… belonged. It stayed with me. Long, tousled hair blowing in the wind, no makeup, cargo shorts and a worn-out shirt, a natural. Completely unassuming, down-to-earth. What we call in the industry a ratings magnet." Tess raised an eyebrow. "A real crowd puller, even with zero television experience. Girls like Kiana are hard to find these days." He smiled again and lowered his head as if reliving a cherished memory. "A year later, bored out of my mind after so much retirement, I put a proposal on the studio's table. Then I had my assistant make her an offer." He crossed his arms at his chest as if to say he was done talking.

Tess stood and Fradella followed suit. "Thank you, Mr. Stone. One final question before we leave." He nodded as he circled the desk to show them out. "Are you aware of any personal enemies or hate mail received from viewers, stalkers, anything like that?"

"Absolutely not," he replied. "I would've started with that." He shook their hands by the door. "But ask Bella. She and Kiana were, um, are close."

27

FLYING

I had a dream of flying.

More like floating, really. Rising above the tree canopies, my arms stretched far and wide, effortlessly leaving miles and miles of greenery behind me, headed for the ocean blue.

It wasn't a dream; more like a wakeful escape from reality, a place I sought refuge. That wondrous place opened its arms and took me in, lifted me on its invisible wings and allowed me to live what I'd only seen on TV before.

It has no name, the world in which I can fly. It's something I learned I can invoke, much like a prayer invokes hope if not actual help, when my reality is just too much to bear.

I remember waking up to bitter tears flowing from my eyes as he carried me inside the house and threw me over the worktable in that dreary, dusty room. I landed face down against the stained wooden surface, feeling the softness of fresh flower petals under my skin. The taste of daisy pollen on my swollen lips.

Several stemless flowers littered the table, crushed under my weight. I recall thinking how strange that was, how much they didn't belong there, but at the same time not caring. In a weakened, exhausted frenzy, I tried to stand, but his hand gripped my nape and forced me down. Panicked, I flailed my arms, trying to grasp the edge of the table and push myself off it.

The wood left splinters in my skin, in my hands and abdomen. A rusty, crooked nail ripped through my skin. Droplets of blood emerged, unable to soothe the searing pain, and seeped down toward the edge of the table, then trickled down onto its crooked leg.

Terror-stricken, I froze, watching my blood, fresh, fill in the old stain lines.

Someone else had been there before me. Had bled there before me. Maybe Carolyn. Or the girl before her, the one who wrote her haunting message on the wall.

I drew air forcefully, a desperate gasp, then pushed myself desperately against the table, trying to reach the ground with my feet and get my bearings. But his hand had a steeled grip on my neck. All I did in my desperation was drive more splinters into my skin. Bruise my ribs against that rusted nail.

And entertain him.

I could hear his breath accelerating, closer, its singe burning my cheek when he drew close.

"My sweet Daisy," he whispered, "why did you leave so soon?"

I whimpered something unintelligible that made him chuckle. Then I felt more than heard his hand fumble with his belt buckle. Then his zipper.

Panic rose the bile in my throat. I choked and gasped for air. I knew I couldn't fight him; I didn't stand a chance. I wanted to, with every fiber in my body. I wanted to scream, but I'd screamed before, and no one heard me but him. And he'd enjoyed it.

In that split second of sheer terror, I made a promise to myself. Even if I died on that table, I wasn't going to play his game.

I squeezed my eyes shut and desperately searched through my memories for something that could help me escape that place. Escape him. I couldn't save my body from his reach, but my mind, that was all mine, and he couldn't touch it.

I would never allow it.

On the wings of a drone filming footage over the Amazonian jungle, I took flight, soaring a thousand feet above the depths of my hell. Then I visited Ireland, floating over its lush pastures of an incredible bluish green. I was tempted to slow my flight and land for a moment, to search for a four-leaf clover, but I felt afraid. What if I couldn't take flight again?

One day, soon, when my reality would be bearable again, I will travel to Ireland and spend days looking for that perfect four-leaf clover. I made that second promise to myself, eyes squeezed shut and dripping with tears, before regretfully leaving Ireland to float over windmills and fields of colorful tulips in the Netherlands.

Then I was floating over Spanish moss-covered trees. I was in Georgia, on the coast near Savannah, flying low over gentle ocean waves that crashed against the sandy shores, sending droplets of salty water against my face.

I could taste the ocean on my swollen lips, each droplet made of tears I'd cried while I was gone, floating freely, out of his reach.

He was long gone when I opened my eyes again.

It was pitch black. The room was shrouded in darkness, not the slightest bit of light coming from the small window. I was lying on the floor, my entire body aching, trembling, weakened. A loud grumble and a sharp pain in my stomach reminded me I was still alive.

I had no idea how long it had been since I had a bite to eat.

Days and nights had started blending together. I was losing track of how many there had been. From memory, I knew there was nothing I could do while in that room. I stood on shaky legs, leaning against the wall for balance, and felt my way to the door.

My hands trembling, I found the handle and squeezed. It didn't budge. Maybe I was too weak. I took another step closer, then squeezed again and pulled hard. Nothing. I remember clearly the door opened toward the inside, but I felt the edges to make sure. Then I tried again, panting, whimpering quietly, afraid he'd come back if he heard me.

The door remained shut.

Resigned, I sat on the floor, leaning against the wall, and hugged my knees. I kept my eyes wide open in the dark, hoping soon I'd be able to distinguish something, but all I could see was blackness, not even vague shapes of the objects in the room. Nothing but the color of absolute darkness.

Outside the room, night critters performed a symphony of sounds in the surreal harmony of the Glades wilderness I was so familiar with. Two owls were hooting in trees nearby, their voices distinctive over the chorus of frog croaks and insect chirps.

I was almost dozing off to the familiar music of nature when something touched my leg.

I flinched and withdrew, then listened intently, holding my breath. After my panic subsided and my heart's rushed thumping faded, I could hear the sound of tiny claws against the wooden floor, scratching, scuffling. Then the critter squeaked, ever so faintly.

A mouse.

Nothing I couldn't handle.

I breathed and stood, then felt my way slowly through the room until I reached the worktable. Its edge was still damp with my blood. It still smelled of crushed daisies. Struggling a little in the darkness, I climbed on top of it and wrapped my arms around my knees.

Then I closed my weary eyes.

Daylight will make things better, I told myself.

It always does.

28

BELLA

Mr. Stone's assistant swayed her hips, walking quickly through endless corridors minimally decorated with custom-made light fixtures and the occasional modern piece of furniture. Two stories down in a quick elevator ride took Tess and Fradella to the studio level, probably one of several. It swarmed with people, all seeming frantically busy as they bounced from office to office, talking loudly in a lingo Tess only half understood.

The assistant stopped in front of an open office door, where a tall and slender brunette was reviewing glossy prints laid out on a glass table. "Bella, I have two FBI agents who want to speak to you about Kiana."

The brunette dropped the prints she was holding and came over to meet them. "Thanks, Marcie. Please, come on in," she added, extending her hand.

"Special Agents Winnett and Fradella, FBI," Tess said, shaking the woman's hand. She had a firm and quick grip, a trait Tess associated with strong, dynamic personalities. She seemed young, maybe twenty-five or so, and kept an honest, welcoming smile on her lips.

"Belinda Santillo, but you can call me Bella. Please, take a seat." She gestured toward the chairs surrounding the glass table covered with glossy prints. Walking over quickly, she started collecting the prints and stacking them neatly into a folder. "I was so happy to hear Kiana is back. They wouldn't let me see her at the hospital," she added, her smile gone, her eyes touched by sadness. "They said she can't receive any visits except for immediate family, but they gave her the flowers at least."

Tess remembered the two dozen red roses in Kiana's room. "The red roses were from you?"

Bella smiled shyly. "Yes. She's my best friend. I miss her so much."

Tess pulled out a chair and sat. It was soft and comfy, the black leather feeling like butter. Fradella closed the office door, then took a seat at the table next to Tess.

"Tell us about Kiana," Tess asked. "What was she like before she vanished?"

Bella's eyes lit up. "She's full of life, strong-willed, and absolutely great at what she does. No one was surprised when the syndication deal happened. And she's the kindest, most understanding person I've ever known." A frown fluttered over her perfectly waxed eyebrows. "I thought you met her."

Tess let that comment go unanswered. "Was there any hint of a romantic relationship between Kiana and Martin Stone?" She'd meant to ask Stone that question but had decided against it at the last moment. His emotional attachment to Kiana, the way he'd talked about her indicated she was more to him than just an employee. At the same time, he'd spoken of her only in past tense, as if she'd ceased to exist the moment she'd stopped hosting *Swamp Secrets*. Maybe the one thing Stone was emotionally attached to was the show and the money it used to make him.

"What? No." Bella seemed appalled at the idea. "Kiana's totally in love with David." She spoke the words in a strangled voice. She looked around the office for something, then stood and retrieved a small water bottle she uncapped with a quick gesture. After taking a quick sip, she sat and screwed the cap back on, before steepling her hands on the table in front of her. "I heard he's, um, he—they didn't find him, did they?"

"Where did you hear that?" Fradella asked, sounding just as frustrated as Tess felt. "This information hasn't been made public yet."

Tess doubted David's parents would've rushed to speak to the media after seeing Kiana and learning of their son's demise in such a heart-wrenching way.

"It was on the news. They cited sources close to Kiana but didn't specify who."

Damned newspeople and their sources. "Still, I sensed Mr. Stone cared about Kiana very much," Tess asked, slipping into the past tense Stone had used.

"He still does. He and Gerry are good friends and fishing buddies." Another wave of sadness washed over the girl's face. This time it stayed, brimming her eyes with tears she tried blinking away. "Or at least they were, until Gerry had a stroke." She sniffled, then retrieved a Kleenex from the box on the table. "A few months after she vanished. He… couldn't take it."

"That's Kiana's father?"

She nodded, patting her nose discreetly. "I heard she's not doing very well," she whispered. Then, without warning, she reached over the table and clasped Tess's hand. "Please, help me see her."

Tess considered the idea for a split second. "Yes, we can arrange that," she replied, gently withdrawing her hand from the girl's grasp. "We can take you there right now, if you'd like."

Bella sprung from her chair and rushed to collect a few personal items. Her purse, car keys, and a small stuffed dog with a red ribbon around its neck she picked up from one of the bookcase shelves. "She loves this little guy," she clarified, her voice fraught with tears. "I'm ready." She opened the door, ready to sprint out, but then froze in the doorway. "Damn… my car is in the shop. I'll have to call an Uber or get someone to drive me."

"We'll drive you," Fradella offered, holding the door for the two women.

"Perfect, thank you," she said, sounding so happy and relieved Tess was afraid she'd lunge and give Fradella a hug. Or worse, both of them.

On the way to Tess's Suburban, they didn't ask too many questions. Speaking excitedly, Bella shared a few points about what their team was like, how well they worked together, what they were doing now that the show was cancelled, and how much everyone missed Kiana. Nothing caught Tess's attention. Whatever her gut had told her to follow there, she couldn't find.

Fradella took the wheel on the drive over to the hospital, while Tess rode in the passenger seat, half-turned toward the back where Bella was seated. The moment the Suburban set in motion, she started asking questions.

"Mr. Stone mentioned something about a snake hunter causing some trouble on the set," Tess said.

"On location," Bella corrected her with an apologetic smile. "We were filming on location, not on set. Snake hunters never set foot here," she added, gesturing toward the building they were leaving behind.

"On location," Tess repeated. "What was the incident about? Were you there?"

"Yes, I was," Bella replied without a trace of hesitation. "It wasn't anything much, just the typical swamp guy comment, something about Kiana's ass," she said, instantly blushing as she said the word. "Nothing she hadn't heard before. Men are such, um, I didn't mean—" She stopped abruptly, looking sheepishly at Fradella's nape. "I'm sorry."

"What happened after the incident?"

"She just went along with a different guy for the shoot, that's all. I'm actually surprised Martin knew. It's not like Kiana to complain about these things. She says they're just as common to the Glades, like mosquitoes and gators."

"She didn't complain," Fradella intervened, taking the interstate off-ramp. "One of the cameramen did, per Mr. Stone's statement."

"That makes sense, yes, I remember that." For some reason Tess didn't understand, her cheeks caught fire again, and she veered her eyes sideways for a moment. "We were all trying to figure out what had happened to her when she didn't—I mean, after she disappeared. That's when Jim mentioned the snake guy comment. The director was there too. Everyone remembered it, but it was just… nothing."

"Tell me about the competitors on the show that day," Tess asked.

"There were seventeen entrants, all your typical snake hunters. Typical to us, I guess. We cover these competitions twice a year. I can give you a list of names and show you photos."

"You have their information?" Fradella asked. "That's helpful."

"Of course, we do." Feeling a little more comfortable, she leaned forward in the space between the front seats. "Each episode has a binder with the storyboards, call sheets, release forms, every participant's background, the works. We do background checks on everyone. We don't want the embarrassment of featuring someone who's wanted for murder or was just released after serving time for dealing crack. It would reflect badly on the show, the network, on everyone." She took her phone out and typed a text message with fast-moving fingers. "Who do I send it to?"

Tess chuckled, while Fradella gave Bella his phone number. The assistant producer had spunk and seemed quite good at her job.

Fradella pulled into the hospital parking lot and slowed down by the entrance. "And did anyone stand out as particularly creepy?"

Bella stared at Tess with widened eyes and a slightly slacked jaw. "Why are you asking me this? Didn't Kiana tell you who took her?" Her voice was a strangled, fearful whisper.

"It's not that simple. You'll see," Tess replied gently. "Maybe you can help."

Pale and a little shaky, she didn't say another word until they reached Kiana's room. Holding the stuffed dog at her chest, she stopped at the door and peeked inside, where Kiana slept. Her breaths were rapid and shallow, her closed eyes moved with the imagery of her night terror, her lips sometimes parted to let out a muted scream. From a few feet away, seated on a small lab stool, Doc Rizza watched over Kiana warily.

"Oh, no," Bella whispered, covering her mouth with her hand. Then she slid open the door and stepped inside. While Tess and Fradella kept their distance and waited by the door, Bella sat gently on the side of Kiana's bed and touched her arm. "Hey, sweetie," she whispered, caressing her tangled hair, removing a strand that covered her face. "It's me, Bella."

Startled out of her troubled sleep, Kiana sat abruptly and looked at Bella with haunted eyes. "Run," she said in a loaded, tense whisper. "Go now, before he comes back." She shoved Bella hard, pushing her off the bed. "Don't come back here, you hear me?"

Doc Rizza didn't intervene. Now standing, he let the scene play out while he watched, ready to step in if needed but otherwise just observing.

"It's okay, sweetie," Bella said, holding Kiana's hand. "You're safe, you're in the hospital." She put the stuffed dog in Kiana's lap. "Here, I brought Mr. Wiggles for you."

Still confused, Kiana stared at her as if struggling to recognize her. "Run," she said, the tension in her voice still high. "You can't be here." She shoved Bella again. "You understand me? Run!"

Stifling a sob, Bella left Kiana's bed. Tess stepped out of her way, but she stopped and clasped her hand. "Please, help her," she cried, looking at Tess, then at Fradella. "Please, promise me, you won't leave her like this."

Before Tess could answer, Bella rushed out of there, sobbing hard. Alone in the dimly lit hospital room, Kiana lay on the bed and squeezed her eyes shut. A moment later, a shudder rattled her frail body, and she whispered, "Don't touch her, you son of a bitch."

29

WORKSHOP

"You had to run, didn't you?" Carolyn's voice was laced with bitter resentment.

The sharp sting of guilt cut through me. She sounded angry at me for trying to escape this hell. In her place, I would've been angry too.

She was sitting on the dirty, wooden floor, staring past me with an absentminded gaze. One eye was almost swollen shut. She had fresh bruises on her arms and back, and her lip was bloodied.

And I couldn't think of anything to say that would really make a difference. Just banalities, even if they were heartfelt.

"I'm so sorry, Carolyn," I whispered. "Please, let me help you." I couldn't think of anything I could've done to ease her pain, but it felt like the right thing to say.

After a moment of silence, she scoffed bitterly. "And what, exactly, do you think you can do to help me, if the one thing I asked you didn't do?"

Her question threw me off for a moment, but then I realized what she meant.

"I had to try," I whispered. "You know I had to." I wrung my hands powerlessly. "I… just can't resign myself to stay here. To give up."

She shot me a weary look and sighed. Then she stood and reached on top of a stack of wooden crates and retrieved a piece of bread. It was dry, crusty, and touched by mold in places. She broke it in two and handed me a piece. I took it with tears of gratitude in my eyes.

We both ate slowly, although I had to resist the urge to wolf it down. I was famished. It had been at least two days since I ate anything, just some scraps from the hunter's table. We had water from the squeaky faucet of a small sink in the workshop, and there was a toilet too, behind a half-wall. But food we lacked almost entirely, and the absence of nourishment had already started to spread weakness and weariness throughout my body. I had to go back out there, if only to get us something to eat.

I had to try again, while I still could.

"Just don't do it anymore," Carolyn warned, crumbs still clinging to her lips moments after she'd finished chewing her bread. "It gets you nowhere but back here, in the devil's workshop."

It was an actual workshop; she was right. Although I'd never thought of naming the room where David had taken his last breath, that name suited it just fine. The worktable now stained with my dried blood was just one of several implements that supported the room's utilitarian function. Several tools cluttered the space, and wooden crates I hadn't thought of rummaging through yet, but I felt I should have. Maybe I could find something I could use. Something with a blade, an axe, a weapon of some kind. The shovel was too heavy and too large for me to wield with any chance of surprising him.

"What was it last night?" Carolyn asked, looking at me with pity in the eye she could keep open.

I turned and stared at her. "What do you mean?"

"Don't get locked in the workshop again," she said instead of replying to my question. "One day, it will break you."

"Carolyn, what are you talking about?" I asked, feeling a chill down my spine.

"He'll try until he finds what breaks you," she replied, her voice breaking at times. "What makes you lose your mind." As understanding was starting to dawn on me, colored in shades of nightmare, she repeated the question. "What was it last night?"

"Um, a mouse, I think. Or a small rat." I stared at her, horror dawning. "You mean, he brings different critters—"

"Yeah," she replied, a barely audible whisper leaving her lips with a long sigh. "Every time you try to escape, he drags you back and tries something else. Until one day, you'll just stay here, paralyzed, afraid of what else he could still do to you, and accept your new life." She wiped a tear with a quick hand movement. "Like me."

Seemingly absentminded, she picked a withered daisy bloom from the worktable and threw it to the floor, then stomped it angrily, crushing the petals under her foot.

Instead of scaring me into staying put, her words fueled my determination to escape. I resisted the urge to bolt out of there through the window that was conveniently left unlocked. I stared at the dirty glass with a new understanding of the man who'd taken us. He was toying with me, baiting me to escape only to give himself the pleasure to hunt me down, defeat me, punish me. Overpower me in a sick game I had already played into unwillingly, until I could fight no more.

He'd already defeated Carolyn. Now it was my turn.

"Each time it's worse than before," Carolyn added, her words an echo of my troubled thoughts.

"Is he ever gone?" I asked, lowering my voice, afraid he might overhear us. "Away from here?"

"Almost every day," Carolyn replied. "He leaves in the morning most days, comes back in the afternoon. As crazy as this sounds, I think the bastard has a job somewhere."

"Then that's when—" I stopped mid-phrase, wondering how come she hadn't thought of it yet. "How do we know when he's gone?"

Carolyn shook her head slowly. Her face was partly hidden behind strands of blonde hair, matted and a little grayish in the faint light. "You don't get it, do you?"

"What?" I asked, drawing closer to her. "Tell me, what am I missing?"

"You think I didn't try?" She looked at me with an intensity I hadn't seen before. Then the flicker vanished. "You can hear his truck's engine from the barn, if you listen hard. But try not to get dragged into the workshop again. The barn's much better. He won't try to break you in there. Only in here."

"Then that's when we leave," I whispered so quietly, she could barely hear me. "When he's gone."

She laughed bitterly, her voice resonating weirdly in the workshop. "He locks everything up before he leaves. He's not stupid."

I wasn't going to give up. "Have you tried?"

"What? To run when he was gone?" I nodded. "Yeah... it didn't work out." She shrugged, as if to say that's why she was still there. "I spent the entire day pushing and pulling at a piece of wood to break out of the barn wall, and I had barely made it out when he caught me."

I closed my eyes, blocking the image that was flooding my mind. Carolyn's body bloodied and hurt, her arms flailing as he threw her onto that table, his hand on her nape, mercilessly holding her down in its steeled grip.

"Rose tried it too once," she added. "He nearly killed her that night."

A beat of desperate silence. "Who's Rose?" I found the courage to ask.

A tear streaked down Carolyn's cheek. "She was here before you. I forgot her other name. She was a student, a beautiful young girl scared out of her mind. She looked just like Amanda Seyfried. I think fear killed her long before he did. She only tried to run a couple of times. By the second night spent in the workshop, her spirit was gone. He'd broken her." She walked slowly to the window and pushed it ajar with her fingers. "She's over there now, with the rest of them." Another tear followed the same path toward her jaw. "I put her there." She drew breath shakily. "I never thought I could do such a thing, dig a grave and bury someone, but at least she's free now."

I looked at the mounds under the old cypress tree, my eyes shifting toward the one with two small branches tied up in a cross with a hair scrunchie. *David, my love, one day I'll break free from here. I'll keep my promise. Or I'll die trying.*

"Don't run again," Carolyn added after a while, disrupting my thoughts like a bad omen. "He always finds you."

30

HUNTERS

"Why didn't you stop her?" Doc Rizza asked in a low whisper, startling Tess out of her thoughts. "It would've been helpful to tell the young woman that Kiana emerges from these dissociated states, and that they're normal for PTS sufferers." He rubbed his nape as if it were stiff or painful. "Although it's a very early and severe onset of PTS, I'll give you that."

Tess stared at Doc Rizza, strangely perplexed by his simple question, unable to say a word. The coroner and Tess stepped outside Kiana's room, sliding the door to a quiet close. He was looking at her in disbelief, while she struggled to find her words.

Really, why hadn't she stopped Bella from storming out of there? Memories of her own recovery, twelve years ago, invaded her mind. She recalled spacing out just like Kiana, reliving her trauma over and over, sometimes with tiny variations from reality, but always so immersive. So strangely captivating, she resented being dragged back into reality, being snatched away from reliving her nightmares. As if watching a movie over and over again, in the hope that one time it would end differently.

With Bella's visit and Kiana's reaction, Tess had been yanked back into her own trauma, reliving pieces of it without realizing. She'd identified with Kiana more than she cared to admit, more than it was useful in an investigation, where keeping one's distance is paramount for clarity and perspective. Now, watching Bella trying to bring Kiana back to reality, she felt like storming in there and telling Bella to leave her the hell alone, because she remembered how it felt when she was pulled back into reality herself.

How incredibly painful it was. Unbearable.

She shook her head slightly, disappointed with herself, doubting her sanity and her ability to continue working the case. Yet no one else was better prepared. Doc Rizza studied her reactions with a hint of worry in his eyes. Then the worry turned into something even scarier.

Understanding.

He'd seen through her defenses, through the wall of denial and faked normalcy she wore like a second skin.

A moment too late, she turned her head away, hiding from the coroner's scrutiny.

"I can call Bella back," Fradella offered. "She texted me the show binder. I have her number."

"N—no," Tess replied. "Let Kiana sleep for now." She sighed and shoved her hands in her pockets, feeling a sudden chill. "I hate to admit it, but she's nowhere near ready to leave this place."

"I agree," Doc Rizza replied sternly. He searched her eyes intently, but she looked away.

After a moment she took to steel herself, to fill her lungs with air and regain confidence in herself, she turned to the medical examiner and asked, "How do we reach her, Doc?"

"We don't," he replied, running his hand over his hair to smooth back the isolated turf still clinging to his scalp. "Not yet."

"Listen, she's the only one who can tell us if there are other women held by this unsub. Only she knows that. Don't tell me there's nothing we can do." She'd drawn closer to Doc Rizza, hands propped on her hips, drilling into his eyes with an angry glare the man didn't deserve. Realizing it, she backed off, a little ashamed.

"Find another way, Tess." Doc Rizza paused for a moment. "Think of her as if she were one of your typical victims. Deceased, with nothing left to say than what you can gather from the evidence found on her body. From my report, from what I can tell you about her demise. You've worked with less. Why can't you do it now?" He drew closer to her, touching her arm with parental kindness in his gesture and voice. "Why are you still here?" Unexpectedly, he wrapped her in a warm hug that brought the threat of tears to her eyes. "Go out there and catch that son of a bitch, all right? I'll watch over this girl for you."

She pulled away and averted her eyes, afraid her tears might show. "You got it, Doc," she replied, glad to hear her voice sounded normal. "Come on, Todd, let's look at those snake hunters."

31

IDEA

A fine white powder had snowed over the wide table, near where Donovan worked on his laptop, barely aware of their arrival. The same powder covered his upper lip and his left-hand fingers, held in midair over an open box of fresh donuts, ready to pounce and grab another. He chewed heartily, then licked his lips with a satisfied groan. A few specks of powdered sugar clung stubbornly to his mouth.

The air in the training room was filled with the smell of fresh donuts, as if the sight of them in the open, inviting box wasn't enough to stir Tess's stomach into demanding sustenance.

"May I?" she asked, grabbing a tissue from the Kleenex box and extracting a huge, mouthwatering cruller from the box.

"Uh-huh," Donovan replied, still holding sugar-stained fingers ready to grab another donut, while typing quickly with only his right hand. "Just give me a minute, let me wrap up the hunters' backgrounds."

Grateful for that minute, Tess sunk her teeth into the fresh donut and chewed with her eyes half-closed. It was delicious.

"You still believe it's one of the hunters?" Fradella asked. "I thought we determined that there's no real connection between that group and Kiana, other than the fact she was held in the Glades somewhere." Hesitating for a moment, he chose a chocolate-frosted donut and took a big bite. A few crumbs landed on his tie, bringing a hint of a smile on Tess's lips. They looked like children, both of them. She probably looked the same.

"They fit the profile. And there's something else," she replied, taking another bite and devouring it. "I mean, other than my gut." Fradella grinned. "I think you know what it is."

He frowned, and the speed of his chewing slowed. "Uh-uh," he said, still chewing. "I don't," he added, after swallowing the rest of the donut and washing it down with half a bottle of cold water from an ice bucket. "I thought we concluded the unsub could've seen Kiana on TV, and that he could be anyone out there with a television and time to spare."

"Correct." She wiped her mouth with the tissue, then dropped it in the trash can. Then she accepted a water bottle from Fradella with a quick nod. "Yes, we know she's been held in the Glades, and these snake hunters spend a lot of time there, but there's something else, a critical tidbit of information we nearly missed."

Donovan raised his eyes from the laptop screen. "All backgrounds are done."

"The snake hunter episode was the only one Kiana hosted as a blonde." Tess drank a bit of water. It felt good, after an entire day spent without taking a sip. She drank some more, reluctant to screw the cap back on. "We have the five missing girls we short-listed, and they're all blondes, right?"

"Right," Fradella said, his eyes glinting. "We narrowed the unsub's time frame to that last episode, whether in person or not. I remember. But he could still be someone who only saw her on TV."

"Yes, it's true the unsub could've never met her in person until the day he took her and her husband. That's an extremely long shot, by the way. Even if he'd originally seen her on TV, he had to locate her, stalk her, figure out when and how to make his move. He didn't just see her on TV, then stumble across her in that parking lot." She stood and walked over to where

Donovan sat. "Right now, we can't look at all those people. We can only look at seventeen snake hunters."

"And what a collection that is," Donovan said, shifting through screens until he displayed a list of names. "All of them have criminal records. Absolutely all of them." He scoffed. "Small stuff mainly, DUIs, a couple of bar brawls, even a manslaughter charge with time served, paroled last year."

"Manslaughter? Which one?"

Donovan crinkled his nose. "Shane Delaney, thirty-two, long rap sheet, although only one charge came with serious jail time. Unfortunately, he was in jail at the time of Kiana's abduction."

"Great," Fradella replied. "It's not like we don't need a break here."

"Wanna hear what for? Not that it matters, but maybe it does."

"Come on, D, cut it off with the suspense," Tess replied. The sugar rush was making her a little irritable. Her analyst didn't deserve it though. She smiled awkwardly, a sort of an apology he pretended he didn't notice.

"They caught him weighing down a python with ball bearings, stuffed down its throat. He won the heaviest snake category, then got thrown in jail for it. They confiscated his boat too, a hundred thousand worth of equipment."

They all burst into a short bout of laughter. People never ceased to amaze Tess. Every time she thought she'd seen it all, there came another one with some crazy, new idea of how to game the system.

"Their average credit score is four-twenty-five," Donovan continued. "I'm surprised it's not less. Only three are married; two have kids. Four of them hold steady, full-time jobs, and only hunt for fun. For the rest of the bunch, this competition is serious money."

"Thanks, D," Tess replied, looking at the list of names. "Do any of them live in the Glades?"

"Almost all of them," Donovan replied.

"Fabulous," Tess muttered, just as the door flung open and Michowsky came in.

"Hey," he said, smiling widely when he saw the donut box. He made straight for it and grabbed the only remaining donut, a bear claw. "What did I miss?"

"I was wondering about you. Everything okay?" Tess asked, not willing to mention his back problem openly.

"Oh, I had issues with my temporary boss. I'm on personal time right now. He had me benched for calling you in on his case without approval. He's investigating it himself, by the way."

Tess rolled her eyes but didn't say anything. If almost all the snake hunters lived in the Glades, she had nothing.

"Do we have a profile yet?" Michowsky asked.

"Barely pieces of one," she said. "We know he's a hunter, because he shot arrows into Kiana's flesh. We know he's more than familiar with the Glades ecosystem, because he was comfortable keeping a kidnapped woman there for seven months. And we mostly assume he's a sexual predator, although Kiana refuses to make any statement to this fact. Anything else I'd say to fill in the blank spaces of this profile would be statistical in nature, not evidence or testimony based."

"But Doc Rizza was right," Fradella intervened. "We've worked with less. Caught unsubs with less."

She tilted her head, considering his statement. "Yes and no. When we have a dead body, the medical examiner is usually able to tell us every piece of the unsub's signature. Every detail of the assault is analyzed, compared, recorded. With Kiana, we just don't know."

"What do you mean?" Michowsky asked.

"For example, was the snakebite on Kiana's leg part of the unsub's signature? Or did that happen when she escaped? Still, the snakebite is older, not recent. So, she escaped before? Why did she go back?"

An incoherent thought started swirling in her mind, bothering her like an uninvited insect. She couldn't tell what it was... something like a hint or an instinctual idea.

"Maybe she went back because that's what she wants to do now," Fradella said simply. "She wants to go back, doesn't she?"

She nodded, thinking through her next moves. "Let's get a warrant for the snake hunter who harassed Kiana on the show. Then you two pay this guy a visit. Maybe we hit jackpot with this guy."

"Dream on. That kind of luck doesn't really happen to people like us." Michowsky wiped his hands with a tissue and took the empty donut box to the trash can in the corner. "Fradella, why don't you put in for the warrant? The FBI is officially handling this case."

"Already done," Donovan replied.

"Awesome," Tess replied. "You guys go ahead, it's almost five, and you don't want to be in the Glades after sunset."

"And you?" Fradella asked.

"I'll go back to victimology. Kiana has made reference to other girls twice before." Michowsky raised an eyebrow. "The latest, with her unusual reaction when her assistant producer came to visit. If Kiana was but one of many taken, then the snake guy on the show probably has nothing to do with it. He might know something about someone, and that's our best shot."

"How are you going to tackle victimology," Fradella asked, "when there's no clear MO, no dead bodies, nothing but eleven missing person cases scattered over five years and an area that is home to over ten million people? Beyond victims' histories prior to abduction, you have nothing. Where would you start?"

Reaching for the door handle, Tess smiled and said, "I have an idea."

32

SNAKE

I must've let a week or so go by. Or was it three? It's hard to remember now, the days and nights blended together in one endless nightmare. With each passing day, I grew weaker, more fragile, more afraid that the next attempt to escape would be my last. Not because I would succeed, but because he would catch me and end my life with one swift blow.

Every day I let pass by without running was an exercise in willpower, not knowing what another day might bring. I fought the urge to escape with every fiber of my being, knowing it would pay off to learn his ways first, his routine, the distant, faint sounds of his comings and goings. How his truck sounded when he pulled over by the side of the house. How oversized tires crunched pebbles and dirt when he left in the mornings. How the sound of the opened fridge door was soon followed by the microwave beeping and the TV turned on. Then, about ten minutes later, a pop marked a can of beer being opened. And another… and another. Then snoring.

I still didn't know when, in all this hellish routine, he locked and unlocked the windows and doors that held Carolyn and me captive. Somehow, he did, silently, without being seen.

The night before I stayed up and tested the barn window every hour or so, pushing it gently with a finger to see if it still opened. It did, then immediately fell back into the closed position, driven by a spring mounted on its frame. Then, about an hour or so after sunrise, I pushed the frame to open it and it stayed closed. I felt I was losing my mind. Angered with myself for not seeing him sneak by to latch it, I paced the room for a few minutes until Carolyn talked me into settling down and staying put. I did so, only because I realized my constant movement gave her a sense of panic.

I sat on the floor, leaning against the wall, looking at the corrugated metal ceiling, wondering if anything was holding it in place. It was too high anyway; I dismissed the thought. Then I noticed tears streaming down Carolyn's face.

"What's wrong?" I asked. It must've been the most ridiculous question in history. Everything was wrong. Every single damn thing.

"I miss him so much," she whimpered, clasping her hands at her chest as if holding something close, something very small or ethereal.

"Is there anyone waiting for you?"

My question ripped a sob out of her chest. She wept for a while, and I didn't ask any more questions. Nor did I rush to her side to comfort her. I knew she still tensed if I hugged her, her body understandably loathing any physical contact with strangers after who knows how many months in this hellhole.

I had withdrawn into the world of my thoughts when she said, "A son. He just turned two." Her voice was fraught with tears still, a whisper wrapped in immense sorrow.

A son. I couldn't begin to understand her heartache. "What's his name?" I asked.

"Brian. I left him with the babysitter and went out to meet with friends." She sniffled and pressed her lips together for a moment. "The first time I went out after having him. That's all it took. One time."

"It's not your fault," I said, uttering the words I knew she needed to hear. "Only one man is to blame." My voice took on inflections of pure hatred as I spoke.

But she didn't pay attention. "He must be with my parents now." She wiped her eyes with the backs of her hands. "I hope he's with them. My husband left when I was five months pregnant. He's a drunk and a piece of shit. For once, I'm glad he's all that."

"How come?"

"Because he wouldn't want Brian to live with him. He's better off with Mom and Dad." Another sob shattered her breath. "Not knowing how he is kills me." She patted her chest a couple of times. "Inside. It's like I'm dying. I can't stop thinking I'm never going to see my little boy again."

I pushed myself over the floor to reach her and took her hand. "I'll get us out of here, I promise." I squeezed her hand, but felt it limp in mine, as if life had already left her body. "Now I know the sounds of the house better. And it's going to happen today."

As if my touch burned her skin, she pulled away. "Please, don't! He'll kill us both." The look she gave me was one of sheer terror.

"Not if I make it out of here and I come back with the cops," I whispered, bringing my lips close to her ear.

Her body shuddered. "You think you can make it out of the Glades?"

"I have to," I replied earnestly. "He's never going to let us go. You know that, right?" I stood and walked over to the window. A fresh, stemless daisy was laid on the sill, a few petals torn, scattered on the floor.

I hated those things.

In the distance, a microwave beeped. A moment later, the TV came on, and some sports announcer said something unintelligible, the exaggerated excitement in his voice the only indication a game was on.

It was time.

After looking at Carolyn once more, I snuck out the unlocked door, careful at every step I took, looking around, listening, making sure I didn't make a sound. I hid myself behind trees, so he wouldn't see me from the house. I chose a different path away from the house, even if that path led me southwest, not directly south from there. But the sky was clear, and I could see the sun between the trees, about two or three hours before setting.

I knew where west was. This time, I could find my way home.

I must've stridden like that for about thirty yards or so, faster and faster, gaining confidence with every step that put distance between me and that place. That's when the sound of a cord snapping taut gave no warning of the net that snared me. Lifted a few feet from the ground, wrapped into a fishing net that smelled of mold and seaweed and rotten fish, its knots digging into my skin, I dangled like a writhing and shrieking human charm on a tree's unlikely piece of rope jewelry.

I had stepped into a snare trap, the likes of which had been used by hunters for centuries to hunt big game. And the hunter who'd laid the trap was laughing a mere ten feet away, his cackles silencing the uncaring wilderness for mere seconds.

Bitter tears sprung from my eyes. "No," I whimpered, grabbing hold of the fishnet, anticipating the fall when he finished cutting the rope.

"I knew you'd make my day, sweet Daisy," he said, his voice coarse and breathless as he cut the rope. "Have you decided to stay after all?"

I landed on the ground hard, still wrapped in the fishnet. I tried to free myself, to get up and run, but the net was tangled around my limbs. I flailed desperately to no end other than serving as entertainment for my captor.

Then I stopped trying to escape, knowing I was defeated. Again.

I knew what was coming, the agonizing routine I had already learned.

First, the workshop table, where rugged, splintery edges cut into my flesh while I waited, eyes desperately shut and mind wandering, for him to finish with me and leave.

Then nightfall in the workshop, while, in the distance, I could hear Carolyn screaming and crying. I waited for him to bring her, but he didn't. The darkest hour of the night found me alone in there, shaking, huddled in the corner of the room, eyes wide open, fixed on where the darkening rectangle of the window had faded to black. Because that's where the first light of dawn would appear, when that window would turn just a little bit lighter than anthracite.

But I wasn't alone.

A snake slithered across my legs, stopping at times. I froze, my heart thumping in my chest so loudly I could only hear the rhythmic whoosh of my own blood. I covered my mouth with my hand to keep the scream locked inside my chest and slowly withdrew with the slightest movement.

The snake didn't run away but didn't pounce either. It stood immobile, from what I could tell, and hissed a couple of times, the sound of its fear.

I forced some air into my lungs and willed myself calm, rational. Had it been a rattlesnake or a cottonmouth, it would've attacked already. Both venomous species are famously quick to pounce. Or would it?

What if I was wrong?

I sat there, frozen, not daring to move again, waiting for it to go away, but it didn't, probably attracted by my body heat. In my crazed mind, I kept imagining things. Was it a python? How large? It didn't *feel* large. I didn't sense much of its weight on my leg. What should I do if it started coiling its body around my chest? What if it was a copperhead? I couldn't remember if copperheads were aggressive or not. That tidbit of information eluded me, driving me insane. What if it was a coral? There's no antivenom for those. Not that the hunter would rush and call 911 for me if I got bitten.

When the snake finally moved, I started screaming, panic so powerful, so overwhelming I couldn't control it. I shrieked until I ran out of breath, then crawled to the worktable and climbed on top of it, sobbing and wondering if the snake would follow me there. It probably would, but it just felt better to not sit on the floor while the creature slithered somewhere unseen.

That's where the first light of dawn found me, on that table, hugging my knees and shaking uncontrollably. After a while, when I could see clearly into the darkest corners of the room, I started looking for the snake, not daring to climb off that table until I'd found it.

Then the door swung open, and the hunter came in, smiling.

My throat suddenly dry, I stared at his strong arms as he approached, then noticed the lustful glint in his cold eyes.

"Hello, Daisy."

33

DAISY

Tess found Kiana awake, eating pudding from a small plastic cup with measured, slow movements. She sat on the bed with her legs folded underneath her. At the foot of the bed, Doc Rizza, seated on a four-legged stool, was telling her a story about something he'd noticed at the farmers' market the week before. She listened without interrupting, without spacing out, occasionally taking a small spoonful of chocolate pudding and seemingly savoring it.

On her way over, Tess had swung by the nurses' station, where a flash of her badge earned their cooperation. One of the nurses printed copies of the missing persons' photos in large color format, then offered a manila folder where Tess could hold them.

With that folder tucked under her arm, she slid the door to Kiana's room open and stepped inside.

"Turns out, bees are capable of recognizing human faces. Did you know that?" Doc Rizza was asking as Tess walked in.

Kiana nodded and took a bite of pudding, holding it in her mouth for a while. "Uh-huh," she replied without opening her mouth. She didn't seem to notice Tess's arrival or mind it if she did.

"Well, that was news to me," Doc Rizza replied, standing up with a groan. "Why don't I give you two a minute?" he added, walking toward the door. He looked at Tess with an unspoken plea in his eyes.

The moment Doc Rizza left the room, Kiana abandoned the pudding on the table, only half-eaten. She gave it a regretful look, then stared at Tess inquisitively. "I guess the fun is over, huh?"

She seemed perfectly lucid, aware of her surroundings, in a state of mind one would consider normal for her situation.

"I have a few more questions," Tess said, pulling Doc's stool closer to the side of the bed and taking a seat. "I'll make it quick."

"Yeah." The condescension in Kiana's voice was unmistakable.

"Will you sit with our graphic artist for a sketch of the man who kidnapped you?"

She turned her head to the side, looking away from Tess. She seemed to be staring at the window. It was still covered by vertical blinds, but someone had opened them partially. Slivers of daylight made it through between slats, sunlight and shade dancing on the wall behind Kiana. In the tense silence, only the faint beep of the monitor could be heard.

"I don't think I can," she eventually replied. "Don't make me. Please."

Tess nodded. "It's all right. We'll go as easy as you'd like."

"Thank you," the girl replied, looking straight at Tess for the first time since she'd arrived.

"Were you sexually assaulted while you were held captive?" Tess asked gently, watching carefully for her reaction.

She caught a glimpse of her pupils dilating before Kiana turned her head toward the window again.

Tess waited patiently. It wasn't an easy question to answer.

When Kiana looked back at Tess, her eyes were ice-cold. "Let me tell you how this is going to work. If I say I was assaulted, all my life, everything I am and I'll ever be, will become about that assault. About what he's done to me. That's what everybody, friends and strangers equally, will see in me. That's what they'll talk about. I will be reduced to what this man has done. Some will pity me, while others will secretly fantasize, visualizing the assault every time they lay eyes on me." She paused for a moment, sounding a little choked. "My answer is no. I was not assaulted."

Tess realized she'd been holding her breath. It was uncanny... Kiana had voiced her own thoughts from twelve years ago, almost word for word. Tess took a deep breath, doing her best to hide the emotions the girl's statement had stirred up inside her.

"Noted," she replied calmly. "We have enough as it is to put him away for a long time." It was the least she could do for that girl.

A flicker of surprise flashed in Kiana's eyes. "Thank you."

Tess set the folder on the bed. "One more question. Could you please look at some photos, and let me know if they look familiar?"

Kiana seemed startled by the request somehow. She turned pale but nodded and reached toward the folder with a trembling hand. Tess opened it and showed her the first photo, watching for her reactions.

The first picture, belonging to a twenty-three-year-old gas station attendant named Alana Munch, got Kiana to shake her head. Although watching closely for microexpressions, Tess didn't notice any flicker of recognition.

She turned the page.

Kiana's facial expression shifted to surprise and grief. Her lower lip quivered, and a tear sprung from her eye. She touched the woman's face with trembling hands and whispered, "Daisy."

Frowning, Tess checked her notes. The woman's name was Carolyn Ladson. She was a waitress from Miami. She didn't correct Kiana. Instead, she turned the page slowly.

The next photo stirred Kiana up worse. She stroked the photo with her index finger as if caressing the girl's hair. Then she whispered, "Daisy."

The woman in the photo was Ashley Nettleton, a hotel receptionist from Hialeah.

"No, Kiana, her name is Ashley. Do you know her?"

A silent tear was the only answer Tess received for a while. Kiana stared at Ashley's photo, seemingly unable to take her eyes off of it, lost in what seemed to be painful memories. "Daisy," she repeated.

That name had to have some meaning Tess didn't understand yet. It had to be more than a name, but what exactly, she didn't know yet. Tess moved on to the next image.

Kiana didn't recognize a woman who'd been taken four years before her abduction, a schoolteacher by the name of Sally Murphy, but hesitated when looking at the fifth image. It was a student by the name of Rose Sandoval. Kiana's hand hovered over it as if unsure whether she knew the girl.

Tess was about to blame Kiana's hesitation on Rose's uncanny resemblance to Amanda Seyfried. But then, Kiana asked, "What's her name?"

"Rose," she replied, surprised. "Rose Sandoval."

Kiana touched the picture briefly and said, "Daisy."

Tess closed the folder slowly and set it aside on the table. "Who is Daisy?" she asked. The women Kiana had called by that name were the three most recent abductions. It couldn't be a coincidence.

Kiana put a hand on her chest and stared into thin air for a moment, completely silent. Then she looked at Tess. "You have to let me go. I must go back."

"Do you know where Daisy is?"

Kiana stared at her hands with the same unusual, eerie expression she had the first time Tess had met her. Her head hung, and tears fell from her eyes, staining the back of her hands as she kept them in her lap, resting on her thighs, trembling slightly.

"Yes, I'll take you back," Tess said, reluctantly deciding to make it happen. Whatever the girl was hiding, whatever it was she couldn't talk about, was hidden there, in the depths of the swamp, and she was willing to take her to it. "Tomorrow morning, first thing," she added after giving it some thought. She hadn't heard yet from Michowsky and Fradella but felt the same urgency as Kiana did. Maybe Ashley was still alive, and she was wasting precious time waiting until the morning.

"No," she said, leaning forward and grabbing Tess's hand. "Now. We have to."

"Is Daisy still alive, Kiana?" Tess asked, thinking of Ashley, the most recently taken of the five missing girls. The unsub wouldn't be the first to give his victims a different name.

"I have to go back," she insisted, letting go of Tess's hand and pounding weakly on the bed with her emaciated fist. Her gesture, albeit forceful in its nature, barely crinkled the sheets.

"I can't take you into the Glades at night. The sun's already set." She paused for a moment, seeing how her words seemed to devastate Kiana.

"I have to go back," she whimpered. "I have to know." She wrapped her arms around her knees and started rocking back and forth, the way some children do when they're left alone for too long.

Then she started singing a children's song, softly, in a shaky voice that could barely carry the tune, sending shivers down Tess's spine.

"Ring around the rosy,
Pocket full of posy,
Ashes! Ashes!
We all fall down!"

34

BOOTS

I'd spent half the afternoon sitting on the damp floor by Carolyn, not making a sound, watching her sleep. I wasn't sure she was sleeping, though. Sometimes she seemed to slip into unconsciousness. Since the hunter had brought me back to the barn, she hadn't said a word to me, nor moved from where she laid. I'd heard her screams the other night; I had no question in my mind about what she must've endured.

Because of me.

Because I'd failed.

There I sat, nursing my feet, pulling splinters and burrs, and realizing I couldn't fail again. But I couldn't wait any more either. There was nothing else to learn about the hunter's routine. It all came down to trying, again and again, until one day I'd make it out.

Maybe instead of breaking out of this place, I should break into it, for starters. Break into his house when he wasn't there and see what useful things I could find. Gather some food, some medicine, get stronger, get Carolyn back on her feet.

I should try to start his truck. Maybe I could manage what I've seen done in the movies, with the wires pulled from under the dashboard. I was hoping it would be an older truck; I was sure the newer ones couldn't be started that way.

Or maybe I could just run past the truck and follow its trails back to the road, instead of risking it by cutting straight through the wilderness. But what if the road he took was a much longer hike, than the straight due south escape route I had planned? Highway 41 crosses the Florida peninsula almost horizontally, running parallel to I-75. Based on the flora and the landscape, I had guessed I was closer to 41 and decided to try my luck going south. The worst possible distance I could be looking at was anywhere between ten and fifteen miles, something I could maybe pull off in a day.

If he didn't catch me again.

But what were my chances, really? He'd placed traps in probably all directions; I had already stepped in two of them. I was afraid to think what else was lying out there, hidden under the thick layer of rotting foliage.

And I was slow, not only weakened by hunger but also having to look where I stepped, and forced to keep to dry, visible ground.

I needed boots.

Tall ones, so I could cut through the shallow marshes without fear of snakes, without hurting my feet at every step.

Carolyn whimpered and shifted in her sleep. I crouched by her side and called her name, then pushed a strand of hair off her face, barely touching it with my finger.

She opened her eyes and looked through me, her eyes dark and haunted. Then she closed them again. "You're back," she whispered, and I wasn't sure if she wasn't disappointed about that.

"Yes, but I have to go now. Do you know if there are any boots around here somewhere?"

She turned her back to me as if blocking me out. After a while she said, "He comes at me after he locks you in the workshop. He says it's my fault you run, because I don't tell you otherwise." A sob rattled her shoulders. "I do tell you otherwise."

"Yes, you do tell me," I said, then foolishly added, "Next time I'll tell him you did. But there won't be a next time, Carolyn. He'll be out there hunting for me, but I'll be long gone. All I need is boots and a knife or something."

Her scoff sounded like she was choking. "I can't believe how naïve you are. He *wants* you to run." She turned to face me. Her gaze was filled with unspeakable despair. "Every time you run, he wins. He loves to hunt. That's what gets him off. Didn't I tell you that?"

She seemed confused for a moment, her eyes veering off to the window, as if trying to remember.

I squeezed her shoulder. "Yes, you did."

My statement brought some comfort to her, as if reassuring her she was still sane. She closed her eyes, seeming a bit more at peace.

"He doesn't care if we die out there in the woods, or if we bleed to death on this damn floor." She swallowed hard and licked her dry, cracked lips. "That's how Rose died, and others before her, others I didn't—"

She started coughing, and I rushed to get her a bit of water in an old can we used for a glass. I held it to her lips and tried to lift her head, but she yelped, and I withdrew. She sat up slowly, wincing with every move she made, then drank a little water.

"How many girls were here before us?" I asked, afraid to hear the answer.

She shook her head. "I don't know," she whispered. "There are graves... but after a big storm, the ground levels. It's hard to say if there are more." A tear rolled down her swollen face. "I dug Rose's grave. You'll probably dig mine."

"No," I snapped, standing as quickly as I could and pacing the room, rejecting the thought of digging another grave with every fiber in my being. "No. You'll help me get some boots and a knife, so I can walk the swamp out of here."

"Listen," Carolyn said, raising her fraught voice just a little. The effort to speak seemed to take all her strength. I stopped in place, looking at her while I swore to myself to not fail again. Even if it killed me.

"He'll catch you again, and lock you in that workshop again, until he finds out what breaks you. Then it's only that... that utmost fear you hold secret inside your soul, the nightmare that is going to haunt you every night until you die." She paused for a moment, urging me with a desperate stare to take her words seriously. "Do you understand?"

I looked at her with conflicting emotions. Every time I ran, and he caught me, this woman paid for it in suffering and blood and tears. And still, I couldn't stop thinking I could save her. I was the only one who could.

I could also get her killed the next time the hunter caught me, or the following time after that. It was a risk I had to take, even if I couldn't spend a single moment wondering what that made me.

Please, forgive me, I asked her in my thoughts.

Then I propped my hands on my hips and said, "Boots. I need boots. Have you seen any boots lying around somewhere?"

35

WARRANT

Michowsky drove the first SUV, with Fradella in the passenger seat. Behind them, a Ford Interceptor bearing the insignia of Collier County Sheriff's Office, had Officer Patchett behind the wheel, a little upset because the sheriff had made it clear he wasn't going to get any overtime pay for this.

It seemed the boss had taken a clear dislike toward Michowsky, despite the fact he'd apologized profusely for calling in Tess Winnett on the Kiana Bayliss case. The man just wouldn't hear it. Michowsky found himself wondering if he'd ever met someone so insecure in a sheriff's role. Now he was taking it out on Patchett, dinging him for overtime pay. Outstanding.

They took Highway 41 heading east, weaving through the rush hour traffic that jammed the narrow highway connecting the Miami metro area with Naples, on the west coast of the peninsula. The sun was setting fast, threatening an arrival in full darkness, a thought that gave Michowsky the creeps.

The suspect, a thirty-three-year-old snake hunter by the name of Joshua Coppinger, was built like a brick house. Six-foot-three and weighing about two-fifty, he was covered in tattoos, mostly all about snakes. He'd served time for a couple of drug charges, cocaine possession ten years ago, and possession with intent the last time he was hitched. This would be his third charge; Michowsky was anticipating some serious resistance the moment they pulled over in front of his hut.

He turned right onto Cross Seminole Trail and slowed down. They were off-road, the trail not a real trail, just tire tracks carved in dried mud. He looked in the rearview mirror and saw a cloud of thick, reddish dust where Patchett's vehicle should've been, but he was coming; he saw a glimpse of the SUV when the trail turned.

Michowsky shot Fradella a glance. The kid had been eerily quiet since his return from Quantico. He looked different, more mature, but also younger somehow. Must've been his hair, or maybe he'd dropped a few pounds over there. He wasn't a kid anymore; he was at least thirty. He stopped being a kid a long time ago, but Michowsky had at least twenty years over him, so the nickname had stuck since he was assigned to him fresh out of school.

"So, tell me, how good is the money?" he asked, looking to break the ice.

Fradella flashed him a grin. "Good enough. We should've done this a long time ago."

"We?" Michowsky laughed. "Isn't there an age limit? Or a weight one?" He patted his round abdomen.

"They'll get you in shape," Fradella replied. "They got me in shape, and that wasn't easy."

"Ha! Explain to me how that wasn't easy when you're lean, fit, and thirty years old, basically a toddler."

Fradella smiled and looked away. Michowsky could swear he saw him blush.

"I bet you're glad to be back," he said.

"Yeah," he replied simply. "This is home."

"And Tess?"

"What about her?"

Michowsky slapped the steering wheel jokingly. "C'mon, man, it's me, your old partner. You think I'm blind or something? There's a spark between you two. You can see it a mile out. And you'd be a damn fool to turn away."

"Slow down," Fradella said. "There it is."

A small clearing opened up to the left of the trail. Michowsky cut the lights and turned into the clearing following the countless tire tracks leading there. Several hundred feet into the clearing, backed against the pines, there was a small cabin, just two windows and a door, and a straw roof. In the distance, the low hum of a generator covered the wilderness sounds.

"Who lives like this?" Michowsky muttered, looking around carefully.

"Apparently, Joshua Coppinger and thousands of others. People like him prefer to live off the grid."

Michowsky stopped a few yards from the cabin door. Patchett stopped on the other side of the cabin and climbed out of his SUV, gun in hand.

Fradella drew his weapon and approached the door. It was weathered and cracked, hanging loosely on rusted hinges, seemingly about to fall apart. He tapped against the wood with the barrel of his HK. "Joshua Coppinger, open up, FBI." He knocked again, keeping his body to the side, in case the ex-con had any ideas to shoot through the door.

But the door unlatched and squeaked loudly as it opened. A man, wearing a sleeveless fishnet undershirt with holes in it, its color uncertain, and a pair of boxer briefs that had seen better days, stood in the doorway. Scratching his beard with dirty fingernails, he squinted in the fading daylight as he looked at them. "Yeah? What do you want?"

"We have a warrant to search the premises," Michowsky said. The apparent confusion on the man's sleep-lined face turned into instant panic. "Step outside, sir."

Coppinger stepped back instead, slowly, appearing ready to turn and run. Patchett reached him in two large, determined steps and clutched his arm.

"Hands behind your head," he commanded. "Now, greaseball. Fingers interlaced."

Coppinger obeyed, his eyes shooting darts left and right as if trying to figure out when and how to bolt. Patchett slipped handcuffs around his wrists quickly and effectively. The snake hunter flinched when the cold metal tightened around his flesh.

"Why are you busting me?" he asked, muttering oaths under his breath.

"Just 'cause I can," Patchett replied coldly, yanking him by the arm and leading him to his Interceptor. He opened the rear door and shoved him onto the back seat, keeping one hand on his head. "You've done time before. You know the drill."

"You son of a—"

The slammed door muffled the man's tirade, just as Michowsky drew a lungful of clean air before venturing into Coppinger's hut.

The man had never taken the trash out, not in recent times, anyway. The floors were littered with food wrappers and old pizza boxes. Empty beer cans and bottles contributed to the mess. The dimly lit place, a mere two rooms, a small kitchen, and a bathroom, smelled of musty garbage and animal feces. In a corner, something moved where Michowsky ventured to step outside a relatively clear path that led from the front door to the kitchen.

"Well, hello," Fradella said, grinning wickedly as he shone the beam of his flashlight on a small, dirty coffee table. Placed in front of a sofa that had seen better times maybe a couple of decades ago, the table's grimy surface held several things of little interest, with one exception: one three-inch line of perfectly white powder. Next to it, an old credit card with bent corners that had been used to arrange the powder just right, and half of a red plastic straw, its end covered in specks of white.

Michowsky sighed as he stared at the table. He'd hoped to find some evidence tying Coppinger to Kiana Bayliss or other women, but there was nothing to point in that direction.

Frustrated, he walked out and took a deep breath, then stepped over to Patchett's vehicle.

"You know what we found," Michowsky said to the perp as soon as he opened the door. Coppinger glared at him and cursed. "Are you willing to bet that stuff on your coffee table ain't powdered sugar you use to keep your rats happy?"

"Go to hell, pig." Coppinger spat mere inches from Michowsky's shoe.

"You first, asshat." He paused a moment, then asked, "It's your third collar, huh?" His voice had empathy inflections, enough to make Coppinger stare at him in disbelief.

"Yeah, but you knew that already, didn't ya? So, why fuck with me, huh?"

"'Cause I could remove those handcuffs and leave you simmering in your own filth if you give me what I need."

Coppinger stared at him, speechless. Fradella approached and smiled politely.

"We'll do you one better," Fradella said. "We'll leave your stash untouched, right there on the table, ready to be snorted."

Coppinger's eyes glinted. "What do you want?"

"Information," Michowsky replied. "We're looking for someone who's holding girls here in the Glades somewhere. Give us a name, and we'll let you go back to your wonderful life."

The man scowled, his face scrunched with hatred and contempt. "I ain't no snitch."

"You ain't too smart either," Fradella said. "You see, for us, it's simple. Someone *will* go to jail today. It can either be you or this other guy we're looking for." He gestured with his hands, illustrating the choice Coppinger had to make. "On one hand, you. You're a three-time loser, going for the VIP extended stay package. On the other hand, him, a man you shouldn't care about, your one-time-only, get-out-of-jail-free card. We don't care... We get paid either way. A collar is a collar."

"Damn right," Michowsky added, rubbing his hands together with mock excitement.

"Is that how it goes, huh?" Coppinger asked in disbelief.

"Pretty much, yeah," Michowsky replied.

"Or maybe it goes like this. I want a lawyer."

"Fair enough," Fradella replied, grinding his teeth. "A man has the right to be stupid. Read him the rest of his rights on the drive over to the precinct," he asked Patchett. "We got our collar for the day. Let's roll."

Then he slammed the car door shut and looked at Michowsky. "Bloody hell... He was our only lead."

36

GHOSTS

The whiteboard in the training room had been wiped clean. Tess stared at the white, glossy surface, black marker in hand, getting her thoughts organized.

She'd never worked with less. Or had she? What if she separated Kiana's puzzling behavior from the evidence on her body? Could she get an inkling of a profile?

For a moment, she considered going back to the office. The federal building was by far better equipped for what she needed to do. She could print photos over there, build a complete victimology analysis on a board she had no fear of anyone seeing and sharing with the press the next day. But the federal building didn't have Kiana.

She wasn't going anywhere, and neither was Tess.

Toward the left corner of the whiteboard, she started a list of everything she knew about the unsub. Hunter: he'd used arrows on Kiana. Glades: that's where he lived or at least had held Kiana hostage. Experienced: had taken women without leaving any trace of evidence, witnesses, not even a recording of his actions on one of the countless video cameras in the city. Stalker? Maybe… definitely organized and a good planner who chose video dark spots to pounce. Power/control oriented.

The squeaking of the tip of the marker stopped for a moment, while Tess revisited the last item written. Did she know enough about the unsub to firmly slap the power/control motive on him? Was he hedonistic? Or a plain thrill seeker?

She wrote another word. Daisy.

Yes, he was power and control motivated. Someone by the name of Daisy was a staple of his past, someone whose actions, or the unsub's perception of her actions, had been the trigger, leading the unsub to start kidnapping, hunting, and killing women.

Her hand froze midair, while her mind searched for another item to add to the list. After a while, she lowered it slowly without taking her eyes from the list.

She needed more. Statistics could give her a few more pieces of the puzzle. He was likely a white male, although this statistic was increasingly unreliable. He was probably in his thirties, maybe late twenties. Traditionally, power/control serial killers had difficulties holding a job or building careers. In many cases, they'd been abused as children and the cycle of abuse had continued, enhanced by the trigger event, taken to a new dimension.

But was the unsub a serial killer? There was no body to speak of, unless she followed her gut and chalked up Kiana's husband to the unsub's list of victims. Yet in her gut, Tess had no doubt about it. Glancing at the list of missing persons that Donovan had narrowed down, she wondered how many of those women had been killed. Were any of them still alive?

Seated at the table, Donovan had dozed off, his head resting on his laptop. Doc Rizza looked at her as if she held all the answers locked in her mind somewhere. She didn't. Lowering her head, she paced the space between the table with her hands shoved in her pockets, her fists clenched. Something was throwing her off her game, and she couldn't even pinpoint what it was.

Stopping for a moment in front of the window, she looked outside. It was dark, and the city lights reflected in the water in shimmering colors. The rising moon smudged a wide swath of yellow, rippled by waves, the serenity of the view breathtaking.

And deceptive as hell.

In a few hours, she and Fradella would head into the Glades with Kiana.

Until then, she had to figure out what to expect.

"Who could Daisy be?" Doc Rizza asked. His voice, sounding a little tired, echoed strangely in the deep silence of Tess's thoughts. Donovan continued to sleep, breathing quietly, his folded arm covering his eyes.

She turned and walked over to the whiteboard and grabbed the marker. Then she wrote quickly the names of the five short-listed missing persons and Kiana's, listed in the order of their disappearance.

Alana Munch, a twenty-three-year-old gas station attendant, missing for five years last month.

Sally Murphy, a twenty-five-year-old schoolteacher, taken almost four years ago.

Rose Sandoval, twenty-three, a student, disappeared two-and-a-half years ago.

Carolyn Ladson, a waitress who'd vanished about a year-and-a-half ago.

Kiana Bayliss, twenty-seven, a TV show host, taken seven months ago.

Ashley Nettleton, a hotel receptionist, taken only three months ago.

He was escalating. Fast.

She looked at Doc Rizza. He was still waiting for her answer.

"Daisy could be the original trigger in the unsub's life. The woman he keeps punishing over and over by hunting and hurting these girls."

"For what?"

Tess shrugged and rubbed her forehead. Tiredness was seeping through her body, claiming its toll. "Who knows for what transgression, real or imaginary. There's no way we could tell, until we establish his identity." She looked at the list of names, noticing none of the girls were called Daisy. The name wasn't as popular as it once was. Could she have been an older woman? A mother, maybe?

"She could be the figment of a seriously damaged mind," Doc Rizza said, speaking softly so as to not wake Donovan. "The victim's," he added.

The notion brought a deep frown to Tess's brow. Regardless of how aberrant Kiana's behavior had been, Tess had never doubted the girl's sanity. But now, she was starting to doubt her own. Was her personal experience as a victim of sexual assault a hindrance in this case? Was her own memory playing tricks on her, keeping her from asking the right questions?

She didn't believe so.

"More likely, Daisy could be a lover who jilted or cheated on the unsub. A wife or a mother. The name used to be more popular with Gen X."

Tess shifted her attention back to the board. "He's taking them faster now," she said, pointing at the board with the marker. "He's escalating, unraveling fast. Something must've changed." Doc Rizza nodded, folding his hands in his lap. "My question is, why did he take Ashley Nettleton if he still had Kiana? How many of these girls does he keep alive at the same time?"

Donovan lifted his head up from the keyboard and rubbed his eyes. A long, hearty yawn and a stretch completed his ritual. "Good morning," he said sheepishly.

"Not morning yet," Doc Rizza replied.

"It's morning to me," Donovan replied cheerfully, adjusting his shirt and tie. "And mornings start with coffee." He walked over to the door but stopped short of opening it. "Any takers?"

"Oh, yeah," Tess replied enthusiastically. "Would love some."

Doc Rizza held his thumb up. A moment later, the door closed behind the analyst, and Tess resumed working on the victims' profiles.

"What do we know about these girls?" she asked, more to herself. She didn't actually expect Doc Rizza to reply. "Donovan worked their backgrounds. Based on his findings, these womens' paths never crossed."

"We don't know enough, then." Doc Rizza smiled encouragingly.

She wondered what he was doing there, instead of going home to get some rest.

"Right. The unsub must've found them somewhere. Or, if we're really unlucky, he could be like Ted Bundy, roaming for victims, constantly on the move." She paced around slowly, trying to keep her frustration in check. Illogical things always frayed her nerves, and nothing was more illogical than Kiana's behavior. "If only that girl would bloody talk to me," she snapped, then walked over and sat, crossing her arms at her chest.

"She's very fragile now," Doc Rizza said. "I appreciate you giving her the time to heal."

She shrugged. "I don't have much of a choice, Doc. What am I supposed to do?" She stood and started pacing again, although she was worn out, her entire body aching. "I swear, if her games cost those girls their lives, I'll throw the book at her."

"Whoa... Where did that come from?"

She turned and looked at the medical examiner, hands propped on her hips. "She refuses to identify the unsub, Doc. If those girls are still alive, they're going through hell right now because of her, and whatever the hell she thinks she's doing. Why can't she talk to me?"

Doc Rizza shook his head slightly, apparently disappointed. "Let me play the devil's advocate here. You're holding this girl hostage, after she's been a hostage for seven months. No due process, just some bogus Baker Act lockup, but without meds or psych consult. I don't even want to know how you pulled that off, to be honest."

Tess gasped at the doctor's tirade. "I'm not—"

He held his hand in the air, and she clammed up, bewildered. "You're not listening to her, and she's telling you what she needs."

"So, you think, taking her back is the right idea? I'm doing it anyway, first thing in the morning."

He nodded patiently as she spoke. "Yes, I'm aware of that. But you'll get nowhere with this girl if you keep ignoring who she is."

"What do you mean?"

"She's a strong woman, Tess. A survivor. Damaged? Yes, no doubt in my mind about that. But she's first and foremost a traumatized and strong survivor. Listen to her."

Tess stared at the doctor, struggling to wrap her mind around his words. When had she not listened to Kiana? What was he trying to tell her?

As if reading her mind, Doc Rizza smiled faintly, then bit his lip, a little unsure of himself from what she could tell. "Who was there for you when you needed it the most?"

Slack-jawed, Tess looked away briefly. He couldn't mean what she thought. It was just in her wild and overworked imagination. She shifted her gaze back to the doctor. "What do you mean?"

"You and Kiana have a lot more in common than you let people know," he said softly, his words a gentle whisper. "I've known for a while."

Tess stared at him in disbelief. He knew? How? Her face caught fire and tears burned her eyes. Desperately blinking them away, she breathed, trying to instill some reason into her panicking mind.

"You knew?" she managed to ask, her voice brittle and faint.

"I wouldn't be much of a medical examiner if I missed all the signs."

"Does anyone—"

"No one else knows," he replied, as always, seeming able to read her mind. "And it will stay that way as far as I'm concerned." He reached out and squeezed her hand gently. "All I'm asking is to draw from your terrible experience and find what you need to help this girl transcend her trauma." He looked at her intently, pleading. "Otherwise, she won't survive."

A tear rolled down Tess's cheek. She wiped it quickly with the back of her hand. "Uh-huh," she whispered, still choked. "I thought I was—"

"And I want you to promise me something," Doc Rizza said. "When you go after the unsub tomorrow morning, don't let your ghosts prevail. Whatever happens."

She paused for a beat. "Is that why you're really here, Doc? To make sure my ghosts don't prevail?" He smiled and nodded shyly, scratching the roots of his rebellious tuft of hair.

"Thank you," Tess whispered as Donovan barged in, carrying a large box of donuts and a carton with five tall coffee cups bearing the Starbucks logo. Hiding her tear-filled eyes, Tess sniffled and smiled.

"What's wrong?" Donovan asked, looking at her with a slight frown.

"Allergies," she replied quickly.

He didn't seem to question her answer. "Ah, yes, victimology," he said, looking at the whiteboard with her handwriting in black marker. "What's next?"

She reached into the box and hesitantly grabbed a donut, aware her stomach hadn't stopped growling since Donovan's arrival had filled the room with the smell of fresh, warm sugary dough and coffee. She had to give him a quick lesson into female metabolism basics sometime, ideally before he developed a habit for feeding her loads of fattening carbs.

"We have until dawn to figure out where the unsub saw these women. Otherwise, come morning, we'll be heading into his hunting grounds with no idea who he is and what he can do."

37

CAROLYN

For a while, I waited and worked diligently at getting ready for the next time I was going to try to run. The thought of risking my life was scary enough, but risking harm being done to Carolyn was unbearable.

During these endless days and nights of terror and pain, I learned to know the sounds he made when he left the house, when he arrived. When he slept, ate, drank, or did whatever else he liked to do. I spent so much time learning his behaviors, studying him, that I'd learned to read his mind almost. I could anticipate, cringing with every fiber of my body, when he was about to come to see me. Of course, "see me" was a euphemism for the things he did to my body I'd rather not talk about. Knowing he was coming and willing myself to sit still and not run out of there screaming, only to be dragged back again took every bit of willpower I could muster.

I'd like to think it paid off.

At first, I started escaping into the house while he was out. Instead of running, I fled the barn via the open window, then snuck into the house, looking for food, for a phone, for things I could use.

The house was cleaner and more ordinary than I'd expected. All I'd seen until that day was the barn, the workshop, and the dimly lit corridor that led from the workshop to the side entrance with the huge stuffed python on the wall. But the house was relatively clean, a two bedroom, one bath, pragmatically furnished. No stuffed snakes anywhere. Of course, there weren't any throw pillows or anything; a man lived there alone.

I had to resist the thought of taking a quick shower. Any scent, any hint that I'd been trolling his house could have serious consequences that I didn't dare risk. There would come a day for a long, soothing bubble bath, scented candles burning, and a wineglass within reach, but that day had not arrived yet.

And there was no phone. I looked everywhere, careful to not leave a single footprint or trace of my trespass. I turned on the TV just to take a peek at the date, and I gasped when I realized I'd been there for three months, one week, and four days. I'd lost track.

The next stop was the pantry. I inspected the shelves for things Carolyn and I could eat straight from the can, without any cooking. The shelves were almost barren, and what I could take I was afraid he'd notice. The only exceptions were a can of peas, two cans of mushrooms, and two cans of beans. Those products were stacked on a lower shelf, and I could extract the ones on the second row, where he wouldn't notice. Yes, at some point, he'd probably notice, but I was sure I'd be long gone by then.

I swiped some Neosporin from the bottom of a drawer, just in case we'd need it, and took the cans back to Carolyn in the barn. That day, we had a party. We ate beans and peas and barely abstained from opening some mushrooms too. Later, she threw up, poor thing. Her stomach couldn't handle so much food after who knows how long.

But that was everything I could take from the house. The following day I raided it again but didn't find much else. A pair of old socks for Carolyn; her feet were always frozen. A frayed, gray T-shirt that would help me hide better in the swamp mist. A half-eaten slice of pizza recovered from the trash can.

I couldn't find the spare key to his truck, even though I looked everywhere. It took me two full days of searching to admit defeat.

Then I waited a day and snuck out the following night, about an hour after he'd fallen asleep, snoring loudly enough for me to hear him from the barn. I took with me a hand saw blade, rusted and crooked, found littering the barn floor near the back wall. It was the only long, thin tool I could find to use as a slim jim in case his truck was locked.

Ignoring the fresh daisy I found on the windowsill, I hopped over and tiptoed toward the truck, careful to not make a sound. It was pitch dark, a moonless night with a clear sky, the stars too far and too faint to shed any light. I felt my way more than saw where I was going, but after a few long minutes I stopped by the oversized front tire of a black Chevy truck. It was an older model, the kind that had a keyhole in its door handle. Did it have an alarm? Soon I'd find out.

I tried to open the door, but it was locked. Grinding my teeth, I remember asking myself, who was he locking his door for? No one would venture that deep into the Glades to steal a damn Chevy. No one would be that desperate. No one, except me.

The thought brought a chill down my spine. Did he know I was going to try to steal the truck? Then I had no chance in hell.

Still, I had to try.

I slipped the tip of the saw blade between the glass and the seal, close to the handle, and felt around with it, trying to grab the wire that controlled the lock. Every few seconds, I stopped, worried the alarm would go off. But it didn't. At some point, I felt the blade meet some resistance toward the tip. Holding it tightly with bleeding fingers and pushing it down as far as I could, I pulled toward the back. With a muted click, the lock pin popped up.

No alarm went off. I breathed again and pulled the blade out of the door, then dropped it on the ground.

I stopped and listened for a while, and nothing moved. Through the closed window, I could hear him snoring faintly. I opened the door slowly, afraid it might squeak, and climbed inside. Then I started feeling under the dashboard for some wires, for anything that could match what I'd only seen in movies.

There was nothing. No cover I could feel the edges to with my trembling fingers. No edge beyond which I could reach to pull at wires. Nothing but smooth plastic as far as I could reach. Some screws, buried deeply into the plastic, so deep I couldn't turn them without a screwdriver. And the steering column with its large bolts and absolutely no wires I could tie together to get the engine to start.

I remember crying bitter tears on the driver's seat of that Chevy, biting on my fist to keep my wails quiet. After a while, I wiped my eyes and climbed out of the vehicle, then stood for a while, thinking about how best to close its door without making a sound. I pushed down the lock pin and brought the door close to the latch, then gradually put my weight on it until it closed fully. I ran my fingers against the gap between the doors' edges and they were level. Then I took the saw blade and started walking back.

When I reached the house, I saw the daisy flower bed by the wall, white and yellow blooms, barely visible in the dark, undulating gently in the breeze. In a fit of senseless, silent rage, I stomped every flower, not giving up until I was completely out of breath and no stem was still standing. Then I hopped the window back into the barn and curled up in a ball, crying softly so that Carolyn wouldn't hear.

The next day, as soon as I heard him snore during his afternoon nap, I slipped on the old, musty rubber boots I'd found in one of the workshop crates and made a run for it. I didn't have a knife, but I took with me a stick long enough to help me feel my way through the swamp.

I didn't take any of the paths I'd taken in the past. On one, I'd stepped in a snare trap. On another, I'd ended up several feet aboveground, dangling by my ankle. I had to try something new, something where he wouldn't follow.

Direction didn't matter. Screw south. Who cared anymore? I would find the way out of the Glades as soon as I'd put enough distance between me and him. Then, five miles or twenty, I could walk them out. If I closed my eyes, I could visualize the map of the Glades just as if I were looking at a GPS screen. I would never get lost in there.

Sea marshes are shallow expanses of slow-moving water on top of limestone bedrock. I could find a shallow path out of there, and hopefully make it to dry land before any alligator could snap me. Gators are extremely fast and dangerous. As I was about to dip my boot into the warm water, they were the creatures I feared the most.

Walking through marshes proved to be slower and more treacherous than I'd thought. The bedrock was slippery under the soles of my boots, slowing me down. There was little to no cover in the low-rising marsh grasses and succulents. After trudging for a few minutes, breathless and sweaty and panicked, I sought the dry land at my left. Once I had put several yards between my boots and the water edge, I found a wide tree trunk and leaned against it to catch my breath.

I heard the arrow coming, slicing the air before it pierced my arm, pinning it against the tree trunk. Then I heard myself screaming against a backdrop of sickening laughter. Unable to move, I looked around everywhere but couldn't see him. While I waited for the inescapable, I kicked off my boots into a nearby bush, knowing well he wouldn't let me keep them.

Then he caught up to me in a disturbing, maddening déjà vu.

I thought I knew exactly what to expect; I'd been through it before, I can't recall how many times. Ignoring the throbbing in my arm while he dragged me back to the house, all I could think of was Carolyn.

He took me to the barn that time, not the workshop, and I was out of my mind with fear. Even the tiniest change makes us afraid. What is change other than a temporary and total loss of control? I remember shaking and sobbing, almost ready to beg him to take me to the workshop, just because the unknown was far more terrifying.

He shoved me into the barn. I landed hard on the ground and yelped. Pain throbbed through my arm where his arrow had torn through my flesh.

He laughed heartily. "My sweet Daisy, how I love your spirit. You're not like anyone I've ever met."

Carolyn watched the scene with a trembling hand over her gaping mouth. The poor woman was shaking. Unable to stand anymore, she sat on the floor and withdrew into the corner, whimpering.

Struggling to get back on my feet, I couldn't keep my mouth shut. "I'll never resign myself to be your prisoner." He stared at me, amused, but I wasn't paying attention. "You hear me, you son of a bitch? Never," I bellowed, out of breath, holding pressure on my wound with my hand, blood trickling through my fingers. "Even if it kills me."

He grinned widely, seemingly satisfied with what I was saying. The thought of playing into his hand drove me insane. I couldn't think of anything else to say that wouldn't make it worse.

Slowly, keeping his eyes riveted into mine, he pulled his gun from his belt and removed its safety. I stopped breathing. Then he walked over to Carolyn. "I don't need her anymore, then, do I, my feisty little Daisy?"

The gunshot ripped through the silence with echoes of my screams.

38

LEAD

The coffee cups had been emptied, then refilled from the hospital cafeteria. Fradella had gone downstairs twice to top them off, while Donovan pledged a run at six sharp, as soon as the local Starbucks opened.

Michowsky and Fradella had returned after ten in the evening, frustrated with the outcome of their visit to the Glades. Tess found it strange that the snake hunter wouldn't take the deal of a lifetime and rat on the unsub, especially since he was looking at his third conviction, likely to come with hard time attached.

Maybe he did know the unsub but was more terrified of him than of spending the next two to five in jail. Then she dismissed the thought as pure speculation. It was just as likely the man didn't know the unsub and had never heard of girls being kept in the Glades. She would've liked a moment or two with the perp in an interview room and had left Pearson a voicemail message to that respect.

At about one in the morning, she finally talked Doc Rizza and Michowsky into going home to get some much-needed rest. She'd had to twist Michowsky's arm to make him go home. He insisted on being part of the incursion into the Glades the next morning. Tess hoped his alarm clock wouldn't go off or he'd somehow not make it. The detective seemed to be in pain, moved with difficulty, and could be a liability on the treacherous terrain of the wilderness.

After a catnap on the corridor couch, shivering under the flow of air conditioning, she resumed working on victimology, her coffee refilled promptly by the enthusiastic FBI rookie, with a hint of a smile on his lips.

The whiteboard was covered in her handwriting, every detail of the missing persons' lives and Kiana's organized neatly in a table, a format she liked to use to easily spot commonalities. Have the missing girls been to the same schools? Shopped or dined in the same places? Worshipped at the same church? Used the same vendors, caterers, lawn service companies? Donovan, appearing as fresh and rested as if he'd been on a long weekend in Vero Beach, readily extracted credit card information, tax returns, phone location data, and everything else she needed to establish if their paths had ever crossed. Here and there, two of the women had crossed paths, never the same two, never more than two. She was looking for something they all —including Kiana—had in common. Chances were that was the place the unsub found them.

A few hours of arduous work later, Tess had nothing except an empty coffee cup, a whiteboard covered in black marker scribbles, and a bitter taste in her mouth to go with the sickening dread she felt in her chest.

The unsub had to have seen them somewhere.

"All right, we got nothing," she said, painfully aware how depressing she sounded. Rubbing her forehead as if to scare the threat of a migraine away, she added, "What do we do when we have nothing?"

"We keep looking," Donovan replied enthusiastically. "Come on, Winnett, don't let this bastard ruin your case stats."

She dismissed the thought with a hand swat. "Oh, no, I won't." Her stats were not what she was thinking of. "What else do we have left?" She pointed at the last column of the victims' table, labeled MISC, all its lines empty. It was reserved for miscellaneous information extracted from case files, bits and pieces of information that couldn't be easily categorized.

"Just case histories," Donovan replied. "Let's divide and conquer." He pushed two stacks of paper toward Fradella, and two more toward Tess, while keeping two for himself. Dr. DiDomenico had arranged for a printer to be brought to their room and a few critical office supplies, like paper and a stapler. The cases didn't have folders or labels; they were just stapled printouts of the information found in the system.

For a while, only the sound of rustling paper disrupted the silence. Tess took a seat while she read, flipping quickly through the case files, but scrutinizing every word in the case interviews conducted by the respective investigators. If they couldn't find what they were looking for in the case notes, they'd have to go back and interview every missing persons' family, friends, and people they'd been in contact with before they vanished. Weeks of work, while the unsub could vanish.

For Carolyn Ladson, the only thing worth jotting down was that she was featured in the TV commercial for her place of employment, a sports bar called Luca's Sports Bar. It was a handwritten note put there by the detective who'd worked her case, with no mention of follow-up. It seemed irrelevant.

Except for one minor detail. Carolyn Ladson had appeared on TV. Just like Kiana.

Tess stood and walked over to the whiteboard, then uncapped the black marker and scribbled *TV AD* on Carolyn's line. Then she added *TV SHOW* on Kiana's.

She was about to go back to her seat and start reading the second file, when Fradella said, "Put *TV INTERVIEW* for Rose Sandoval. She was invited on a talk show to speak about USF students on social media and their concerns for privacy."

Goosebumps prickled Tess's skin. She jotted the words quickly, then rushed to the second case file, flipping through the pages quickly.

"Sally Murphy was featured with her class on local television when they won some singing contest. It was about a couple of months before she vanished." Donovan pushed that file aside and walked over to Fradella, who kept turning pages furiously.

Tess kept perusing the notes in Ashley Nettleton's case. Buried at the bottom of a page, in hard-to-read cursive, there was a one-liner that had her heart thumping.

Featured in news piece about hotel opening.

She walked over to the whiteboard and added the two notes on the table, *TV Contest* for Sally Murphy and *News—Hotel* for Ashley.

"Come on, guys, let's make it six out of six," Tess said. "You know what this means. We got him."

"I got nothing," Fradella said, pushing aside the case file. It slid over the table and stopped against Donovan's laptop. "And I don't know what you think we got." He stood and stretched his arms, then looked at the whiteboard with a frown. "We've already established he could very well be someone who watches TV. We knew this from Kiana. How is this different from what we already knew?"

"Were these women the only blondes featured on local television during this time frame? A span of five years? Definitely not. But these were the taken ones."

"An assumption," Fradella interrupted. "We assumed—"

"It's no longer an assumption for three of them, once Kiana recognized them, Todd."

"True," he admitted, seemingly embarrassed just a little.

"So, the question is, why these blondes out of the very many featured on TV during this time?"

Donovan still perused the Alana Munch case file, mumbling something under his breath. The analyst was worse than a pit bull. And she loved that about him. If anyone could find the bit of information she needed, it was him.

Fradella didn't reply; just shrugged.

"From seeing someone on TV to actually knowing where that someone is to stalk and kidnap her is a big stretch. Most TV pieces don't speak of locations, but some do. The hotel piece with Ashley, yes, the unsub could've found her based on that. Luca's Sports Bar, easy to find. Sally's school was probably named in the news piece. I'll make the same assumption about Rose Sandoval, once it was mentioned that she's a USF student. Yes, the unsub could've gone to the University of South Florida to find her." She walked over to Fradella, unable to hide her excitement. "But nothing explains Kiana."

"So, what are you saying?"

She smiled widely and tilted her head a little. "We've been looking at this all wrong. It's not a snake hunter. It's someone who works in television." She looked at Donovan with a tinge of disappointment. "If only we could confirm six out of six. Then we could really narrow down the people who were attached to all six shoots."

"I'll find the son of a bitch," Donovan muttered. "There's no mention of anything TV in Alana's file," he added, slamming the case file down. "But the detective who worked it is an old high school buddy of mine. I'll give him a call."

He fished his phone out of his pocket and started thumbing through names.

"It's four in the morning, D," Tess said weakly. She didn't want him to back down. She needed to know if Alana had been on TV, even if it meant waking up a cop.

"Whatever," Donovan replied, grinning. The call went unanswered, but he tried again. Then he tried one more time. "Oh, so that's how you wanna play it, huh?" he mumbled, starting to type incredibly fast on his laptop's keyboard. "I'll turn your ringer on, Freddie-man."

The next attempt was successful. Tess listened intently but could only hear Donovan's side of the call. He didn't put it on speaker, but after a few endless moments, Donovan's thumb went up. He ended the call and said, "I took a lot of expletives, but now we know Alana won *Miss Mermaid* the year she was taken, an event featuring female divers. It had about five minutes of coverage time across multiple news channels."

"Yes," Tess said, holding her hand up in the air for Donovan's high five. "We got him."

He sat at the table and interlaced his fingers, then stretched them until his joints popped. "We ain't got him yet, Winnett; hold your rabid horses. TV crews and everyone involved in a shoot, you're talking thirty, forty, maybe even a hundred people, and teams overlap a lot."

She patted him on the shoulder. "Nothing you can't sort through. Remember he's a hunter and the name Daisy carries an important significance."

"It will take me a while." He sighed and started typing. "And you owe me big. My man Freddie will never speak to me again."

Tess grinned. "When's the last time you two spoke?"

"Oh, that was a few years ago, when he invited my girlfriend to the prom before I could ask her. She said yes, I punched him in the eye, then we never spoke again."

Laughter erupted in the room as the sun peeked over the horizon. It was time to go.

She grabbed the phone out of her pocket and looked at the time before calling Pearson. He needed to know they were heading into the Glades, but she was determined to leave him a voicemail instead of asking Donovan to remotely bypass the phone's silent settings.

Or maybe she was better off not calling him until after the fact. He'd told her specifically not to take Kiana back, not to endanger the surviving victim. And what was she going to do? The exact opposite, something known as defying direct orders. In other words, a career killer.

No... there were moments in life when it was best to ask for forgiveness rather than permission. This was one of those moments.

She slipped the phone back into her pocket and looked at Fradella.

"Ready, partner?"

39

SPIDERS

I don't remember much of the days following Carolyn's demise. I mourned her as if she were my sister. Her senseless death left a hollow in my heart.

And a disturbing thought.

On some surreal level, I was glad she was gone. I could plan my escape without having to think of her, of what pain or suffering my failure would inflict on her.

I didn't like who I'd become. Her blood was on my hands, just as David's. Even now, when I look at my hands, I see bloodstains. And the blackness of the damp earth I'd covered their bodies with, clumped and sticking to my flesh like a leper.

Those days were spent in a haze of sheer terror, the nightmares renewed, never-ending, haunting. When awake, all I could think about was how to run again and not get caught. What could I do differently this time? What was I missing? How did he know I was gone, when I always waited for him to fall asleep before running? It didn't make sense. It felt as if the entire universe was conspiring against me, telling on me the moment I made a move.

Every day I found fresh daisies somewhere in my space, and I never knew how they got there. I hated the damn things… I'd stomped his flower bed, yet he had fresh flowers to lay on the barn windowsill, creeping me out to no end. He never mentioned the damaged garden. Maybe he thought a bear rolled in it or something.

But there was something about his obsession with daisies that chilled me to the bone. Whoever the original Daisy was to him, she sure as hell screwed him up pretty badly. I only regretted she didn't finish him.

The stolen Neosporin worked wonders on my wound. It was sealing nicely, and I kept it wrapped with a strip of my old blue satin dress so he wouldn't notice the greasy layer on my skin.

Then it ran out.

I snuck back into the house when he was away, and took with me the old used tube, planning to only take some cream if I found another one. I didn't. I swiped another can of beans that lasted me three days and regretfully stopped there. Only two were left, the shelf almost empty now. Soon he'd figure out I'd been stealing supplies, and there was no telling what he could do to me for that.

My arm had started throbbing again, the crust on my wound surrounded with a reddish, telling sign of infection. I racked my brain trying to think what I could do. Seminoles used to call the Glades their home before anyone else, and they used medicinal plants and herbs to heal their wounds. I'd read somewhere they used yarrow to help heal their wounds and keep infection at bay. But yarrow rarely grows in swamps; it likes dry land with a bit of sunshine. Only I had it in the back of my feverish mind that I've seen a couple of flowering plants invading the flower bed. The exact same one I had stomped into oblivion.

I waited for nightfall and the sounds of the hunter's hearty snoring, then snuck out and walked stealthily over to the flower bed, keeping close to the house. In the faint moonlight, I could see some daisies had recovered from my furious treading. Many blooms faced the sky, although some did so from the ground level, their stems broken, forever downed. Yet the blooms survived, as if fed by the same frenzy that kept my captor hooked to the idea of Daisy. Whoever she was, I couldn't blame her for not being there anymore. For wounding that son of a bitch the best she'd known how.

I was right. Toward the far end of the flower bed, a couple of yarrow plants had been downed with the daisies. One had died, its leaves withered, almost dry. I picked that one, and just a few leaves from the other that still stood crookedly, refusing to die.

Back at the barn, I soaked the dry leaves in water until I could chew them. If I remembered correctly what I'd learned in botany, the plant contained salicylic acid, the active component in aspirin, and had strong antibiotic properties. It tasted something terrible and scratched my throat with its pubescence, but I didn't care. Then I took the fresh leaves and applied them to the wound, hidden under the strip of once-blue silk I used for a bandage.

And I waited.

Every night until I healed, I snuck out to the flower bed for fresh yarrow leaves. The reddish circle slowly faded, the throbbing waned. Soon I'd be ready to run again, although I still didn't know how he knew precisely when I did, and how he'd be out there, hunting me, when I'd left him in the house, snoring like a drunken sailor.

Maybe I had to escape at night. Better yet, toward four in the morning, when it's known people sleep the soundest. The moon was waxing. A few more days and it would be almost full, shining brightly right above my head if my prayers for a clear night would be answered.

But lately, I'd become obsessed with his uncanny ability to sense my moves. Were there motion sensors in the barn? Some kind of technology that alerted him to my moves? Then how come he didn't seem to know I'd tried to steal his truck? Or that I'd stomped his damn daisies? This man wasn't the forgiving kind, quite the opposite. He relished the opportunity to punish even the slightest of transgressions with brutal assaults followed by nights of psychological torture in the workshop, where he released a new critter every time, hunting for my deepest fears.

I had made up my mind to run that night, at about four in the morning, when the barn door opened, and he shoved a young girl inside. She was sobbing uncontrollably, scared out of her mind. She seemed dizzy and kept taking her hand to the back of her head, then staring at her blood-smeared fingers.

He looked at the two of us from the doorway, then said, "You two have fun." Then he left, and the girl's sobs turned into heart-wrenching wails. I approached, feeling compelled to give her some comfort, although I resented her presence, and I wished her gone.

Sometime, between that last dinner with David and the present time, I'd turned into a sociopath. I'd lost all my empathy, my conscience, under the constant barrage of terror and urge to escape. I didn't need that girl, heaving and shuddering under my merciless stare, to hold me back. To make me doubt every step I took. To fear for anyone else's life but my own. To make me care about her, then die on me like I hadn't lost enough already.

I drew closer, just one tentative step, studying her. She was a thin blonde with long, wavy curls and manicured fingernails. She wore a hotel uniform of sorts with a gold name tag that read *ASHLEY* in black, etched letters and a logo I recognized. Something was deeply disturbing about her, something that stirred the hollow in my chest without a clear explanation at first.

It was her smell.

Clean, fresh, scents I recognized. Shampoo, shower gel, a hint of perfume. A whiff of dryer sheet, lavender, I believe.

Oh, Ashley, welcome to hell.

I took another step toward her, but she withdrew, the fear in her eyes unmistakable. I looked at myself, dressed in rags that must've offended her nose, wounded, bruised, and dirty. For a moment, I felt tempted to turn and leave her to process her new reality all by herself, but she didn't seem able to.

So, I stood there, trying my best to smile.

"Honey, I'm not the one you should fear."

She nodded fearfully, the way you do when you accept statements at gunpoint.

"Listen, if you keep your mouth shut and don't expect too much, you should be fine, for a while. And if he comes for you... don't fight it. It makes it much worse."

Her eyes rounded through a blur of tears. Blue irises disappeared under the black of her expanding pupils. She hugged herself and heaved, trying her best to keep her sobs locked inside her chest.

"Shh... don't make so much noise. He hates it." And I hated myself for being the unwilling ambassador of his savage brutishness as if I condoned it. "Most of all, don't try to run," I added, giving her frail body a good sizing. That chick wouldn't last a minute out there in the swamp.

No. If this girl had a chance in hell of surviving, it was up to me to make it out of there and come back for her with cops and guns and whatever else they use on predators like him. Maybe they shoot people like him from helicopters, like they hunt for wild boar in Texas. I got lost for a moment in that fantasy, visualizing the hunter running for his life through the Glades while helicopters swarmed above his head, taking shot after shot at him until he—

"What do I do?" Ashley asked in a timid, fraught voice, yanking me back into the grim reality.

I shrugged and pointed at the small cot in the corner. "Go sit there." It would take her some time. It had taken me days... maybe weeks. "Whatever you do, don't let him kill your spirit," I added, maybe out of a sense of duty, because I could see the advice would be lost on her.

"What do you mean?"

How could I tell her what that meant in a place like this? How could I explain how I let my mind wander, I forced it to, while he took my body, an empty shell discarded while he was using it, while my spirit soared, free as it would always be, until the day and time I drew my last breath?

"Just hang in there, okay? I'll make it out of here and come back with help."

Same as I'd told Carolyn, more than once.

Then I'd dug her grave.

That night, after pleading and encouraging Ashley to keep her wits about herself, I snuck out, barefoot, absolutely convinced this time I was going to make it. I kept telling myself that, wishing hard for it, planning for it to the best level of detail I could.

With the moon above my head and just a faint hint of daylight on the horizon, I started walking as quickly as I could, headed for the bush where I'd dumped my boots.

Alas. That night was destined to hold answers, not freedom. Right before he snatched me again, I caught a glimmer of light reflected into something up in the tree in front of me. Squinting hard in the dim moonlight as he clutched my arm with a steeled grip, I recognized the object that was pinned up there.

A trail cam. That's how he knew every time when I tried to run. The damn things must've alerted him somehow. Maybe they pinged his phone when they registered any movement.

The following night, locked in the workshop, bloodied and bruised and covering my ears to not hear Ashely's screams, I waited to see what critter he had planned for my punishment.

Then I saw them, their eyes tiny reflective dots one could barely see in the deep darkness, pierced by a hint of moonlight stabbing the night between wallboards.

Wolf spiders. Lots of them.

Relieved, I grinned in the dark. This time, I had the upper hand. I grew up hunting wolf spiders in the wetlands behind our house, with other kids my age, but I was one of the best. Flashing a light against dark underbrush after sunset made their eyes glow. Easy pickings.

If the hunter thought wolf spiders would break me, he was dead wrong.

But maybe he didn't have to know that. As the idea bloomed in my mind, I felt an invigorating rush of adrenaline, of hope that I could turn the tide and have the upper hand for a change.

The time had come for me to start controlling my destiny, one tiny little bit at a time. If the hunter wanted to know what my biggest fear was, he was about to find out, as I decided to give myself a severe case of arachnophobia.

I waited for an hour or so before letting out a concert of shrieks and wails that would've made my television director proud. I kept going for as long as I could draw breath. Then I fell asleep on that sickening worktable, three feet above the stained floor crawling with spiders.

40

BACK

Hospital mornings started early, but not early enough for Tess. As soon as the new day started filling the training room with horizontal, yellowish rays of sunshine, she wandered over to the nurses' station and asked about breakfast.

It would be served in about an hour, but they were able to offer her a small cup of green Jell-O and a plastic spoon. She took those like prized treasure to Kiana's room.

The girl was already awake, and she'd been up for a while. She'd taken a shower and washed her hair, then tied it up in a ponytail. She was fully dressed, new sneakers and all. The only thing left behind was the sweatshirt, folded neatly on the bed by her side.

"Good morning," Tess said, offering her the Jell-O. "Enjoy."

"I'm not hungry," she said, waving her off. She stood and stretched her legs, then her arms in quiet preparation for who knows what. Seeing her get ready with such diligence gave Tess a chill down her spine.

"Not negotiable," Tess said coldly. "Either this, and we can be on our way as soon as you're done, or I'll ask my colleague to go to Starbucks and grab you a croissant or something. It will take him about an hour."

She pressed her lips together in an uncensored expression of frustration, much like a child's but not really, not when Tess took into account the sadness in her haunted eyes and the scars on her body.

Pinning Tess with her glare, Kiana took the Jell-O and downed it with three or four determined gulps. Then she threw the cup and spoon in the trash can by the door. "Now, can we go?"

Tess hesitated for a split moment, once again second-guessing herself. Was it wise to take her back? Maybe if she gave Donovan several more days, he would zero in on the unsub, starting from the list of television crews and support staff. Or perhaps she should call Pearson after all and take his advice instead of shunning his years of experience and seniority in the field.

It would've been the smart thing to do, the logical one, but her gut disagreed.

Kiana's hospital hold would expire that morning at ten.

Tess knew very well that Kiana would go back into the Glades the moment they would release her from hospital, and she'd go at it alone. What chances did she really have to survive the unsub for a second time? Out of time and out of choices, Tess slid open the door and gestured an invite.

Kiana walked through the door hesitantly, like an animal being released back into the wild after a long period of captivity. She didn't say a word until they climbed into the SUV pulled up at the entrance by Fradella. Then she whispered, "Good morning," politely, calmly, as if she'd known Fradella for years and their morning together was just routine.

The inner, steel core that had kept Kiana alive all those months was starting to shine through. In between moments of post-traumatic dissociation and confusion, Tess recognized a bit of herself in the young woman, undefeated and untamed after seven months of torture. Although she had to wonder, while a shudder rattled her to the core, if she would've survived had she been in Kiana's place.

The SUV set in motion and Fradella drove off, quickly merging into the light morning traffic. "To the scene, right?"

"Yeah," Tess replied. "Take us to where Kiana was found."

She kept her eyes on the girl's face, sitting sideways in the passenger seat, her head slightly turned toward the back. Kiana didn't seem to notice. She appeared lost in her thoughts, tense, a little shaky. As the SUV wove its way through the heavy downtown traffic, her eyes lit with a sort of determination, something fierce Tess couldn't read. At the same time, she seemed scared, skittish, and restless, quite normal under the circumstances.

She was scared of going back. Yet she was adamant about it. This had to be about someone else, someone Kiana had left behind when she'd escaped.

"Who's Daisy?" Tess asked, hoping this time the girl would trust her enough to confide in her.

"I am," she replied softly, lowering her eyes and kneading her fingers.

"That's not your name," Tess said gently. "Did you forget your name?"

A flicker of anger lit Kianna's eyes. "No." Her fingers clasped and unclasped the hem of her T-shirt, tugging and pulling. "To him, I was Daisy." She swallowed hard, her lower lip touched by a tremor. "So was everyone else."

"I see," Tess replied. Kiana's statement confirmed what she'd thought about the use of the name. The unsub was recreating the trigger event. In every woman he took, he sought to punish someone by the name of Daisy. She might've hurt him badly, or the injury might've been a figment of his diseased mind. Either way, the name was relevant to the unsub, something Donovan could use to narrow his search. "How were you taken?" she asked, encouraged by Kiana's articulate answers.

She took a trembling finger to her mouth and bit her fingernail, scrunching her eyes shut. Tears flooded her lashes. She didn't say anything for a moment, and Tess didn't push. It must've been painful for her to remember.

"He, um, stopped and asked for directions," she eventually said, her voice fraught with tears. "He seemed oddly familiar and genuinely lost." A sob shuddered her breath. "He was asking about a boat ramp, and David and I put our heads together looking at the phone." As she spoke, her hand clutched the fabric of her T-shirt over her chest, twisting it as if she wanted to rip it off. "That's all it took," she added faintly. "He hit David first, then me, before I could scream." Still tugging at the T-shirt, she shook her head, seeming lost in memories too painful to endure. Tears flowed down her face while she stared into nothing, her brief contact with reality now broken.

"It's all right," Tess said, "we can stop now. I won't ask you any more questions. But you know you can talk to me about anything." She squeezed the girl's hand, but she didn't seem to hear a word nor sense Tess's touch.

Tess's phone rang loudly. She swallowed a curse. It was Donovan. She took the call eagerly, hoping he had the unsub's identity.

"A new missing person report just hit the system," Donovan said, skipping over the greeting. "It came straight into your email."

"Who?" Tess asked, the stress in her voice getting Fradella's attention. "And why my email?"

"Because it's Bella. You know, Kiana's assistant? And because the unsub left a message this time."

Something cold and ominous unfurled in Tess's gut, filling her with dread. "What message?"

41

GAME

I'd inched some more toward becoming a sociopath. Or so I believed at that time; now I'm not so sure.

The pang of guilt that stabbed my disappearing conscience lasted less than a split second.

As I dressed Ashley's wounds and then reluctantly held her in my arms while she sobbed, I didn't consider mentioning she'd been punished for my failed escape. I preferred her quietly rooting for me, instead of clinging to me and begging me to not try again, the way Carolyn had done.

I felt surprisingly comfortable lying to Ashley, while at the same time knowing my relentlessness was the trigger for the hunter's bouts of violence. Yet I couldn't look her in the eye, knowing I was about to try again. Knowing she would probably die if I failed, and still, I had to try.

What did that make me? Was I just as guilty as the hunter was or a mere puppet in his game? If I resigned myself to stay put, would he stop assaulting us? Killing us?

Never.

He thrived on our pain, inflicting it on our defiled bodies and fractured minds to find his release. He dozed off while we wept and bled and screamed and starved. When we stopped being entertaining for him, he discarded us like old, bedraggled dolls.

Perhaps I was rationalizing, trying to ease the already waning sense of guilt I had over jeopardizing another woman's life. But what was I supposed to do, each day when I woke up with a start from my restless, haunted sleep? Wish for a quick and painless death? Or plan my escape, again and again, however many times it would bloody take?

Ashley was better off not knowing what my failure stood to bring her. I gave her trembling body a critical look and pressed my lips together. The thin, pale girl wasn't going to last long. I had no time to waste.

Yet seeing her sob incessantly, curled up on her side on that miserable cot by the wall, filled my heart with rage and self-loathing.

I better not screw up again.

I knew the hunter had trail cams installed, probably more than one. Leaving at night was no longer an option, because I didn't know where they were, and their motion sensors worked in the dark. I had to try again when he dozed off in the afternoon, while the sun was still up, and I had the tiniest chance to see them.

I didn't expect those cameras to extend too far into the wilderness. They were probably mounted in the vicinity of the house, over two hundred feet or so. If I managed to breach that unseen wall of surveillance, I could finally make it.

I waited for the snoring to start. It took him longer that time, fraying my nerves as he drank beer after beer and cheered along with some stupid ball game. But eventually, he dozed off. I listened to the sounds of his snoring for a few minutes, reassuring Ashley I'd come back for her. Then I slipped over the windowsill, barefoot.

My boots were in the same bush I'd thrown them after he'd put an arrow through my arm. That's where I needed to go first.

Unlike before, I didn't sprint into erratic movement. Instead, I stood calmly, looking for the trail cam, my eyes scanning tree after tree, bush after bush. It was hard to spot, hidden between several branches that knotted several feet aboveground in an old cypress. Based on its angle, I was able to figure out a path I could take without triggering it.

It took me about ten minutes to walk three yards.

Then I stopped again, scouting for the next one. Even if I didn't see it, I couldn't be sure it wasn't there. I just kept looking for it, afraid to make a move, to take another step. Eventually, eyes riveted on tree branches and trunks, I took another step. I didn't look where I stepped, didn't scan the terrain before setting my bare foot down.

The black racer pounced, sinking its teeth into my calf in rapid sequence before disappearing into the underbrush. I shrieked and fell to the ground, holding my calf with my hands and praying the hunter didn't hear me scream. A few minutes later, when I could barely walk, I limped back to the barn and snuck in through the window.

Then I saw him.

The hunter stood by Ashley's body. It was lying lifeless in a pool of blood. A crushed daisy had landed in the slowly spreading puddle, white petals in stark, ominous contrast with the red. He stared at the girl with disgust and disappointment on his face, a grimace of contempt like I'd never seen before.

"No," I whimpered, frozen by the window with my back against the wall. The senseless waste of life crushed me, opening a hollow in my chest I didn't think possible. "Why?" I asked, feeling tears starting to flood my eyes. "I wasn't running away this time. I was looking for saw palmetto berries to eat. I swear."

He drilled his eyes into mine with a strange expression that chilled me to the bone. "She was whining too damn much, that's why." Then he drew closer and grabbed my chin between his fingers, lifting it up until I could feel his breath searing my face. "And don't you fucking lie to me again. You'd be long gone if that snake hadn't taken a bite out of you first."

Our eyes locked in an intense stare, but I didn't back down, I didn't look away. An unfamiliar feeling swelled my chest. An urge more than a feeling, something all-consuming and demanding.

Lust.

For his blood.

Whatever evil he put in his glare, I matched with mine. He wanted to kill? So did I. He wanted to hear me scream? Looking him straight in the eye, I fantasized about cutting into his flesh and making him bleed, while looking into his irises, seeing them dilate, the heady feeling sending shivers down my spine. The connection between us, sickening and deranged, was electric. Enthralling. As if staring into an abyss that was also a mirror. As if I looked into the future, but that future could go either way. His way. Or mine. Regardless, it would end in blood and screams and death.

Without another word, he broke off and walked over to the door, then grabbed the shovel and threw it toward me.

"Get busy," he said, while the shovel clattered on the floor, stopping against Ashley's body.

"No." The word came off my lips firmly, in a cold voice.

He shrugged and gave me a good sizing up with eyes that felt sticky and wet on my body. "Would be a terrible waste of such a fine piece of ass, but either you dig or I get someone else and have her dig two holes instead." He sucked his teeth and licked his lips. "Take your pick, sweet Daisy."

A crooked smile tugged at the corner of his mouth as I gaped at him in disbelief. Then, profoundly and acutely defeated, I picked up the shovel and walked past him, headed for his personal burial grounds outside the window.

He didn't follow.

After the shovel dislodged the first spade of moist earth, I let bitter sobs escape my chest.

It was his game. I was never going to break free. Not like that.

Not unless I twisted it, turned it into my game instead.

42

NOTE

"Turn the car around, Todd," Tess said quietly.

Fradella threw her a quick glance, then turned on the flashers and flipped a U-turn in the middle of screeching tires and blaring horns. "Where to?"

"Near the TV station, there's a small plaza with a coffee shop. That's where we're going, fast as you can."

"Copy that," he said, looking briefly at Kiana in the rearview mirror before taking the on-ramp.

"What are you doing?" Kiana asked. She seemed disoriented, but in touch with reality to some extent. It could've been the horns that drew her attention, or maybe the sudden turn, but she was coming out of her dissociative state with an expression of fear on her face.

Tess reached back and squeezed her hand. She withdrew. "You promised," she said, her voice fraught with tears.

"I know, and I'll take you there." She didn't seem reassured. Fidgeting in place as if trying to figure out how to escape the moving vehicle, she kept wringing her hands nervously and looking out the window left and right. "Something happened," Tess added.

Her face turned a sickly shade of grayish pale. "What's wrong?"

Tess hesitated, thinking how best to tell the disheartening news. "The man who took you, he took someone else."

Kiana frowned a little, as if struggling to process the information. "No," she said, shaking her head violently. "It's impossible. You don't understand."

Tess refrained from asking questions. "It's Bella," she said gently, as the SUV turned into the coffee shop's parking lot, where several Miami-Dade police cars had surrounded the place.

"What do you mean, it's Bella?" Her pupils had dilated in sheer panic. Her lips trembled and her voice was shattered and breathless.

"He took Bella," Tess said as gently as she could.

"No!" Kiana shouted, pounding against the window with her fists. "Oh, no, not Bella," she wailed. "Let me out of here."

As soon as Fradella stopped the vehicle, Tess climbed out and opened the back door. Kiana got out and stopped inches away from Tess with her hands propped on her hips.

"It's your fault! I told you to take me back." She paced in place, turning sideways, irrationally looking for Bella, perhaps in the onlookers kept at a distance by yellow tape. She took one hand to her head, rubbing her forehead forcefully as if nursing a blinding headache. Then she turned to Tess with pleading, tear-filled eyes. "You don't understand. Bella isn't strong. She won't make it. Please let me go. Please... she's just a kid." She sobbed with her mouth open, mumbling words Tess didn't understand.

Tess wrapped her arms around the girl's heaving shoulders. "We're both going, okay? But I wanted you to see something first." Kiana pulled away and stared at Tess with an intensity she didn't expect. "This time, he left a message."

"Show me," Kiana said, her voice cold and steady, as if now she was a different person than moments before.

"Come, let's have a look." Tess led the way to the café's patio. On one of its four-by-four posts, a handwritten note had been stuck with an arrow at about five feet aboveground.

Slipping on a pair of gloves, Tess removed the arrow with some difficulty. It was a broadhead, consistent with Kiana's scars. After unscrewing the point, she pulled the paper gently toward the tip and extracted the note without tearing it. She dropped the arrow pieces into an evidence bag held open by an officer, then looked at the note.

The message was written in rushed, slanted block letters that sent a chill through Tess's blood.

GOT YOUR ATTENTION NOW, SWEET DAISY?

She felt Kiana's hand gripping her arm, her thin fingers digging into her flesh. The girl's eyes veered from the note to Tess, her face scrunched in anger and despair.

"What have you done?" she cried. "You don't even understand. I shouldn't've left. I was there, and I was going to go back, but you people took me." She looked at the uniformed cops with grievous anguish, as if the cops who found her on the side of the road were there, among the ones working the scene. "Why? You don't understand... you killed her."

Tess watched her behavior, trying to make sense of what seemed like completely erratic behavior. Was she delusional? Out of her mind with grief and despair? Or was there some truth to her statement? In a scenario that her going back to the unsub would've prevented Bella's kidnapping?

They would soon find out.

Fradella beckoned a detective who seemed to be in charge of the scene and showed him his badge.

"Special Agents Fradella, Winnett, FBI," he said. The man nodded. "How did it happen?"

"He took her in broad daylight, about an hour ago," the detective said. "Witnesses say the vic climbed into his truck on her own. It's quite possible she knew him."

"Do you have a description? Or a tag?" He looked around, squinting in the sunlight, probably looking for the coffee shop's surveillance cameras.

"Working on it still," the cop replied. "No tags on the truck, but we have make and model. An older Chevy Silverado, black or dark blue. The only consistent bits of description we have so far is he was white, in his thirties, wore a beard, and walked with a heavy limp."

Tess looked at the detective, intrigued. "If she got into his truck on her own, why was the abduction reported?"

"Oh, because of this," the cop replied, gesturing at the note Tess held in her gloved hand. "The moment he stuck that piece of paper up on that post and drove off, one of the patrons called us in."

After she slipped the note into a transparent evidence pouch offered by the detective, Tess peeled off her gloves and touched the post where the broadhead arrow had pierced the solid wood. The steel tip had penetrated at least one inch. "He shot his bow in the middle of a parking lot?"

"Nope. Witnesses say he drove the arrow in with his bare hand. In plain view of the folks having their coffee over there," he gestured toward the patio tables, "like he didn't care."

That must've taken some serious strength. The unsub seemed to be filled with rage, most likely at Kiana for escaping his grasp. He didn't care that witnesses saw his vehicle or could easily pick him up from a lineup. Nothing mattered anymore. He was devolving, spiraling out of control.

"He wanted us to know the moment he took her," Tess whispered. "Any idea why?" she asked, turning to Kiana.

She nodded. "Because he wants me back."

That much she knew already. "Thanks," Tess said to the detective, turning to leave.

"You bet," he replied, staring at them with a puzzled expression on his face as they climbed into her Suburban.

Fradella drove quickly, siren and lights on, heading toward the Glades. It gave Tess an eerie sense, but it wasn't déjà vu, because they'd actually driven the same roads going in the same direction only an hour earlier.

Only this time, the sentiment in the vehicle was entirely different. Tess called Donovan first thing after the SUV set in motion, giving him the additional details gathered at the crime scene. The make and model of the unsub's car, the descriptive elements, even the precise time the kidnapping had taken place, in case the analyst wanted to access Miami's vast network of traffic cameras and get a tag.

It was only a matter of time until Donovan would have the unsub identified. But Bella didn't have that time, and neither did Tess. If the unsub was devolving, there was no telling how quickly he could snap and take Bella's life.

"We need to call Pearson for backup," Fradella said, as soon as she ended the call with Donovan.

"Right," she said, retrieving the number she had stored for the special agent in charge.

"No," Kiana said, putting her hand on Tess's shoulder. "You can't call anyone."

Tess turned to look at the girl, expecting to find her tearful and scared. She was everything but. The same unusual intensity Tess had seen before lit her eyes. Kiana was tense and focused as if getting ready for a fight, but Tess wasn't going to let her engage the unsub. She just needed the girl to point her in the right direction, then she and Fradella would take care of the son of a bitch while she waited in the SUV.

"Why not?" she asked, her finger hovering above the call icon.

"He'll see you coming a mile out, and he'll kill Bella. I can't let you do that." She pressed her lips together as if steeling herself before taking a leap into the unknown. "I'll have to go by myself."

Fradella shot Tess an inquisitive glance.

"That's not going to happen, Kiana," Tess said calmly.

"I don't want to hear that," she shouted, tugging at Tess's shirtsleeve. "You don't know what you're doing."

"Even if I have to handcuff you to the steering wheel, you're not going back into those woods," Tess said. Much to her surprise, Kiana didn't reply anymore. She just stared at the road ahead, an expression of sheer determination on her face.

Whatever Kiana thought was going to happen, wasn't. That simple. With that thought, Tess pressed the call button. Pearson answered the call immediately.

"Winnett," he said, "where the hell are you?"

"On the way to the Glades, sir. With the… um, with Kiana." The man always made her second-guess her choice of words. "We're going in after the unsub."

"Didn't we have this conversation? You're not going anywhere."

"He took someone else today. We can't afford not to follow this lead."

A moment's silence, more ominous than Pearson screaming at her and threatening her with disciplinary action. "Does Donovan know where you're going?"

"Yes, sir."

"I'll send some backup." Pearson sighed. "You better know what the heck you're doing, Winnett. It's not just your life you're gambling with."

"Understood," she replied. "Please tell the team they are not to enter the Glades before I give the go signal."

Another moment of tense silence. "All right. You'll get details shortly." The call ended. She stared at the phone in her hand, trying not to see Pearson's threatening glare in her mind. Then she slipped the phone in her pocket and checked her weapon for ammo.

"They'll never find her alive," Kiana said calmly. "You just killed Bella."

Grinding her teeth, Tess willed herself to stay calm. Kiana was a traumatized victim, someone who was afraid for a loved one's life, someone who'd been through months of hell. She deserved some slack.

"Do you know where he is?" Tess asked, instead of scolding her like she'd intended.

"Yes."

"Do you know *who* he is?" Tess looked at Kiana, watching her reactions carefully. She shook her head slowly, her eyes downcast, heavy. There was no sign of deception in her gestures or the expression on her tense face.

"I believe I've seen him before," she whispered, looking out the window. Fradella turned onto Highway 41. They were getting close. "I don't remember who he is, his name, or where I've seen him before. I just can't remember." She punctuated her statement with her hand pounding against her forehead angrily. "I was never good with faces," she chuckled bitterly. "I can recognize a voice years after I hear it, I'm great with names, but if I see you tomorrow at the mall, I won't recognize you. It's called prosopagnosia."

"Face blindness," Tess said. "It's more common than you think." She felt sorry for Kiana, seeing how troubled she seemed over her inability to remember. "Most witnesses can't describe a suspect properly, you know."

"What if we cross-reference the name Daisy with the seventeen snake hunters?" Fradella asked.

"What snake hunters?" Kiana asked, turning slightly pale.

"The ones on your show."

"He's not one of them," Kiana said firmly.

Tess frowned slightly. If she had face blindness, how could she be sure? "You're positive about that?"

"Yes. All those snake hunters had tattoos on their arms or necks. He doesn't. I tend to remember these things, because I can't remember faces. Tattoos are different."

"Ah," Tess replied. It made sense.

Fradella slowed as they approached the spot where Kiana was found.

"One more thing I'd like you to tell me," Tess said, looking straight at Kiana. "Before Bella was taken, why did you want to go back?"

She lowered her eyelids for a moment, staring at her hands and rubbing them as if trying to shake some stuck-on dirt, then looked at Tess with an unspoken plea. "To get closure," she whispered. "To make sure he pays for what he's done."

43

READY

I cried while I dug Ashley's grave. I cried and talked senselessly, to myself, to the girl whose body lay at my feet, to anyone who would hear me. To my father, even though he wasn't there, and I was deeply grateful for that. How could someone like this hunter be allowed to live, to prey on innocent girls? All those principles I'd learned growing up were pure garbage. The bad guy always won, like in a movie no one would watch without booing.

The sandy, moist soil was easy to dig into, or I was getting better at digging graves, because I made quick work of burying Ashley. Once she was covered with earth, I stopped for a moment, leaning into the shovel, trying to think of a few words to say.

Nothing came to mind, except a whispered, "I'm sorry."

Then I left the shovel stuck in the ground by the foot of her grave and went looking for some more yarrow in the flower bed by the house. Daisies were standing tall again, some on crooked, fractured stems, but still striving to reach the sky. More blooms had opened, a cheerful sight for anyone else but me.

At the far end of the flower bed, a sole, tall yarrow ceded a few leaves. I left it standing, because it was the last one, and my wound wasn't. After healing my arm, the leaves served to prevent infection in my calf where the racer had sunk its teeth three times. Standing by the flower bed, I looked at the expanse of green surrounding me, and thought of karma, for the second time that day. I loved everything about the Everglades passionately, yet the place didn't love me back. I would've never thought it possible to find such anguish, such misery in the place I loved so much.

I took the shovel and returned to the barn, then waited, fear paralyzing me. I knew the routine that followed each failed escape attempt; I knew what was coming and I trembled, anticipating the agony, my entire body screaming in apprehension. I was expecting him to drag me into the workshop for another night of punishment, but that didn't happen. Probably killing Ashley had him satisfied for a while, sated in his sickening urges. I spent the rest of the day dozing off in anxious tension, only to flinch awake at every sound, every bird cry, and every toad croak.

That night I waited for him to fall asleep. I listened intently, holding my breath, until the sound of his snoring was loud enough, then I snuck out the window, taking the shovel and the old, rusty saw blade with me. It was a humid night, warmer than usual, and myriad insects welcomed the scent of fresh blood. I didn't mind the countless stings; all I could think of was where to dig, how deep, and how many holes I needed.

But first, I had a trail camera to deal with.

I knew where it was; I remember the tree it was strapped on. I didn't know much about trail cameras, only what I remembered from my dad using them to map wildlife behavior patterns, but I knew they weren't equipped with the same fail-safes as security cameras, because they were built for wildlife, and wildlife doesn't know how to remove batteries.

I snuck carefully toward that tree and approached it from outside the camera's field of view, then turned the camera off. It had a side slider that made my job easier than removing a battery. Then I started digging.

After the bear pit was just right, I took the saw blade and wrapped one end in a strap of fabric torn from one of the rags I'd found in the barn. Then I started sawing off a few slash pine branches, sharpening both their ends. I stuck them in the ground at the bottom of the pit, then collected several fallen palmetto fronds and loose leaves to cover the pit. When I was done, grimy and sweaty and bloodied by insect bites, I stared for a moment at the pit, wondering if one was going to be enough. What if he took a different path to chase me?

Only three paths led from the house into the swamp; I needed two more pits. Before I could dig them, I had to venture out during daytime and locate the other trail cameras. As eager as I was to finish what I had to do, it couldn't be done that night.

I crawled back into the barn and spent the night wide-eyed, leaning against the wall, planning the next move. And fearing his visit more than ever, his punishment that could so easily go too far, now when I was getting so close.

He drove off that morning, early, about an hour after first light. I tried to leave the barn, but the window was locked. I'd been awake all night, watching, listening, and heard nothing. He didn't sneak up outside the window to lock it. I would've sensed him; I would've heard something. Yet the window remained hermetically closed, despite my efforts to pry it open.

For a while, I played with the idea to break the glass with the shovel, but I wasn't ready to execute my new escape plan just yet. But what if I broke it and just ran as fast as I could, trail cams be damned, because he wasn't there to hunt me down? Energized and ashamed at the same time for not thinking of it sooner, I picked up the shovel and slammed its blade into the glass pane, expecting it to explode in a million shards.

Nothing happened. I tried again and again, until I gave up, out of breath. I wasn't going anywhere. Not yet, not like that.

With him gone, I lay down on the cot and slept, recharging my batteries for a long afternoon and an even longer night.

The sun was still high when he came back. He didn't follow his routine; instead, he came straight to me, lusting and enraged by something I didn't understand. Squeezing my eyes shut, I let my mind wander, I forced it out of its realm and willed it to transport me far away from that place, somewhere where I was safe and he was dead, bleeding at the bottom of a freshly dug bear pit.

That time, my fleeting consciousness was dragged abruptly into the moment, and it nearly killed me. He grabbed my hair and forced my head around.

"Open your eyes, Daisy dear, and look at me," he growled, tugging harder and harder until I complied. "I will never let you go; you hear me?"

I stared at him, while at the same time blocking the sight of him in my mind, willing it gone. But then that strange feeling returned, swelling my chest with an urgent need to see him writhing in pain, so intense I could sense the smell of his blood.

That feeling must've come across in my eyes, because he shoved me away, laughing heartily, and said, "That's my Daisy." Then he left and slammed the door shut behind him. He was still laughing when I heard the padlock click.

It took me a while to recover. I don't know how much time I spent lying there on the floor, my entire body throbbing in pain and horror, the memory of his touch more sickening than ever, now that I'd seen it with eyes wide open.

Then I heard the sounds of his usual afternoon; the microwave, the television, the beer cans popping open, then light snoring in the armchair while the TV rambled on. It was time to get up.

The window, now open, had several fresh daisy blooms on the sill. Repulsed by the sight of them, I swiped them off the sill and stomped each and every one of them to a pulp. It didn't matter, but it made me feel just a little bit better.

That afternoon, I found the other trail cameras that overlooked the two remaining paths. The following night, I dug two more bear pits, and nearly split my hand sharpening slash pine branches. Then, crawling on all fours, I started feeling the ground of the snare trap I'd stepped in, the one with the net. I recalled exactly where that had happened, and I knew the netting had to be hidden somewhere under the foliage. I felt around for it, careful not to trigger the spring.

After a long time spent on my hands and knees, feeling for rope under layers of rotting foliage and torn palmetto fronds with sharp thorns on their edges, I found it. Now I knew precisely where it was, but so did he.

It was starting to break daylight as I considered my options. I could dismantle it, but I didn't have the physical strength to bend a sapling to spring the trap someplace else, where he wouldn't expect it to be. All I could do was slide the netting a couple of feet closer to the house, on the other side of the bent sapling that served as a spring.

I knew I could make it irresistible for him to hunt me down, to follow me wherever I'd go. Then I'd make him bleed. Slowly.

As I dragged the netting carefully to the other location and toiled to cover it with foliage and debris, I thought of my father. Would he be proud of me? Or would he be horrified by my thirst for this man's blood?

I didn't know that, but one thing I knew for sure.

I was ready.

44

GONE

Tess got out of the Suburban, her hand on the grip of her holstered weapon, her head on a swivel. Fradella had stopped the SUV by the ditch, leaving two wheels on the asphalt as a tourist would do. The black Suburban, unmarked, had flashers embedded in the grille and the rear bumper, but from a distance, could easily pass for a civilian vehicle.

Kiana pounded against the window, but Tess didn't turn her head. She was scrutinizing the edge of the woods, wondering what to expect.

"He'll see you coming and pick you off one by one," Kiana shouted.

That got Tess's attention. She opened the door and let her out. "What are you talking about?"

The girl bit her lip, hesitating for a moment. "He's got trail cams, and he shoots one of those automatic crossbows that looks like a gun."

"Rambo stuff, huh?" Fradella asked, frowning despite his failed attempt at feigning lightheartedness.

"Okay, noted," Tess replied. "Now get back into the vehicle and wait."

Kiana didn't budge. Tess grabbed her arm, but the girl resisted. "There are bear pits. I know where they are."

Tess let go of her arm, swallowing a curse. Bear pits and automatic crossbows, and Little Miss Sunshine didn't think to mention it until now? Her empathy for the young woman was wearing thin, but they didn't stand a chance without knowing the terrain like she seemed to.

Pearson was going to have her badge.

"All right," she conceded, running her hand quickly through her hair, where countless tiny, invisible mosquitoes were prickling her skin. "You're coming with us. But don't even breathe unless I say so, is that clear?"

Kiana didn't reply. Instead, she took off her white T-shirt and reached into the ditch for a handful of mud she smeared over her face, arms, and chest. Standing casually in her bra and gray sweatpants and continuing to apply mud on her arms, she looked at Tess critically. "I suggest you do the same."

"Oh, hell, no," Tess replied coldly. "What the hell are you doing?"

She shook her head slightly. "You're not dressed right for the swamp. You guys wear wide-cut pants. You see?" She tugged at the sides of her sweatpants. "Mine are tight around the ankles. Countless critters might want to crawl up your pant leg."

"Whose fault is that?" Tess snapped. "You know this wilderness like the back of your hand, yet you didn't find it necessary to say anything. For three days now, you refused to answer my questions. I'm really tempted to slap an obstruction charge on you, now that Bella is missing. You're willingly withholding information, and you're putting every single one of us at risk, including Bella."

After she said the words, she thought about it again. What if she called HRT instead of venturing through miles of wooded swamp with an unstable, traumatized victim and a rookie agent? It would be the logical thing to do. But it didn't feel right. She'd trusted her gut this far; it was too late to turn back now, when Bella was in the hands of a devolving sociopath.

She couldn't trust Kiana with much; so far, she'd proven to be closed off, even manipulative. But one thing she got right. Bella's life was in immediate danger. Would the unsub kill his new hostage if he saw the cops coming? There was no doubt in Tess's mind. At that point, he'd have nothing left to lose. Perhaps Kiana's strategy was the best, approaching the unsub stealthily, without being seen, led by someone who'd managed to escape once. It was just so frustrating and incomprehensible the girl refused to cooperate with them. Tess just couldn't get it.

"Why don't you give me some straight answers?" Tess asked. "What kind of game are you playing?"

"It's not my fault you can't be trusted," Kiana replied, under Fradella's stunned stare. "Are you ready? Figure out those pants... you'll thank me later."

Tess looked at her navy slacks, grinding her teeth. Critters or no critters, she wasn't going to troll through the Glades in her underwear.

Kiana gave Fradella a long stare, then pointed at his shirt. "You wear white, and your blue isn't much better," she added, touching briefly Tess's shirtsleeve. "You can see these colors from a distance out there. If he can see you, he can shoot you." Her voice sounded confident, reminding Tess of the episode of *Swamp Secrets* she'd watched. Kiana was at home in that wilderness, even if she seemed a bit off, driven to return to where she'd been held, while at the same time afraid, horrified even.

"And you didn't think to say anything before we left the city?" Tess repeated to hide the embarrassment she felt because she hadn't thought of it. For some reason, she'd imagined the unsub's house would have a street address with a road leading to it. "Whose side are you on?" A chill traveled down her spine when she remembered Doc Rizza's comments about Stockholm. What if Kiana did have Stockholm, and she'd turn on them at the last minute, sell them out to the unsub?

One problem at a time.

Pulling hard at her socks to stretch them, Tess managed to slip them over the hems of her pants. At least for a while, critters wouldn't crawl up her pant legs. Just the thought of that was giving her the creeps.

"Look before you step and stay clear of the water. Just stay behind me and do as I say," Kiana said, seemingly not caring to answer any of Tess's questions as she started to walk briskly toward the wooded swamp. "Whatever crawls on you, don't flinch and don't shriek. You'll die if you don't hold it together. Get my attention, quietly, and I'll deal with it."

Wonderful. Tess fought the sense of dread that was coursing through her veins. She must've been insane to let herself be talked into this incursion. It was reckless, stupid, and every other adjective that Pearson would rightfully throw at her the first time they met. It was also Bella's only chance.

After exchanging a quick look with Fradella, Tess drew her weapon and removed the safety, then stepped hesitantly into the thick greenery that lined the ditch. Something moved about a foot away, rustling though the grass away from her. She froze and held her breath for a moment. Damn crawlers. She didn't even want to know what that was.

"How far do we have to go?"

"About six miles."

"What?" Tess stopped, looking around in dismay. The woods seemed endless; the highway they had barely left behind almost completely obscured from view. "You have got to be kidding me," she muttered, doubting her judgment call again. They should've brought ATVs, gear, water, and a satellite phone. It was beyond reckless.

But Kiana marched quickly, expertly using the terrain for cover. She stopped behind larger trees and listened, waited, apparently planning her every move. Then she lurched some more or sprinted at times, resting only with her body against a tree trunk.

Tess was about to question that, when she recalled the scars on the girl's body. She'd taken two broadhead arrows. It probably taught her a lesson in survival.

She kept up with Kiana, but not too close, choosing to stay a few yards behind her and give herself some reaction time in case something unexpected happened. Fradella was walking a few yards behind her, his white shirt visible from a distance, standing out against the sunlit scenery. Every minute or so, she looked over her shoulder to make sure he was still coming. Neither of them was ready for what they were about to do.

About an hour and a half into the brisk, breathless walk, Tess stopped, leaning against a tree trunk like she'd seen Kiana do. She looked over her shoulder, checking on her partner, but the white shirt was nowhere to be seen.

Holding her breath, she looked everywhere, listening for any noise that didn't belong. Fradella had vanished without a sound. No bullet zipping through the air, no arrow either. No thump when his body had fallen. Nothing, just the eerie, constant buzzing and chirping of critters in the swamp.

Feeling panic invading her jittery mind, Tess pulled out her phone to call Donovan and ask for a trace on Fradella's phone. There was no signal, not even a single bar. She tried the call anyway, obstinately refusing to admit defeat. It failed.

Then she felt something touch her arm and nearly jumped out of her skin.

"There's no point in going back for him," Kiana said calmly, her hand tentatively touching Tess's forearm. "He never lets the men live. He has no use for them."

"Don't you dare tell me that," Tess said angrily, starting on the way back. She breathed heavily, her chest heaving, her heart thumping against her ribcage, while she continued walking and scrutinizing the wilderness she'd left behind. Where was he?

Kiana didn't follow. She just stood there and shrugged. "Suit yourself, but your partner is gone."

45

TRAP

The swamp fell quiet when I screamed.

My clipped cry, quickly smothered as my shaking hand rushed to cover my gaping mouth, left the stage open for the concert of crickets, frogs, and countless other critters. Within half a heartbeat, the cacophony of sounds was back in full force as if I was never there.

Gasping for air, I leaned against the thick trunk of a bald cypress covered in Spanish moss and listened intently. Not too far behind, I picked up the sound of a twig cracking.

He followed me. He was hunting for me. It's what I wanted, what I'd planned for. And yet, my hands were shaking, and my heart was beating in the rhythm of sheer panic. What if something went wrong?

"Where are you, sweet little Daisy?" His voice, coarse and lewd and repulsive, seemed tinged with laughter, but I knew better. It's the anticipation of the hunt, the excitement that rushed through his veins at the thought of seeing me bleed, writhing in pain at his feet, begging for his mercy. Then submitting to his will, utterly defeated.

He was drawing closer with every step, crunching rotting leaves and palm fronds under his boots, seeding unspeakable fear in my blood. It took every ounce of willpower I had to not dash away from there screaming and running as fast as I could.

I stood still, holding my breath, knowing that when I set foot out in the open and he saw me, he'd strike me down mercilessly.

He never missed.

I had the scars to prove it.

Only this time, I had what it took to turn the tables on him. If I could only hold it together long enough to see it through.

Zigzagging from one tree to another in quick darts, deathly fearing his arrows, I lured him onto the path where I'd dug a pitfall two nights ago. As I approached it, I whimpered loudly, even cried once as if I'd twisted my ankle or stepped on something, barefoot as I was.

Stopped behind a tree trunk, I watched him approach. He walked steadily, holding the middle of the path, no reason for him to hide. He held the crossbow up, ready to fire, aimed at wherever his eyes were looking, his hand steady, his finger on the trigger. Before he got too close, I darted again, leaping over the bear pit. I waited less than a second, then bolted again, gaining some distance, enough to entice him to walk faster.

I cried out again, a cry of feigned pain released on a shattered breath, pure spice for the lure set in front of him. He tilted his head slightly, listening, then stomped forward, almost running.

Three steps, and he fell into the bear pit, yelping loudly. The crossbow clattered on the ground, slipping out of his hand when he flailed reaching for something he could grab to break his fall.

I approached slowly, ready to bolt if he made an unexpected move.

He'd crushed most of the slash pine stakes under his weight, but at least one was drawing his blood. It had ripped through his flesh above the knee and kept him from moving.

"I'll enjoy killing you, bitch," he growled among a slew of invectives. "I'll take my time until you beg me to end you."

I grinned, eyeing the crossbow. It was on the other side of the pit. I had to walk around to get to it, and I was just about to, when he snapped the stake that ran through his leg, screaming in pain, then pulled the piece that stabbed him with one swift move. Blood gushed from the wound.

Then, panting heavily, he started lifting himself up, clawing at the ground to escape the pit.

I hadn't dug it deep enough.

That mistake cost me the chance to get the crossbow away from him. Within seconds, it was within his reach. About a minute later, he'd pulled himself out of the pit, bleeding heavily from his injury, and shouting almost all the time.

"Doesn't feel that good, now does it?" I said, disappearing quickly from his view, hidden behind a tree, watching. He was looking for me, hunting for me, walking with a heavy limp, slightly bent forward so that his hand could put pressure on the wound. Then he saw me advance quickly in short bursts across the path.

"Gotcha," he shouted, still panting. He dragged his right foot as he walked, visibly in pain. I felt joy at the sight of his suffering, unabashed pride at the sight of blood dripping down his leg. And a strong desire to hurt him more.

But things could still go wrong. He was advancing far too quickly, fueled by rage and adrenaline, and was almost caught up with me.

Fear choking me, I shifted in place without realizing it, crunching dry leaves under my feet. The noise, barely noticeable under the cover of myriad critters bustling in the falling night, caught his attention from yards away. He froze in place, visually searching for me, turning only his head and with it the sights of that wretched crossbow.

I held my breath.

And waited.

Seconds went by, seeming like hours. Insects claimed their blood meal from my skin, but I barely noticed them. My eyes stayed riveted on the silhouette I could barely distinguish beyond layered curtains of moss. The wind picked up just a smidge and shifted the moss chains near me gently, quietly.

One tendril touched my face, and I nearly flinched but remained still, watching him, waiting for the right time to bolt.

"Come on, dear girl, show yourself." His voice was almost convincing. "Can't let the night crawlers hunt you." A throaty chuckle. "You're mine."

He took a few steps farther down the path and stopped again, his head slightly tilted, probably listening intently. I looked at the dirt I had picked up in my hand, planning my throw.

Seeing the black dirt on my skin choked me. The smells of damp earth, of bog and mist and saltwater and death, snatched my weary mind and filled it with memories too painful to endure.

A sob climbed forcefully from my chest, demanding to be heard among other creatures' agonizing calls. I managed to stifle it, covering my mouth with the back of my hand and blinking away tears.

I filled my lungs with humid, sticky air and found the courage to throw the fistful of dirt across the path, aiming at a cluster of thriving palmettos where I could've easily hidden.

The hunter froze in place the moment he heard the sound. Slowly and quietly, he turned in place and took two steps toward the palmetto bush, studying it intently.

That's when I bolted.

I tried to move as silently as I could, but he still heard me. By the time he fired his arrow, I'd reached the cover of a big cypress, fighting to slow my breathing just a little.

"Sneaky, my little Daisy girl," he shouted. Some of the earlier excitement in his voice was now replaced with budding anger. "Enough games for tonight. It's getting late, and I have plans for you." His lustful, bloodcurdling cackles silenced the frogs for a moment. "Boy, do I have plans for you... You'll love every minute of it."

His words filled my heart with terror. Whatever he promised, he delivered tenfold. I'd learned that the hard way.

His words were paralyzing me like the stare of a deadly snake right before the lethal bite.

The last remnants of daylight were disintegrating quickly like gossamer blown in the wind, and I could barely see a few feet ahead of me. Moss tendrils waved gently in the calm breeze like ghosts haunting the forest from hell.

My knees suddenly weak, I held on to the tree trunk and steadied myself. "Snap out of it already," I told myself, an angry whisper escaping between clenched teeth.

I'll make it. I know I will.

I have to.

He was almost close enough to grab my arm when I ran as fast as I could, zigzagging between trees, holding my breath, and willing myself to not look back.

"Ah, there you are," he said, sending shivers down my spine.

He followed, closing in despite his limp. I didn't look back; I just heard his breath and heavy footfalls as I dashed desperately left and right, knowing it was my only chance to escape his arrows.

The sound of a cord snapping taut ripped through the air like a whip.

I shrieked and fell to the ground, breathless.

"Yes," I shouted, lifting my arms in the air and looking at his body, dangling several feet aboveground, wrapped in the net trap. "I got you, you son of a bitch!"

He bellowed from up there, bloodcurdling threats and curses and hatred dripping from his words like pure venom. It only made me laugh, a hysterical, high-pitched guffaw that echoed through the woods, scaring wildlife into a mere instant of shocked silence.

The crossbow had landed a couple of feet away, under a palmetto bush. I reached under there and grabbed it, then I stood up, taking aim at him from behind a tree.

"Drop your knife," I called. He always carried a knife at his belt, the one still stained with David's blood.

He laughed derisively in response. "You think you got me? You miserable little piece of shit, when I'm done with you, they won't be able to identify your body." He scoffed and cussed, but he wasn't scaring me anymore.

"Drop that knife, or I'll shoot." I trained the heavy crossbow on his body, holding it with both my hands. My weakened muscles trembled under its weight. "I'm not good at this... I might get you in the eye."

He wasn't laughing anymore. A moment later, the knife clattered against the ground when it landed. "There, happy?"

I lowered the crossbow, left the cover of the tree trunk, and just stared at him. He was still dangling, swaying less and less and spinning slowly. How long would that contraption hold him? Someone like him had to have a way out of there, even without a knife.

But for now, I could relish the newly found sense of freedom. And make him pay for David's life, for all those girls who lay buried by the house. And for my own suffering.

That unfamiliar feeling resurged in my chest. "I'll stay here and watch you rot alive, motherfucker," I said, my teeth grinding as I said the words. Then, in a bout of blood thirst, I raised the crossbow and pulled the trigger.

He screamed and grabbed his thigh with both hands, cursing fiercely.

"How do you like your little crossbow now, huh?" He didn't reply, just breathed heavily with his mouth open, spreading droplets of saliva with every breath. If I didn't know better, I could've sworn he had tears in his eyes.

And yet, seeing him suffer, hearing his cries didn't soothe me. It was as if my pain was unquenchable, unwilling to be healed or avenged.

"I'll watch you bleed and won't stop until you give back every bit of blood you spilled in your sorry life," I added, walking away toward the house with a spring in my step. I was hungry and finally I could eat.

Or so I thought. I didn't find much food at the house, only the two cans of beans I'd spared before and some leftover cheese in the fridge, already touched by mold. But I was determined to endure, to watch him until he drew his last breath. The next day, after retrieving the boots I had stashed aside the bush, I went looking for some palmetto berries to eat and found the highway.

And the cops found me.

***

The last time I saw the hunter, he was dangling from that tree, wrapped in a spring net, nursing the wounds I gave him. I wanted to go back, to witness his demise, to be there when he'd hopelessly scream his agony, and let the sound soothe the pain in my heart.

I couldn't.

Once again, I'd lost my freedom senselessly, this time at the hands of a federal agent who was supposed to be on my side. But I couldn't tell her what I'd done, nor risk having her stop me from finishing what I'd set out to do.

She wouldn't understand.

Those days spent in the hospital, when nightmares faded and gave me some respite back into the realm of reason, I had time to think. Why didn't I take the hunter's truck and return to civilization, let the cops deal with him? Why didn't I leave that forsaken place behind me and go back to whatever was left of my life?

The answer was simple.

David.

He's the reason I wanted to stay, to see the monster who ended his life pay for what he'd done. The image of my husband's shallow grave, earth covering his pale face, the twigs tied into a cross placed at his head, it all still haunts me. I can't leave him alone there, in that hell. I can't just walk away.

Now the hunter has Bella, and I know why, even if I don't know how he managed to escape the trap.

Because, you see, the moment I learned how he took her, I realized where I'd seen him before.

46

DARKNESS

Kiana's words froze the blood in Tess's veins. Todd Fradella couldn't be gone... not like that, vanishing senselessly in the middle of that endless swamp. Not without a fight, a chance to defend himself. Not when he'd just reentered her life, shining a light on what she'd been missing all that time.

Faltering, she stopped in the middle of the path, still scouting for Fradella in the depths of the woods, as far as she could see through gently waving tendrils of Spanish moss like see-through curtains hanging from the trees.

"Don't just stand there," Kiana whispered angrily. "Take cover."

Kiana's words had the effect of a cold shower, startling Tess back into awareness. The moment she set in motion, she heard the arrow slicing through the air. It pierced her right arm above the elbow, severing her muscle to the bone. She dropped the gun and shrieked, falling to the ground, holding her arm with her hand where the arrow pierced her flesh.

Then she felt Kiana's unexpectedly strong grip grabbing her collar and dragging her to the nearest tree.

"I can't believe you didn't hear a word I said," Kiana mumbled, examining Tess's wound. "He's hunting for us; do you get it now? Do you understand?"

"Uh-huh," Tess replied between clenched teeth.

"Go back," Kiana said, examining her wound quickly. "You have no business here."

"The hell I don't," Tess replied, pulling herself up into a sitting position and wincing from the pain. She threw Kiana a menacing look, an unspoken warning she was starting to lose her patience. Where did that girl get off telling her what to do?

"I need to remove the arrow," Kiana whispered, looking around in the grass for something. She retrieved a small piece of wood, a section of a dried pine branch. "Here, sink your teeth into this." Tess looked at the piece of wood but didn't take it. "Fine, have it your way, but whatever you do, don't scream. He'll follow your voice and catch us."

Tess bit the side of her left hand, tricking her brain into not feeling the pain in her wound so acutely. Kiana removed the arrow quickly, the pain bringing Tess to near fainting. It was obvious she'd done it before. Then she ripped a section of Tess's shirt and wrapped it tightly around the wound.

"There," she said, tying the stretch of fabric with a double knot. "Now do me a favor and go back. You don't belong here."

Tess looked at the girl's wary features, trying to understand her behavior. She'd seen Kiana battling the nightmarish throes of early onset PTS, then lucid only moments later. She'd seen the girl's wounds, some of them badly healed. Her scars, horrible stories of torture and pain at the hands of a ruthless sociopath. She'd witnessed her anguish when she was disoriented by trauma and thought she was back with the unsub.

And yet, there she was, willing to go back and face him again.

"And you do?" Tess asked, keeping her voice a low whisper.

Kiana nodded, sadness clouding her eyes. "I'm not done with this place yet. And he's got Bella. That changes everything."

"How did he know to take Bella?"

Kiana didn't reply; just stared at the woods, probably planning her next step.

"He knew who to take to hurt you, didn't he? To get to you?" Still silence. "Something tells me you didn't confide in him with the list of people you care about, complete with their names and where they could be found."

She nodded slowly. "What do you want from me right now?" She stood and looked carefully around. "Do you think this is my fault? Any of this?"

"No, I—"

Kiana put a finger to her lips, and Tess fell silent. She listened closely but didn't hear anything other than the sounds of nature.

"He's coming," Kiana mouthed more than whispered. "Let's go. We have to stay ahead of him."

Tess went back to where she'd been shot and felt in the grass for her gun. It felt strange in her left hand. Then she withdrew quickly back to the cover of a tree trunk and nodded for Kiana.

The girl started to advance in short sprints from one tree to the next. Tess followed, grunting and panting. The rhythm of the run was gruesome, physically demanding in ways she hadn't trained for. The entire experience of being in the Glades to hunt for the unsub had been humbling, humiliating even. She'd never felt so ill-prepared to do her job before.

Then, sprinting from one tree to the next, she saw a house, partly shielded from view by moss tendrils. It was small and looked relatively old. A barn stood to the right of the house, toward the water. Between the two buildings, a small garden with white flowers, some trampled over but some still standing.

Daisies.

It made sense, if the unsub was obsessed with that name to use the symbolism of the flower as a homophone.

They had arrived.

Tess looked for Kiana but didn't see her anywhere. She waited for a while, thinking the girl must've been hiding in the underbrush before sprinting again, but nothing moved. Her left hand gripping the gun, ready to fire, she dashed another thirty or forty feet, sideways, the way she'd seen Kiana do. It made sense to do that; she'd learned the same technique in her physical fitness training at Quantico.

She was almost at the house, and there was still no trace of Kiana. She was about to make a final run for the side of the house, when the barn door opened and a man came out halfway, holding Kiana in front of him like a shield, his arm around her neck in a chokehold.

"I know you're out there," the man called. "Come out and drop your weapon, or she dies."

Tess aimed at the man, but then lowered her weapon. She was too far away, and she could hit Kiana instead. Her left hand wasn't as precise as her right; she couldn't risk it.

She stayed still, holding her breath, wondering what her chances were with a devolving serial killer on the verge of a psychotic break. Could she reach him? Not from where she stood.

The unsub's gun went off and Kiana screamed.

"No one said she has to die quickly," the man shouted. "I can make it last."

Holding her weapon by the barrel, Tess left the cover of the tree and walked over to the unsub slowly, with her hands up, taking in as much detail as she could.

The man was tall and well built. The arm that held Kiana's neck in a grip was thick and muscular, the kind of upper body strength one could see in special forces operatives. And snake hunters, from what she'd learned watching Kiana's show.

"Drop it," he said.

She crouched and placed the gun on the ground, then kicked it toward him, forcefully enough for it to slide over a few feet in his direction and put his fears at ease. Then she stood and raised her hands in the air. "You're in control," she said calmly.

"Damn right I am, and I don't need you to tell me that." He shoved Kiana to the side, then approached Tess with a blood-chilling grin on his face.

Her head exploded into a million green stars, then nothing. Just darkness.

47

ARROW

The first thing Tess noticed when she opened her eyes was the blinding throbbing in her head. Something trickled down slowly on her temple, perhaps blood, or maybe a small insect; she couldn't tell.

Then, the smell. The most nauseating mix of mildew and wood rot and blood, a sticky stench that seemed to get worse and worse as she breathed it.

Finally, the sharp pain around her wrists. They were tightly bound with plastic zip ties fastened over a wooden chair's armrests. Her ankles were bound also, tightly secured against the chair's front legs.

She couldn't move an inch.

A couple of feet to her left, Kiana was bound the same way and whimpered quietly, watching the unsub's blooming grin. Tess turned and looked at Kiana, sending her what she meant to be a reassuring look.

But panic rose in her chest, almost suffocating, triggered by memories she thought were long gone, never to resurface again. She couldn't begin to understand how that girl had mustered the courage to return and face the unsub after all she'd been through. Twelve years after she'd been assaulted, Tess still recoiled from the trauma. It felt fresh and painful and terrifying as if it had been yesterday.

If she wanted to survive this, the unsub couldn't feel her fear.

She breathed slowly, forcing air into her lungs methodically, holding it for a couple of seconds, then breathing it out just as slowly. Meanwhile, she scouted the room, looking for something she could use.

Two fresh daisies lay flat on a wooden, decrepit, bloodstained worktable. Two women, two daisies... it made sense. By that worktable, on a low bench, he'd abandoned his tactical crossbow, several arrows still loaded in its compact body. In the corner of the room, on a dusty crate, Tess saw her gun, the magazine still in. Several tools hung on the wall by the door, while others littered another crate, this one missing a couple of slats. Several nails stuck out, forced almost loose when the slats had broken off. Next to that crate, on the floor right by the door, an old, rusty saw blade had its edge wrapped in stained, blue satin, as if to form a handle that wouldn't hurt the person who'd used it. A plethora of tools she could use.

If she could get to them.

The man approached Tess, the glint in his eyes bringing a sense of dread. She'd seen eyes like those before. In killers she'd interviewed. In predators and sociopaths she'd put away, either in jail or into the ground. She knew very well what that look meant, even before he spoke.

"Well, hello, new Daisy," he said, trailing Tess's lips with his thumb. She couldn't help a shudder.

"Hello, Jim," Kiana replied calmly.

She knew his name. Unbelievable. Anger rushed through Tess's blood furiously. She glared at the woman, but she wasn't paying attention to her. She was focused on the man.

"You're not where I left you," Kiana said.

Jim walked over to Kiana. He was limping badly, and the torn pant leg revealed an ugly puncture wound with ragged edges that looked familiar. She had one just like it on her right arm, above the elbow, and it hurt like hell.

The hunter had taken an arrow to his thigh. The blood on his pant leg had dried, and the wound had started to crust over, but was swollen and seemed infected. Tess looked at Kiana with admiration this time. She didn't think the girl had it in her.

"You couldn't help shooting me," the hunter laughed, but his eyes threw Kiana a deathly glare. "Arrowheads are sharpened steel. Just what I needed to cut myself out of that net. But you didn't think of that, did you, sweetheart?"

Jim ran his fingers through Kiana's hair, and she didn't flinch. "You smell nice, my sweet Daisy. And you brought me a present." Something icy glimmered in his eyes as he took a handful of Kiana's hair and wrapped it around his hand, yanking her head back until she yelped. "Did you miss me?"

"Where's Bella?" Kiana asked, panting heavily.

The man twisted his hand a little more, pulling harder. "I knew you'd come for her."

"Yes, Jim, I came for her," she replied calmly. "Not for you. For her." She threw him a glance dipped in poison. "For you, I would've sent the feds to finish what I started."

"Is that right?" he asked, raising his hand. Kiana instinctively cowered.

"When did she leave you?" Tess asked.

Jim's hand froze in midair. He turned with difficulty, wobbly and unsure on one leg. His face was scrunched in anger, his eyes throwing darts of venom her way. "You don't get to talk about her," he growled. His hand came down without hitting anyone, just limp as if he'd lost all steam. But Tess wasn't fooled; it was just a momentary respite, his rage boiling underneath the surface, ready to explode.

"Ah," she said enigmatically, watching carefully the microexpressions on his face, the flashes of rage in his eyes, the moments his pupils dilated. "It still hurts, huh?"

"Shut the hell up," he bellowed, leaning over her and bringing his face inches away from hers.

"She messed your world up so badly, you can't keep yourself from punishing her over and over again, can you?"

He clenched his fists so hard, Tess heard his knuckles crack. She was almost there, close to getting him so enraged he'd start making mistakes. Anger makes people impulsive, slightly disoriented, and clumsy. She needed him like that.

"But I guess it doesn't feel anything like punishing the real thing, does it?" Tess whispered. Kiana stared at her with her mouth slightly open, shocked. "What would you do to get your hands on Daisy?" A beat. "The real one, not me or her. We're just... fakes. Surrogates."

The question took him by surprise. "She's gone." His joints crackled again.

The woman wasn't dead; she'd just vanished. Otherwise, he would've been more resigned about it.

"Of course, she's gone," Kiana said, surprising Tess. "No woman in her right mind would be with you, Jim. Not unless she wants to kill you so badly, she can almost taste it."

Ah, hell, Tess thought. *Now or never.*

Jim turned toward Kiana, his hand raised again, getting ready to strike. In turning toward her, he'd exposed his wounded leg to Tess. Pushing herself as hard as she could, she threw herself in his direction, head-butting his thigh with all her strength.

He screamed and fell to the ground with a loud thump that shook the entire house. Tess didn't waste any time. Still bound to the chair, she hobbled awkwardly on her toes, bent forward, until she reached the wall, then slammed the chair forcefully against the wall.

It didn't break.

On the floor, Jim struggled to get up, screaming profanities and holding his hand over his leg wound. Blood trickled between his fingers.

Desperate, Tess slammed the chair against the wall again and again. Eventually, the handle broke, and her left hand was free to reach out and grab a pair of wire cutters. She moved quickly and freed herself of the chair, just as Jim was getting back on his one good foot, dragging the other and coming at her hard. She rushed over to Kiana, kicking Jim's wounded leg in passing and sending him to the ground once more. Only this time, he grabbed her shirt and brought her down with him. The wire cutters slid on the floor until it stopped against Kiana's chair leg.

Tess fought the man as best she could, but he was massive and his arms were like steel, strong and unyielding. He wrapped his hands around her throat, choking her, but she reached for his eyes and scratched hard, flailing more than taking aim.

He shouted and let go of her throat, one eye half-closed, blinking erratically. Tess crawled away from him and reached for the gun, then turned toward him as he was about to pounce. She pulled the trigger twice, just as an arrow hit him in the throat.

He fell on his back, the wounded leg folded underneath him, his eyes wide open, staring at the ceiling. His fingers moved spasmodically for a moment or two, then stiffened.

Kiana was standing, her legs still tied to the chair, holding the crossbow with both her hands, ready to fire another arrow. She seemed inexplicably sad, depleted.

"He's dead," Tess said, after crawling over and putting two fingers on his neck to search for a pulse.

"I know," she replied, dropping the crossbow on the floor. She stared at the man's face with lips pressed tightly together, visibly dejected.

Could it have been Stockholm after all?

"What's wrong?" Tess asked in a croaking voice, frowning slightly as she got up, holding on to a crate for support. Her entire body ached, and her throat felt swollen and dry.

Kiana shook her head, still staring at the body. Her nostrils flared and her lips, still pressed tightly together, moved as if words were trying to escape her mouth but she wasn't letting them.

"It's over, Kiana," Tess said gently. "He's dead."

The girl shot Tess a scrutinizing look as if trying to ascertain if she could be trusted. "I wanted to kill him so badly," she eventually said. "That's why I wanted to come back. To kill him. I'd wounded him and caught him in a trap... he was mine to kill. I... needed to."

Tess looked at Kiana, a bit surprised but not really. She understood perfectly what the girl felt. Then she leaned over the body, pretending to examine the wounds.

"What are you talking about?" Tess asked, hiding a fleeting smile. "My bullets missed his heart. Your arrow killed him."

"Thank you." Kiana breathed and closed her eyes. Tess watched her body starting to relax as she reached down and cut the zip ties around her ankles.

"Now let's find Bella," Tess said, taking her gun and the crossbow.

She left the workshop frowning, gun in hand, steeling herself for a grim task she wasn't ready for: finding Todd's body. Just the thought of it brought the burn of tears to her eyes and a sick, nauseating feeling in her gut, as if the hunter had punched her in the stomach.

Kiana rushed ahead, not giving a crap about anything Tess had to say. She seemed to know her way around that hellhole really well, while Tess flinched at the sight of the python mounted on the wall.

She caught up with Kiana and pushed her aside as she was about to enter the barn. She opened the door and peeked inside, weapon in hand, then blinked in disbelief. Todd was on the floor, bound with zip ties around his hands and legs, his mouth covered with a stretch of duct tape. He wriggled and mumbled something she didn't understand.

He was alive.

"Oh, no, Bella," Kiana said crying, holding Bella's limp hand. She was lying on a miserable cot, by the wall, and wasn't moving.

Tess removed Fradella's restraints. He sprung to his feet. "This is embarrassing," he mumbled. "She was like that when I got here," he added, gesturing toward the cot.

Tess searched for a pulse and found one, weak and fast. She elevated the girl's head and called her name a few times, increasingly louder. Eventually, Bella opened her eyes.

Tess smiled to hide her emotion seeing Kiana's tears of joy.

"Welcome back."

48

SCARS

I won't cover my scars.

The decision comes easily as I wander through the patch of wilderness that used to be my prison, my own brand of hell. I thought I could never think of coming back to the Glades, but no. My love for this place saved me. As for the man who tore my life apart, he wasn't part of the habitat; he was just a piece of vermin, a parasite, nothing but a venomous snake I happened to step on.

He's dead now.

The thought fills my chest for a moment, then it disintegrates, and the hollow inside returns.

I keep meandering between cops and crime scene technicians who are swarming the place, packing it up in neatly labeled plastic pouches and carrying it out of here in loads atop ATVs.

I see my prison in a new light. Inside the barn, I break down into tears, remembering Carolyn's last moments, while the lyrics of that children's song swirl in my brain. "We all fall down," the song plays in my mind. Well, maybe not all of us fall. I didn't. I get to walk away from here.

Outside, I examine the window carefully, and figure out how he locked and unlocked it without me sensing anything. A thin wire controlled an electric lock on the top edge of the frame.

Had I stopped for a moment to look at the window the first time I slipped out, I would've broken free a long time ago. But I won't blame myself, even if that's hard at times, remembering all the lives lost.

No... I won't hide what happened to me. I won't lie about it, and I won't brag either. But I'll walk with my head up straight wherever life will take me. Most of all, I won't let that monster ruin my love for the Glades, for nature, for the place I grew up in.

The thought of my father comes slashing though my mind, and the hollow in my chest reopens. I gasp for air and try not to imagine Dad alone in the house, distraught after my disappearance, having a stroke with no one around who could've helped him. I've killed the venomous snake who took my father's mind.

I can start grieving in peace.

Tomorrow.

For now, I'm still here, and can't walk away.

I stop by David's grave and crouch down to straighten the improvised cross. A few rainstorms have almost leveled the ground, but that cross is still standing.

How can I leave?

They've taken Bella to the ambulance with an ATV. She'll be all right, they said. That fed woman kept asking questions and giving directions. She wanted the entire place taken into evidence, when setting it on fire would've been just as good, if not better. Fire purifies. This place needs it.

I straighten the cross and tighten the knot that holds the two twigs together. Tears fall down my cheeks, and I don't even feel them. All I feel is love for my husband, and he's not there to receive it. My love has no place left to go.

"We'll make arrangements to have his body buried properly," the fed says, taking me by surprise. I'm still jumpy at times, as if the hunter could somehow come back to life and resume chasing his prey through those woods. Other times, my mind just drifts away, lost in a whirlwind of memories, some too painful to bear, others I relive, over and over as if I could somehow rewrite history.

"Thank you," I whisper, looking at the row of graves that spans from the water line almost to the barn.

"All their bodies," she adds quickly, as if reading my mind.

I just nod and let my mind wander. I don't want to talk to her. To anyone.

"I could throw the book at you," the fed says. I'm not afraid; her voice doesn't match the harshness of her words. "You lied to federal agents. You obstructed the investigation into Bella's kidnapping. You endangered our lives, and that's just for starters." The fed sighs as she looks at my tear-streaked face. "Why not tell me who he was and where to find him?"

I think she earned herself the right to know the truth. She was willing to die for me. "He got off easily," I whisper, suddenly feeling the need to put some distance between myself and David's grave, as if he could hear what I'm about to say. As if he'd be ashamed of what I have become. "He worked with us on shoots, but who pays attention to the cameraman, right?" I shake my head, disappointed bitterly with myself. "Who, other than Bella? She was into the guy, but he didn't seem to know she existed. That's why she got into his truck, on her own. All he had to do was smile in her direction. But I didn't remember him. I didn't know who he was until he took Bella. That's how I knew. It had to be someone familiar with how close we were Bella and me, someone from the crew, yet someone Bella would follow." I chuckle silently. "There aren't too many men like that. She's fiercely independent."

I stand and take a few steps to the side. The fed follows. Tess Winnett is her name, or something like that. The Tess part I'm sure about. She waits patiently for me to continue, and I respect her for that. "I wanted him to pay. For a long time. I wanted him to suffer, for months and months, and die a slow, agonizing death."

Surprise colors her scrutinizing gaze. "What, and live here, in this godforsaken hell, just to watch him suffer?"

I nod, unable to say another word. Something climbs from inside my chest, choking me.

"For how long?" she asks, her voice tinged incredulous.

I swallow hard and blink away tears. "Until my grief would fade." I look at my hands and still see the earth clumps sticking to my skin like a cancer, although they're clean to the naked eye, when memory doesn't overlay images from the past. Then I shift my gaze to the line of graves I've dug. "I killed them," I whisper. "It was my fault. Now I have to live with it."

The fed takes my hand and squeezes it. I look at her through a vale of tears. I see something in her eyes I didn't expect. Understanding. A connection that wouldn't exist unless she—

"Listen," she says quietly, "you are not the villain here, but you aren't a victim either."

Unless she's been through some version of what I've endured.

I hold her strong, reassuring gaze and feel empathy for her, an unexpected connection. I'm willing to listen to what she has to say, because she survived and put it past her somehow. I need to learn how to do that.

I nod and respond to her hand squeeze ever so slightly. "I— I don't know how—"

"You're a survivor," she says, her voice uncompromising. "None of this was your fault." A tinge of sadness washes over her face. "It won't be easy, but you survived much worse. Now it's time to rebuild your life. Don't let the bastard take your destiny to the grave you put him in."

She lets go of my hand and wraps me in a hug that somehow instills energy into my weary soul. Then she pulls away gently and slips her business card into my hand. "Call me sometime, all right? I'll be there, night or day."

I watch her walk away. She's immediately surrounded by her people. The other agent, he's seriously into her, I can tell.

And there's another guy, younger, who doesn't stop talking about the hunter, reading from a laptop equipped with satellite internet connection. I overhear him say the hunter's name was James Brickner, and his father was a famous snake hunter.

That's all I hear from a distance. I'm back by David's grave, there to stay. I have no other place to go, not until we take him home. They say grief is the final form of love. But my love isn't final; it doesn't end. It never will.

In the distance, the coroner's people are loading a black, zippered body bag onto an ATV.

"See?" I whisper, hoping David will somehow hear me. "I kept my word. I survived." I pause for a moment, knowing we have all the time in the world. The sun is low, the insects are starting to come out and the frogs are in full concert. Wind sways moss tendrils gently. "If they'll take me back, I'll continue making *Swamp Secrets*," I say, and only the wind answers, caressing my face with a cool breeze. "But I won't hide my scars."

49

SOMEONE

Tess was quick to leave the doctor's office, cleared the next morning after the concussion she got from Brickner. Unlike Fradella, the night before she hadn't been forced to spend the night in the hospital. After a doctor examined her, he let her go under the promise she'd come back the next morning for a second exam, just to be sure. Then she went straight home and took an endless shower, to wash off the grime, the blood, and the bad memories Brickner had stirred up in her.

She slept for twelve hours straight, only occasionally awakened by shreds of nonsensical nightmares, mostly involving snakes and other swamp critters. The smell of mildew and wood rot and blood had stayed with her, in her mind, unwilling to fade away until she rinsed it off with a couple of glasses of wine.

The following morning, the sun shined brightly, shattering her bad memories, burning through them as if they were clumps of ocean fog.

She hadn't heard from Pearson yet, and she was putting off the moment she'd have to face him. She'd disobeyed his direct order and knew there would be hell to pay.

But first, he'd ask her if she'd been cleared by medical, so she started her day with a visit to the hospital, eager to get that pain in the rear done with. Secretly, not even admitting it to herself, she was looking for an excuse to pay Fradella a visit. His concussion was more severe; he'd spent a couple of hours unconscious. The doctors had shown concern the night before but sent her home without too much ceremony when she offered to stay the night by his side.

Walking briskly through a corridor busy with people, she found the nurses' station and asked where she could find Fradella. The young nurse was reluctant to give her the room number, even after showing her badge. She didn't hesitate one bit to extract it out of her as she would've done with a perp locked in the interview room. Maybe a bit more polite, yet just as quickly and effectively. Maybe she was new or something; usually staff gave room numbers to law enforcement without much fuss.

She walked to Fradella's room quickly, dragging a Get Well balloon she'd picked up from the flower shop downstairs. Her mind was devoid of any concern as to why she was almost running or why her heart was thumping in her chest with worry. When she reached the room, she slid the door open without knocking.

Fradella was awake, sitting on the side of the bed in a short, open hospital gown that showed his muscular torso. Flustered by her sudden arrival, he grabbed the covers and pulled them over his midsection, grinning awkwardly. His cheeks caught on fire.

"Hey," Tess said smiling, relieved to see him awake and his normal self. "I see you're up."

"Yeah." He fumbled with the covers some more. "I'm sorry. They didn't seem to care much for clothes covered in blood and swamp muck."

She just stood and smiled, a little uneasy. What was she doing there? Maybe it was a mistake. Her smile waned and she took a step back. She was obviously making him uncomfortable.

"Aren't you going to give me that?"

"Huh?"

He pointed at the red balloon.

"Oh, yes, sorry." She took it to him and handed him the string. Their hands touched briefly, sending an electric charge through her body.

"Thank you." He made quick work of tying the string around the bed railing, then smiled at her, seeming a little nervous. "I'm a hostage here… no phone, no clothes. Do we still have a job?"

She drew air abruptly. "Well, I don't know yet." She pulled out her phone and stared at the screen. It was almost ten. "Let's call Pearson and find out."

She made the call with the phone on speaker.

Pearson took the call almost immediately. "Winnett," he said, his usual greeting. "One day, I swear to God, I'll kill you myself."

"Good morning, sir," she said calmly. "I have Fradella here with me."

"Hello, sir," Fradella said, but Pearson cut him off.

"Awesome," he blurted. "Maybe he needs to hear this too." A moment of silence, while Pearson breathed heavily, probably trying to contain his anger. "You broke all the rules in the book, Winnett," he said, his voice a bit steadier. "And some rules that were never written, including my direct order to you. I seem to recall I told you specifically not to risk the victim's life."

"But sir, you knew I was going—"

"You gave me no choice!" His shouting made Tess cringe, and she shot Fradella a concerned look.

"Sir, we—"

"Winnett," he said, and Tess clammed up promptly. "This entire case, everything about the way you handled it, was off somehow. Usually you're colder, more rational, procedural to an extreme. This time… what happened?"

She couldn't tell him she'd identified with the victim to the point where she didn't question her statements enough, choosing to believe her when no other agent would've given her the time of day. Instead, she simply said, "I followed my gut. This wasn't a typical case. There's no book for situations like Kiana's."

"So you say," Pearson replied, seeming thoughtful. "I'm tempted to choose this case for a formal review, but Doc Rizza seems to think it's a waste of everyone's time. He said he witnessed your interview with the victim and stated you made the best out of a terrible situation."

She breathed slowly, smiling weakly. "Yes, sir." Good Doc Rizza. She knew exactly why he'd stepped in for her.

"Fradella," Pearson said, and Todd stiffened. "Would you have handled the investigation any differently?"

He cleared his throat quietly. "Probably not. We had several factors to consider, including the negative media exposure for the bureau if Kiana left the hospital on her own and returned to find the unsub unassisted. It would've been a mess of epic proportions."

A moment of silence. "Were you two cleared by medical?"

"Yes, sir," Tess replied.

"All right. Stay out of my sight until Monday morning, is that clear?" He ended the call without giving them a chance to reply.

Tess grinned happily. An entire weekend off. She could think of a few ways she could spend it. Her eyes wandered over Fradella's naked torso, only for a moment, before she looked away.

The door slid open, and Donovan came in. Just like a few days earlier, he carried his laptop and a shopping bag filled with some clothing items. This time, he wore a pair of sunglasses propped up on his head.

"Hey," he greeted them cheerfully. "Ready for the world out there, mate?"

Fradella caught the bag thrown by Donovan. Several items fell out, scattering on the bed.

"This is my stuff," Fradella said. "How did you—?"

"You really have to ask?" Donovan quipped. "I'm a federal employee, an analyst, one of the better ones. Your address is easy to find, and your lock is a sad joke, man. But you're welcome."

Fradella extracted a black, Metallica T-shirt from the pile and slipped it on. It was taut on his body. Tess hid a smile.

"I haven't worn this since high school," Fradella said. "It's good you got me the right pants, or it would've been really interesting."

They all burst into laughter.

"I have the full back story on the perp if you want the deets," Donovan said, sitting on the floor with his legs crossed and firing up his laptop.

"Yes, give," Tess replied.

"I give you James Brickner, he was thirty-four years old. He was born and raised in the Glades, the son of John Brickner, the famous snake hunter. Famous to some, 'cause I've never heard of him," he added, his eyebrow raised and his lip curled. "Jim Brickner was married to a girl from Texas named Daisy, as you might've guessed. But she left Jim and their two-year-old son one day and just vanished. Rumors had it she went back to Texas and lived on a horse ranch."

Tess listened, fascinated. There it was, the event that threw Jim Brickner off into a spin. But there must've been something else. People don't turn into serial killers just because their wives leave.

"Jim's son died a couple of days later," Donovan continued, "right where that creepy daisy garden was. A cottonmouth got to him when Jim wasn't looking." He flipped through some screens. "We all know who Jim Brickner blamed for the death of his son. He was charged with negligence causing death and stood trial for it. That's the only other time Daisy appeared in his life. Visibly distraught, she testified about the Glades, about what a treacherous environment that could be. She also said she left him because he had violent tendencies. The media chastised her for abandoning her child with a brutal man. Quite unexpectedly, he was found not guilty, and his son's death was ruled accidental. That's when Daisy vanished, after that verdict."

"She moved back to Texas?" Tess asked, frowning. Something didn't add up.

"No, I mean, I couldn't find her anywhere," Donovan replied, his voice tinged with embarrassment. "And you know how well I can dig. She's gone. Like, really gone."

Tess wondered why she'd left her son behind with a man she knew to be brutal, in a place as treacherous as the Glades. "Unless she didn't run away," Tess whispered. "Maybe she *escaped* and wanted to come back with help and get her son. Only she didn't manage it fast enough."

"So, you're thinking, he was doing to his wife what he did to Kiana and the others?" Fradella asked.

"No," Tess replied. "Not yet. He hadn't evolved to that stage yet, but he wasn't far from it." Donovan looked at her, seeming intrigued. "You and me, if we lose a spouse or a child, we grieve, we get counseling, and so on. We don't murder people; we don't kidnap and torture women who resemble someone who's done us wrong. That's pathology. Even before Daisy left him, he was a psychopath, only he hadn't been fully triggered yet."

"So, you think Daisy's in hiding? I'll look some more," Donovan offered.

She hesitated for a moment. "No. My guess is if you dig under that flower bed, you'll find the original Daisy." She bit her lip, remembering how she'd looked Brickner in the eye and had concluded Daisy was still alive, because he seemed still raw about what she'd done. "I also believe Brickner was a narcissistic injury collector, not only a psychopath."

Fradella frowned and looked away, while Tess paced the room. "Sometimes I think I should go back to school," he said, his voice tinged with a hint of frustration.

"An injury collector, while not an official term listed in the *DSM-5*, is what some behaviorists call the narcissist who is unable to forgive and move on past the trauma or injury they suffered. Instead, they hold on to it, reliving the negative feelings associated with the injury, because it gives them something they relish. In Brickner's case, it motivated his power and control urges that brought him release."

Donovan looked at her with a slightly slackened jaw, then slammed the lid on his laptop and stood. "Whatever you say, Winnett. I gotta go... Pearson gave me the day off, so I'll be working on my tan." He waved from the doorframe, then stepped back into the room as if he'd remembered something. "Forgot to say, we were right to look at TV crews for our unsub. Brickner was a freelancing cameraman. Several networks used him. That's how he picked his victims." He grinned and lowered his sunglasses on his nose. Then he waved at them and disappeared after sliding the door shut.

Tess stood silently for a brief moment, then plunged her hands into her pockets. "I should be going too."

Fradella started to get off the bed, but remained seated, holding on to the covers with his hand. "How about dinner?" he blurted, a certain urgency in his voice. "I think I know just the right place. It's in the Glades. They serve gator meat and grilled snake." His chuckle told Tess he was joking.

She stuck her tongue out in the universal grimace of nausea. "Sorry, I'll pass. On everything Glades. For a while, at least." He laughed. "For like the next fifty years or so."

"Some other place then?"

She lowered her eyes and shook her head. "I can't, I'm sorry. Not tonight."

"Tomorrow?" he asked, his smile waning, replaced with a hint of worry.

"Not tomorrow either."

Her answer silenced him for a long, uncomfortable moment. "Is there someone else?" The glimmer of sadness in his eyes swelled her heart.

"Yes," she eventually admitted with a tinge of humor in her voice. "There's someone else. And I have to go now." A flutter of a smile tugged at her lips. "But if you're up for a burger when they let you off the Jell-O diet, come find me at Cat's tonight."

Fradella hopped off the bed, still holding the covers wrapped around his waist, trampling and stumbling on them. He was hilarious. And heartwarming.

"Is he the someone?" he asked, but Tess didn't reply. She slid open the door and stepped outside. "Come on, tell me," he shouted from the doorway as she walked away. "Is Cat the someone?"

Still walking away, she shrugged, then flashed him a cryptic smile.

50

DANCE

Tess wore an apron over her jeans and T-shirt, a black one with a crescent moon embroidered on it and the name of the bar in blue cursive font: *Media Luna.* It was quite busy, understandable for a Friday night. Only a couple of tables were still empty and not a single one of the bar stools.

She'd tied her hair back in a ponytail, to keep it off her face when she worked, but a couple of blonde locks had escaped. She moved quickly, serving drinks, running tabs, rinsing glasses, opening bottles. She wasn't much of a mixologist, but the patrons didn't complain; they were the beer-and-a-shot kind of crowd anyway.

Cat worked the grill. He moved a little slower, his back hunched a little more than she cared to admit. He'd lost a bit of the fire in his eyes, but he was still the same Cat, wearing his signature Hawaiian shirts, top buttons undone to show the tiger tattoo on his chest that had earned the Vietnam vet his nickname.

She opened two bottles of Stella Artois for a couple of old coots, then wiped her hands and went over to Cat. Without warning, she wrapped her arms around his neck and buried her face in his shoulder.

"Thank you," she whispered, soaking in the sense of comfort and security he gave her.

"What for?" he asked, his voice a little raspy, the way it sounded when he was tired.

"For my life," she replied, still hiding her face to keep the unwanted tears her secret. "For rescuing me." He caressed her hair with knotty, arthritic fingers. Her shoulders heaved. "I would've never made it without you."

They stood silently for a moment, the warm hug giving Tess balance and strength.

"Hard day at the office?" he asked with parental concern overlaid on top of the humor meant to encourage her.

"You could say that," she replied, pulling away and sniffling quietly.

"Aren't they all?" he groaned. "I don't know how you do what you do, kiddo."

She took a credit card from a patron and ran it, printed the receipts, and handed them back to him with a pen. Then gave Cat a look and frowned. He was pale and seemed a little shaky. "Why don't you sit down? I'll handle the rest of the stuff." He opened his mouth to protest, but she held her hand up. "Uh-uh, don't want to hear it."

She took his hand and dragged him to the recliner she'd squeezed behind the counter, by the supply room door.

"I could at least do the grilling," he protested.

"Nope, you're grounded." She rinsed a few shot glasses quickly, then wiped her hands and opened a new bottle of Grey Goose. "Plus, I have helpers if I need them."

She nodded toward Michowsky, who was seated toward the end of the bar, nursing a bottle of Heineken. He signaled with his finger at the ear and toward the two men seated next to him that their conversation was interesting. He seemed visibly entertained by his eavesdropping, a glimmer of amusement sparking in his eyes while he kept a straight face.

She grabbed a rag and went over there, wiping the counter clean of peanut shells and bottle circles within earshot of Michowsky's source of amusement.

"Heard the place is run by cops or something," one of the men was saying. Both him and his companion were almost at the limit where she'd stop serving them and call them a cab.

"Nah, man, no cop here. I've known this guy for decades." He slurred the words just a little, although she'd only filled his brandy glass twice. He must've come already pickled from someplace else.

"How about her?" the other guy asked, making a head gesture that almost made Tess burst into laughter. She pretended she didn't hear anything and took a couple of steps to the left, loading more beer bottles into the fridge.

"She's just his niece or something," the man replied, seeming sure of himself, while Michowsky struggled to contain a smile. "Helps the old man on the weekends."

"Then, I guess I could snort a tiny bit right here, huh?" The man took out a cigarette holder that most likely contained drugs, not smokes.

That was where she drew the line. She walked over to the two drunks and pulled her apron aside just a little, enough to let them catch a glimpse of the badge clipped on her belt. "Sorry, guys, it's true what they say."

"Oh, fuck me," one of them shouted, hopping off his stool and stepping back as if he'd seen a snake. Michowsky burst into laughter.

"We're about to close now," Tess said, looking straight at them, then at the door.

The two men didn't need more. They stumbled toward the door and clashed, eager to get out.

She turned to Cat and mouthed, "I'm so sorry." She walked over to him with a freshly opened bottle of Coors, his favorite. "I'm killing your business more than I'm helping."

He smiled. "I wouldn't still have a business if it weren't for you, kiddo." He took a couple of thirsty gulps, savoring them. "I don't like druggies either. I always kick them out of this joint. They can get me in trouble with the law." He raised his bottle toward Michowsky, who did the same.

Several other people left in a hurry, leaving cash on the counter. She went over there to collect it and clean up, not paying much attention.

"Hello, Tess."

Fradella stood at the bar, smiling slightly.

She felt a wave of warmth engulfing her. She'd given up turning her head each time the antique brass doorbell chimed, thinking he wasn't going to show after all.

The loud chatter of the late-night patrons seemed to fade away when she looked into his eyes and smiled. "One burger with everything, coming up," she quipped. "Beer?" He nodded. She popped open a bottle of Stella.

"Thanks."

She took care of another patron, who needed a cab more than another shot of tequila, then returned to find Michowsky and Fradella seated side by side, chatting loudly.

"And you couldn't call me?" Michowsky was saying. He sounded seriously pissed. "You went out there by yourselves, no backup no nothing? What brand of stupid is this?"

"We left early, and it could've been dicey," Fradella replied. "You got kids, for crying out loud."

Michowsky didn't seem to hear anything he said. "Is it a fed thing, now? Like, if I'm not a fed, I don't get to play?"

"This is ridiculous," Fradella said, looking at Tess as if asking for support. She pretended not to notice and started making an order of fries for his burger. "You're being an idiot."

"And where were you?" Michowsky asked. "It's almost ten. I thought you were bailing on me."

"I was busy," he replied.

"Doing what?"

"Proving her right again," he said, looking straight at Tess.

She walked over, leaving a patron holding a credit card to call after her.

"What are you talking about?"

"I took a crime scene team at the site with a GPR, and it's there, just like you said."

"What's there?" Michowsky asked.

"A body, buried underneath the flower bed." He tilted his head ever so slightly at Tess. "A woman's body. Just like she called it."

She smiled and mouthed, "Thank you," then took the patron's credit card. Someone else kept her busy after that, then she took Fradella his dinner, and went in the back to get more beer. Michowsky came to help her with the cases of beer.

"I'm going to leave right after I help you close up," he said, then winked. "You don't need me here."

There was a hint of innuendo in his voice, but she didn't mind. She was among family.

Music filled the barroom with the gentle rhythm of Lonestar's "Amazed." Surprised, Tess looked around for the source and saw Todd Fradella walking back from the digital jukebox.

He reached for her hand over the counter and asked, "May I have this dance?"

Cat smiled and closed his eyes, seemingly content. Tess took off her apron, abandoning it on a chair, and pulled off the scrunchie that held her hair. Then she walked around the counter until she landed in Todd's arms, swaying with the sweet tones of an acoustic guitar and a voice that sounded just like his.

Her body found his and moved with it easily, effortlessly as if they'd danced a thousand times before, telling her she belonged in his arms.

Somewhere in the distance, the blue *OPEN* sign got turned off, the last few customers were charged and thanked for their patronage, and then Michowsky left.

Then Cat went upstairs, not before putting that song on repeat.

And they danced.

Did *The Girl Hunter* keep you on the edge of your seat as you raced through the pages, gasping at every twist? Meet Special Agent Tess Winnett of the FBI in another unmissable Leslie Wolfe serial killer thriller.

Read on for a preview from:

Dawn Girl

A short-fused FBI Agent who hides a terrible secret. A serial killer you won't see coming. A heart-stopping race to catch him.

THANK YOU!

A big, heartfelt thank you for choosing to read my book. If you enjoyed it, please take a moment to leave me a four or five-star review; I would be very grateful. It doesn't need to be more than a couple of words, and it makes a huge difference.

Join my mailing list to receive special offers, exclusive bonus content, and news about upcoming new releases. Use the button below, visit www.LeslieWolfe.com to sign up, or email me at LW@WolfeNovels.com.

Did you enjoy *The Girl You Killed*? Would you like to see some of these characters return? Which ones? Your thoughts and feedback are very valuable to me. Please contact me directly through one of the channels listed below. Email works best: LW@WolfeNovels.com or use the button below:

If you haven't already, check out ***Dawn Girl***, a gripping, heart stopping crime thriller and the first book in the Tess Winnett series. If you enjoyed *Criminal Minds*, you'll enjoy *Dawn Girl*. Or, if you're in a mood for something lighter, try ***Las Vegas Girl***; you'll love it!

CONNECT WITH ME!

Email: LW@WolfeNovels.com

Facebook: https://www.facebook.com/wolfenovels

Follow Leslie on Amazon: http://bit.ly/WolfeAuthor

Follow Leslie on BookBub: http://bit.ly/wolfebb

Website: www.LeslieWolfe.com

Visit Leslie's Amazon store: Amazon.com/LeslieWolfe

PREVIEW: *DAWN GIRL*

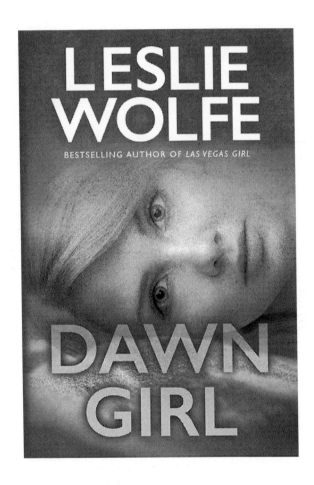

CHAPTER ONE
READY

She made an effort to open her eyes, compelling her heavy eyelids to obey. She swallowed hard, her throat raw and dry, as she urged the wave of nausea to subside. Dizzy and confused, she struggled to gain awareness. Where was she? She felt numb and shaky, unable to move, as if awakening from a deep sleep or a coma. She tried to move her arms, but couldn't. Something kept her immobilized, but didn't hurt her. Or maybe she couldn't feel the pain, not anymore.

Her eyes started to adjust to the darkness, enough to distinguish the man moving quietly in the room. His silhouette flooded her foggy brain with a wave of memories. She gasped, feeling her throat constrict and burning tears rolling down her swollen cheeks.

Her increased awareness sent waves of adrenaline through her body, and she tried desperately to free herself from her restraints. With each useless effort, she panted harder, gasping for air, forcing it into her lungs. Fear put a strong chokehold on her throat and was gaining ground, as she rattled her restraints helplessly, growing weaker with every second. She felt a wave of darkness engulf her, this time the darkness coming from within her weary brain. She fought against that darkness, and battled her own betraying body.

The noises she made got the man's attention.

"I see you're awake. Excellent," the man said, without turning.

She watched him place a syringe on a small, metallic tray. Its handle clinked, followed by another sound, this time the raspy, telling sound of a file cutting through the neck of a glass vial. Then a pop when the man opened the vial. He grabbed the syringe and loaded the liquid from the vial, then carefully removed any air, pushing the piston until several droplets of fluid came out.

Dizziness overtook her, and she closed her eyes for a second.

"Shit," the man mumbled, then opened a drawer and went through it in a hurry.

She felt the needle poke deeply in her thigh, like it was happening to another person. She felt it, but distantly. She perceived a subdued burning sensation where he pushed the fluid into her muscle, then that went away when he pulled the needle out. She closed her weary eyes again, listless against her restraints.

The man cracked open ammonia salts under her nose, and she bounced back into reality at the speed of a lightning strike, aware, alert, and angry. For a second she fought to free herself, but froze when her eyes focused on the man in front of her.

He held a scalpel, close to her face. In itself, the small, shiny, silver object was capable of bringing formidable healing, as well as immense pain. The difference stood in the hand wielding it. She knew no healing was coming her way; only pain.

"No, no, please…" she pleaded, tears falling freely from her puffy eyes, burning as they rolled down her cheeks. "Please, no. I… I'll do anything."

"I am ready," the man said. He seemed calm, composed, and dispassionate. "Are you ready?"

"No, no, please…" she whimpered.

"Yeah," he said softly, almost whispering, inches away from her face. "Please say no to me. I love that."

She fell quiet, scared out of her mind. This time was different. *He* was different.

CHAPTER TWO
DAWN

"What if we get caught?" the girl whispered, trailing behind the boy.

They walked briskly on the small residential street engulfed in darkness, keeping to the middle of the road. There were no sidewalks. High-end homes lined up both sides, most likely equipped with sensor floodlights they didn't want to trip.

She tugged at his hand, but he didn't stop. "You never care about these things, Carl, but I do. If we get caught, I'll be grounded, like, forever!"

The boy kept going, his hand firmly clasping hers.

"Carl!" she raised the pitch in her whisper, letting her anxiety show more.

He stopped and turned, facing her. He frowned a little, seeing her anguish, but then smiled and caressed a loose strand of hair rebelling from under her sweatshirt's hood.

"There's no one, Kris. No one's going to see us. See? No lights are on, nothing. Everyone's asleep. Zee-zee-zee. It's five in the morning."

"I know," she sighed, "but—"

He kissed her pouted lips gently, a little boyish hesitation and awkwardness in his move.

"We'll be okay, I promise," he said, then grabbed her hand again. "We're almost there, come on. You'll love it."

A few more steps and the small street ended into the paved parking lot of what was going to be a future development of sorts, maybe a shopping center. From there, they had to cross Highway 1. They crouched down near the road, waiting for the light traffic to be completely clear. They couldn't afford to be seen, not even from a distance. At the right moment, they crossed the highway, hand in hand, and cut across the field toward the beach. Crossing Ocean Drive was next, then cutting through a few yards of shrubbery and trees to get to the sandy beach.

"Jeez, Carl," Kris protested, stopping in her tracks at the tree line. "Who knows what creatures live here? There could be snakes. Lizards. Gah…"

"There could be, but there aren't," Carl replied, seemingly sure of himself. "Trust me."

She held her breath and lowered her head, then clasped Carl's hand tightly. He turned on the flashlight on his phone and led the way without hesitation. A few seconds later, they reached the beach, and Kris let out a tense, long breath.

The light of the waning gibbous Moon reflected against the calm ocean waves, sending flickers of light everywhere and covering the beach in silver shadows. They were completely alone. The only creatures keeping them company were pale crabs that took bellicose stances when Kris and Carl stomped the sand around them, giggling.

"See? Told you," Carl said, "no one's going to see us out here. We can do whatever we want," he said playfully.

Kris squealed and ran toward the lifeguard tower. In daylight, the tower showed its bright yellow and orange, a splash of joyful colors on the tourist-abundant stretch of sand. At night, the structure appeared gloomy, resembling a menacing creature on tall, insect-like legs.

"It looks like one of those aliens from *War of the Worlds*," Kris said, then promptly started running, waving her arms up in the air, pretending she was flying.

Carl chased Kris, laughing and squealing with her, running in circles around the tower, and weaving footstep patterns between the solid wood posts.

"Phew," Carl said, stopping his chase and taking some distance. "Stinks of piss. Let's get out of here."

"Eww…" Kris replied, following him. "Why do men do that?"

"What? Pee?"

"Everybody pees, genius," Kris replied, still panting from the run. "Peeing where it stinks and bothers people, that's what I meant. Women pee in the bushes. Men should pee in the water if they don't like the bushes."

"Really? That's gross."

"Where do you think fish pee? At least the waves would wash away the pee and it wouldn't stink, to mess up our sunrise."

"Fish pee?" Carl pushed back, incredulous.

"They don't?"

They walked holding hands, putting a few more yards of distance between them and the tower. Then Carl suddenly dropped to the ground, dragging Kris with him. She squealed again, and laughed.

"Let's sit here," he said. "The show's on. Let's see if we get a good one."

The sky was starting to light up toward the east. They watched silently, hand in hand, as the dark shades of blue and gray gradually turned ablaze, mixing in dark reds and orange hues. The horizon line was clear, a sharp edge marking where ocean met sky.

"It's going to be great," Carl said. "No clouds, no haze." He kissed her lips quickly, and then turned his attention back to the celestial light show.

"You're a strange boy, Carl."

"Yeah? Why?"

"Other boys would have asked me to sneak out in the middle of the night to make out. With you, it's a sunrise, period. Should I worry?"

Carl smiled widely, then tickled Kris until she begged for mercy between gasps of air and bouts of uncontrollable laughter.

"Stop! Stop it already. I can't breathe!"

"I might want to get on with that make out, you know," Carl laughed.

"Nah, it's getting light. Someone could see us," Kris pushed back, unconvinced. "Someone could come by."

Carl shrugged and turned his attention to the sunrise. He grabbed her hand and held it gently, playing with her fingers.

Almost half the sky had caught fire, challenging the moonlight, and obliterating most of its reflected light against the blissful, serene, ocean waves.

Carl checked the time on his phone.

"A few more minutes until it comes out," he announced, sounding serious, as if predicting a rare and significant event. He took a few pictures of the sky, then suddenly snapped one of Kris.

"Ah... no," she reacted, "give that to me right this second, Carl." She grabbed the phone from his hand and looked at the picture he'd taken. The image showed a young girl with messy, golden brown hair, partially covering a scrunched, tense face with deep ridges on her brow. The snapshot revealed Kris biting her index fingernail, totally absorbed by the process, slobbering her sleeve cuff while at it.

"God-awful," she reacted, then pressed the option to delete.

"No!" Carl said, pulling the phone from her hands. "I like it!"

"There's nothing to like. There," she said, relaxing a little, and arranging her hair briefly with her long, thin fingers. "I'll pose for you." She smiled.

Carl took a few pictures. She looked gorgeous, against the backdrop of fiery skies, pink sand, and turquoise water. He took image after image, as she got into it and made faces, danced, and swirled in front of him, laughing.

The sun's first piercing ray shot out of the sea, just as Kris shrieked, a blood-curdling scream that got Carl to spring to his feet and run to her.

Speechless, Kris pointed a trembling hand at the lifeguard tower. Underneath the tower, between the wooden posts supporting the elevated structure, was the naked body of a young woman. She appeared to be kneeling, as if praying to the rising sun. Her hands were clasped together in front of her in the universal, unmistakable gesture of silent pleading.

Holding their breaths, they approached carefully, curious and yet afraid of what they stood to discover. The growing light of the new morning revealed more details with each step they took. Her back, covered in bruises and small cuts, stained in smudged, dried blood. Her blue eyes wide open, glossed over. A few specks of sand clung to her long, dark lashes. Her beautiful face, immobile, covered in sparkling flecks of sand. Her lips slightly parted, as if to let a last breath escape. Long, blonde hair, wet from sea spray, almost managed to disguise the deep cut in her neck.

No blood dripped from the wound; her heart had stopped beating for some time. Yet she held upright, unyielding in her praying posture, her knees stuck firmly in the sand covered in their footprints, and her eyes fixed on the beautiful sunrise they came to enjoy.

~~~End Preview~~~

Like *Dawn Girl*?

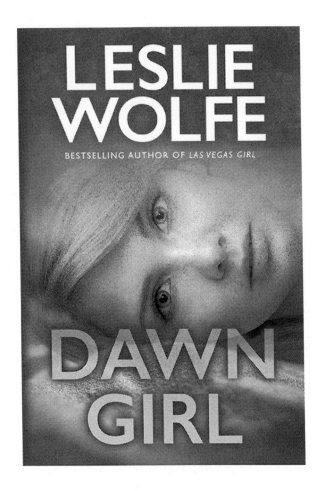

Buy It now!

ABOUT THE AUTHOR

Meet Leslie Wolfe, bestselling author and mastermind behind gripping thrillers that have won the hearts of over a million readers worldwide. She brings a fresh and invigorating touch to the thriller genre, crafting compelling narratives around unforgettable, powerhouse women.

Her books are not only an adrenaline-packed ride, but they're also sprinkled with psychological insights, offering readers an immersive, authentic experience that goes beyond conventional suspense.

You might know her from the Detective Kay Sharp series or have been hooked by Tess Winnett's relentless pursuit of justice. Maybe you've followed the dynamic duo Baxter & Holt through the gritty streets of Las Vegas or plunged into political intrigue with Alex Hoffmann.

Recently, Leslie published *The Girl You Killed*, a psychological thriller that's pure, unputdownable suspense. This standalone novel will have fans of *The Undoing, The Silent Patient,* and *Little Fires Everywhere* on the edge of their seats.

Whether you're into the mind games of Criminal Minds, love crime thrillers like James Patterson's, or enjoy the heart-pounding tension in Kendra Elliot and Robert Dugoni's mysteries, Leslie's got a thriller series for you. Fans of action-packed writers like Tom Clancy or Lee Child will find plenty to love in her Alex Hoffmann series.

Wolfe's latest psychological thriller, *The Surgeon*, will have you racing through the pages gasping for breath until the final jaw-dropping twist, delighting fans of *Gone Girl* and *The Girl on the Train.*

Discover all of Leslie's works on her Amazon store, at Amazon.com/LeslieWolfe. Want a sneak peek at what's next? Become an insider for early access to previews of her new novels, each a thrilling ride you won't want to miss.

- Email: LW@WolfeNovels.com
- Facebook: https://www.facebook.com/wolfenovels
- Follow Leslie on Amazon: http://bit.ly/WolfeAuthor
- Follow Leslie on BookBub: http://bit.ly/wolfebb
- Website: www.LeslieWolfe.com
- Visit Leslie's Amazon store: Amazon.com/LeslieWolfe.

BOOKS BY LESLIE WOLFE

TESS WINNETT SERIES

Dawn Girl
The Watson Girl
Glimpse of Death
Taker of Lives
Not Really Dead
Girl With A Rose
Mile High Death
The Girl They Took
The Girl Hunter

STANDALONE TITLES

The Surgeon
The Girl You Killed
Stories Untold
Love, Lies and Murder

DETECTIVE KAY SHARP SERIES

The Girl From Silent Lake
Beneath Blackwater River
The Angel Creek Girls
The Girl on Wildfire Ridge
Missing Girl at Frozen Falls

BAXTER & HOLT SERIES

Las Vegas Girl
Casino Girl
Las Vegas Crime

ALEX HOFFMANN SERIES

Executive
Devil's Move
The Backup Asset
The Ghost Pattern
Operation Sunset

For the complete list of books in all available formats, visit:

Amazon.com/LeslieWolfe

Made in the USA
Monee, IL
29 September 2023

43654314R00176